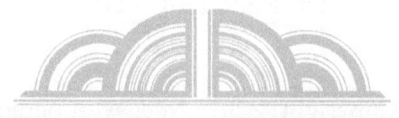

NATIVE SPECIES
A Tale of Two Civilizations in 1928 Los Angeles

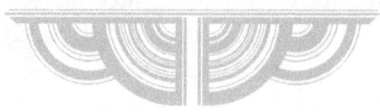

MICHAEL ALBERGO

Published by ELECTRIC TORCH PRESS

Copyright © 2026 Michael Albergo
All rights reserved.

ISBN: 979-8-9938527-0-6
First published in the United States 2026
This paperback edition published 2026

ELECTRIC TORCH PRESS, and the ELECTRIC TORCH PRESS logo are trademarks of Michael Albergo

This is a work of fiction. Any references to historical events, real people, or real locales are used fictitiously. A list of such people and locales is included in the appendix. Other names, characters, places, and incidents are products of the author's imagination, and any resemblance to actual events, locales, or person, living or dead, is entirely coincidental.

All rights reserved. No part of this publication may be reproduced or transmitted in any form or by any means, electronic or mechanical, including photocopying, recording, or any information storage or retrieval system, without prior permission in writing from the publishers.

Cover photo used with permission of The Biltmore Los Angeles. Graphic design by davidomiller.com

CONTENTS

1. The Scientist *1*
2. A Sudden Sabbatical *4*
3. In the Company of the King *7*
4. A Calling *14*
5. The Enemy *19*
6. A Change of Seasons *26*
7. To the Surface *31*
8. Golden Gate *39*
9. Strangers in a Strange Land *44*
10. Name and Address *48*
11. Southbound *52*
12. City of Angels *58*
13. The Departed *65*
14. The Docent *69*
15. Inquiry to the Inquisitor *75*
16. The Professional *82*
17. A Night to Remember *89*
18. A Night to Forget *97*
19. Leads *107*
20. Magnate *116*
21. Secrets Revealed *119*
22. Citizen Kane *127*
23. Meeting of the Minds *134*
24. Post-Partum *141*
25. Chinatown *148*
26. Damn Tourists *155*
27. Source of Power *162*
28. Valley of the Damned *170*
29. Lone Pine *173*
30. The Horror Beneath the Earth *179*
31. The Sagebrush Lodge *185*
32. Forked Tongues *195*
33. Recovery *202*
34. Arrangements *210*
35. Point of Entry *215*
36. Old Friends *224*
37. Confinement *232*
38. Convocation *240*
39. Five Minutes *248*
40. Audience *254*
41. A Place to Sleep *259*
42. A Look Forward *265*
43. Reckoning *270*

For Leslie

CHAPTER

1

THE SCIENTIST

Shila Ghiss

I have never seen a sunrise or a sunset, though our histories say they are beautiful. The light of the Father, they call it. For this brief time, at the beginning and end of each day, one may look upon his face without becoming forever blind. Imagine living beneath something so bright that to look at it is to be blinded!

I don't believe in the Father. But one day, I hope to see a sunrise, and a sunset, and all the bright day in between.

My own father awaits me. As I do every morning, I enter his study, murals of my ancestors judging me as I pass. I approach his enormous desk—real wood, a priceless artifact—and fill his ancient cup with water. A gesture of respect, if not love. All in the colony have pinned their hopes on him, their great scientist. All except me, his daughter. My hopes are different.

I am also a scientist: Warden of Dreamers. A position of importance, if not recognition.

My hope is this: that I will not spend the rest of my days watching Dreamers sleep.

His eyes meet mine as I approach with the pitcher. He watches as I pour the water carefully, without spilling a drop on his precious papers and notebooks. He does not know that I have read them all, that I am shamed each time I do so. But if shame is the price of hope, I will pay it.

He bobs his head in acknowledgment, then returns to his writing. I begin the long trek down my private shaft to the Chamber of Dreamers and my charges.

Before my time comes to sleep, I will see the day.

I slip into my father's study. It is cool and dim, with a taint of mildew. I cannot make out the scenes on the murals, but I know they depict a ruined citadel and my ancestors fleeing during The First Retreat. His journal and research notes are there, on his desk.

I freeze. My father is here, after all. He sprawls across the old wood unnaturally, his current journal beneath him, pen in hand, parchments, inkpot, and cup pushed aside. I forget my purpose and fear of being caught. I rush to his side.

He is dead.

My muscles uncoil. Shock ripples through me, then a flood of regret. I will not say I loved him. He was hard and rigid, like his brother, the king. But he kept my unwanted suitors at bay when I was young, and for that he deserves my thanks.

How did he die? I see no marks, no blood, no signs of violence. Did he accidentally ingest the pathogen that he was creating for our enemies? No, he was cautious. Besides, I know it could not harm us. It is more likely that his ancient body just gave up. Repeated cycles of waking, working, and hibernation, over eons, take a toll. I know this. It is my specialty.

Carefully, shamefully, I prise the journal from beneath his head, his eyes staring vacantly as I do so. *What kind of daughter does such a thing?* But there is no time for shame. I must look through his desk, his shelves, before it is too late. I do not know if his work will be taken from me. I find a satchel and quickly fill it with journals, notes, and papers.

Impulsively, I take his empty cup—the glazed brown clay cup, with its three seals: the red circle of the Father, the yellow crescent of the King, and the blue circle of the Mother. The cup I fill for him each morning and whenever I see it empty. My gesture of respect. Somehow, I feel he would want me to have it; he has left me nothing else.

I have no suitors, siblings, children, or friends. Now I have no parents. No one will ever fill this cup for me.

I must tell the king that my father is dead. The thought fills me with dread. He will not be pleased.

CHAPTER

2

A SUDDEN SABBATICAL

Horace Jennings

In February 1928, after many years of teaching, I took my first and last sabbatical. I was considering retirement, and I thought a sabbatical would help me decide if it was time.

Of course, 55 is hardly retirement age for a professor of physics. Many of the greats in our field teach well into their 70s. Even the mediocre among us often teach a decade or more after it would have been wiser to leave the lectern behind, much to the consternation of our department chairs and students.

I, Horace Jennings, am not one of the greats. In fact, I may not even be one of the mediocre. But I do love teaching: the ever-present smell of waxed wood and chalk; the echoes of voices during discussions and scratching pens during tests. I love the power and elegance of physics, and the cleverness and utility of engineering, which I also teach. I enjoy parsing and presenting the accumulated knowledge of great thinkers and seeing its impact on the faces of brighter students, when I am fortunate enough to have them.

But most of all, I enjoy the students themselves: the new faces every semester; their youthful vigor; their insightful and often droll questions; their passions, problems, perplexities, and pursuits of the latest sport or trend. They push me, without realizing it, to be better than I am. Youth keeps me young.

So why retire?

Brown is a beautiful campus: stately old brick buildings, well-kept lawns, graceful walkways, and ancient, soaring trees…

One beautiful wintry day, the trees and campus clothed in white, I received a call. An old colleague of mine, Charles Ellis, a professor at the University of Illinois, asked if I knew of any good field geologists. He was performing the structural engineering for the planned Golden Gate Bridge in San Francisco. He needed a field geologist to help conduct test borings. Drilling was expected to begin in the spring.

Instantly I knew the right person: one of my former students, Mateo Martinez. Mateo was an outstanding graduate geologist from San Francisco and had an excellent knowledge of the local strata. The work would help him support his family; and I knew that having this premiere project on his resume—a bridge surely destined to become a national icon—would be helpful in advancing his career. He gladly accepted, thanking me profusely.

That was more than a year ago, in January 1927. I received several letters from him those first few months. He described his life as being filled with breathless energy and endless possibility. I was happy for him.

Soon, though, things changed. Ellis reported that Mateo seemed distracted and made several uncharacteristic mistakes. He began missing work. Finally, six months ago, he disappeared altogether, along with the Martinez family car.

His mother called my office herself, convinced that he had driven all the way back to Providence to finish some project here at the university. I assured her he had not.

"Professor Jennings…maybe that girl?" she asked in a thick Spanish accent. "You know, the one he was seeing. The geologist. He is with her? They went somewhere together, maybe?"

"No, Mrs. Martinez. Helen Parker is working on other projects. I have spoken with her, and she assures me that she has not seen him."

The call was short and awkward. But Mrs. Martinez seemed certain that Mateo would return soon. "He is a good boy, Professor Jennings," she said. "He will come home soon."

But weeks passed, and he did not return. Eventually, I received an even shorter and more awkward call from Ellis. "I'm sorry, Horace," he said. "These soil borings can't wait. We need them to progress the design, and we're already falling behind schedule. I'll need to find someone else to lead the field work." He didn't ask me for any more recommendations, nor did I offer any.

I am ashamed to admit it, but somehow my concern for Mateo was overshadowed by my frustration, and yes, perhaps anger, at how he had squandered this opportunity. He let down his family, Ellis, and the project, and he let me down as well: his mentor and advocate, who now bore some of the blame and loss of reputation. It tasted of betrayal. Yet Mateo was a steadfast, thoughtful, dependable fellow; what foible, fancy, or female could have led him to do such a thing?

Well, he was a young man, and I know that young men often do foolish things. But I would learn from this. That day, after the call from Ellis, I resolved never again to recommend a student for a job opportunity. I would put the whole sorry mess behind me and move on.

But I couldn't move on. Malaise had set in. The spring 1928 semester was nearly upon us, but I found myself unable, or unwilling, to prepare for it. When I looked out my office window, I saw only a dreary quadrangle and a clouded sky. Ahead of me: nothing. No youth, no energy, no desire, and no reason to be here. Perhaps it was finally time to retire.

I informed the department chair and staff that I could not teach this spring; instead, I would take a sabbatical. They were shocked, of course, with no previous mention of a sabbatical in nearly 20 years of teaching. The more questions they asked, the more ill-tempered and impatient I became. If Mary were here, she would know how to deal with me. Our department chair, a good man, had never seen me in such a state. Bewildered, he said simply, "Jennings, if you need the time, take it. But please, do yourself this favor: put it to good use. Look inward as well as outward. And come back when you are ready."

CHAPTER
3

IN THE COMPANY OF THE KING

Shila Ghiss

The King's Hall is said to have been carved by the Mother herself, sending her hot, red blood in a torrent to melt the stone. I wish I could believe this, but evidence suggests that something else carved it long ago. Something less wholesome, and far more frightening.

The Hall has been altered since last I was here. Lights have been strung along the smooth, black stone walls and vaulted ceiling—lights of the kind used by our enemy. They shine so brightly I must close my eyes, lower my head. I know who is responsible for these lights.

I make my way past the broad, low ceramic tables with their painted maps, where the Commander, lines of gold scales shining, and the Science Master, a small, jet-black shadow, bob their heads and fret, planning a war against hopeless odds—but one that our enemy does not know is coming. Under the dazzling new light, the colors of the maps are more vibrant than ever, illuminating a world I have never seen: deep green forests, emerald fields, turquoise rivers, brown mountains and deserts, and a sapphire line depicting the great ocean. Settlements, blood red, have grown on the maps like a cancer.

Sesh, my former rival and now our newly minted Inquisitor, meets me at the edge of a shadow, where the unblinking brightness of the electric lights gives way to the dim lichen luminescence preferred by our king.

"May the Father watch over you," he says.

"May the Mother nourish you," I reply.

The formalities over, he pauses, eyeing me with his head cocked to one side. "What do you think of our new lights?" he asks, smoothing his scarlet Inquisitor's vest, his teeth on full display.

"I think you are a clever thief," I say. "Where did you get the electricity? Surely our batteries are not wasted on this?"

"No," he says. "The enemy has a power plant at the end of the canyon, not far from here." He surveys the Hall, pleased with himself. Then his eyes return to me. "It has been long since I have seen you." His tongue flicks out, and his green irises widen.

When I do not reply, his visage cools, and he slithers away. "Come," he calls. "He awaits you."

The tang of incense burns my tongue as I taste the stifling air near the king's seat, carved in gray stone above the far end of the hall. I stand below him, the stone beneath me uncomfortably hot. The huge bulk of the Commander and the poison fangs of the diminutive Science Master flank me as if I were a prisoner. Their usual false courtesies are nowhere to be found.

Sesh perches close by the king, his head raised above us all.

The king is terrible to behold, more so when he frowns, as he does now, fangs exposed, his enormous head bent low in his lofty seat, his crescent painted in gold above his eyes. A devout apostle of the Father, he is always angry, impatient, and intolerant, especially where science is concerned. He leans forward on an ancient, gnarled staff. His mantle and robe are nearly colorless with age, their symbols long faded, but their authority as absolute as if he were crowned yesterday. I do not meet his gaze.

"May the Father watch over you, my king," I manage to say.

"He watches over us all," he grumbles, "as I do. And especially over those who wear their faith as a skin, to be shed when it no longer serves their purpose." His yellow eyes narrow. "Shila Ghiss, you say that you do not know the cause of your father's death? How is it that an expert in the sciences of life and sleep does not know how her own father died?"

"I suspect it was simply his time, Uncle," I say, "but I cannot be sure. Not unless I open his body and test it. Have I your permission to do so?"

Sesh looks down at me and hisses like a snake. "Shila Ghiss, your impudence never fails to amuse. Your king demands an answer, yet you reply with a request."

The king silences his Inquisitor with a wave of his claws. I look up into his yellow eyes, wondering what he will demand next.

"I will not see my brother's remains desecrated, nor his work delayed." His gaze shifts to my right. "Science Master!"

"Yes, Majesty?" she hisses, and her breath is almost as deadly as her poison.

"Search the codex for a new Master of Life Sciences. Provide the name to our Warden of Dreamers. Shila, you will wake him, so that he can carry on your father's work."

My father's work. Develop a disease to eradicate two billion sentient beings. Perhaps it is best he is dead, his work unfinished. This is the end of my hope. I will spend the rest of my days watching thousands sleep, perhaps never to see them awaken.

The king's great head descends and his yellow eyes meet mine, close enough to see his black, slitted pupils widen and twitch forward as he focuses on me.

"See that your father's work is turned over to the Science Master. And do not delay. Our future may depend on it."

The oil lamps shine brightly in my father's study—my study now, I suppose. But though I have brought light and rid it of mildew, I feel it will always be his.

The satchel that I have filled with his journals, notes, and cup sits atop his desk. I had intended to take it and—what? Hide it? Flee with it? A childish fantasy. The Science Master would soon be here to collect it. All of his work—years of labor—would pass to her. No doubt she would take credit for it.

I rise from his desk to inspect the murals. Father always said they remind him of his purpose, but I have no need of them. As I draw near, I see they are not so faded as I had thought. And the detail is remarkable. In "The Destruction of the Citadel", the gates are rent where the great lizards entered and trampled our warriors beneath their feet. The day our dominance ended. But theirs would end as well, eventually.

In "The First Retreat", long lines of my ancestors wind their way up into the mountains, then down into Mother Earth.

A third, smaller mural is painted in the corner of the office. It has no title. It shows our life in the caverns, eons later, and our first sleep chambers. I inspect this one carefully, as I have not truly examined it in the years since becoming Warden of Dreamers. A crack circles the largest sleep chamber at the bottom of the mural, as if to disconnect it from the rest of the colony. At the very top edge of the mural is a detail I have never noticed. What I had thought to be a painted border is a line marking the surface world; and what I had thought were mildew stains along that line are tiny figures. Our enemies: the apes.

My father's fascination with them led him to study their biology, which he documented meticulously, and which I read secretly.

I suppose it was this fascination that led him to collect this great wooden artifact on which he worked. It drew scrutiny and reproval from his peers, until ultimately, they tasked him with using his knowledge to eradicate the apes.

It must have been a terribly sad day for him, forced to put an end to them. If so, he never showed it.

A hiss at the entryway tells me the Science Master has arrived. I amble over, in no hurry to see her.

"Royal One," she says. The words drip mockery. Her breath has the odor of rotted fish.

"Master," I reply. There is no talk of the Father or the Mother.

"Has all been made ready?"

"Yes. My father's research is there, on the desk. I have collected it for you. His laboratory is beyond the far door, should you care to see it."

"Indeed?" She crawls in, and a carrier crawls behind her, its motor humming softly. "Ah, this ancient tree," she says, rising beside the desk. "I was appalled when your father insisted it be brought down here." She brings her head and forelimbs down to its smooth surface, then opens and examines its drawers. "But now I rather like it. Would you mind terribly if I take it for my own?"

What?

"After all," she hisses, dropping the satchel onto the carrier with a thud, "your father won't be needing it. Nor will you."

I envision crushing the life out of her, and the thought both calms and excites me. "I suppose that's true," I reply. "Take it, if you like. Though you may need a bigger carrier."

"Hmm. Yes, I believe you're right. A future task, then. Now, is there anything else here I should have?"

She slithers up against each shelf, knocking things over, tongue flicking. Her claws find a strange metal fork with three prongs. "This, for instance?"

"I do not know what that is. My father's notes do not mention it."

The Science Master turns her head to hiss at me. Suspicious, no doubt; but it is the truth. She turns the fork over in her tiny claws, considers it, then throws it on the floor and moves on. "And these jars?"

"Rapid healing ointment. Antivenom. Black lotus powder."

"Yes." She sweeps them all onto the carrier, then moves on to the other shelves. Soon the carrier's basket is full of jars and artifacts. "These may be useful on the surface. One never knows what mischief these wretched apes may cause."

"The surface?" The words escape me before I can recall them.

She twists away from the shelf and slithers towards me, the carrier humming after her. "Yes. I am to accompany Sesh to help plan humanity's end. He has already secured one of them for me. It is in a holding cell near the surface."

I realize then that I should not envy her. "So you will…"

"Yes," she says, and for a moment, we are united in disgust. "Revolting, I know. But there is no other way."

"May I ask what you know of this human?"

"A female," she says. "She studies other humans and their cultures."

"A human—who studies other humans? Why in the world would they study each other?"

"I don't know!" she snaps. "Sesh called her an 'anthropologist.' He tried to explain it, but like most human endeavors, it makes no sense."

I am amused, though she is not. Then a thought comes to mind. A very foolish thought.

"A human who studies other humans seems unfit for a Master of Science. Would you not be better served by a great scientist? Or a leader? Or perhaps a military commander?"

She joins me in the corner of the room, gazing at the mural with the tiny humans at the top and the sleep chamber at the bottom, lost in thought.

Eventually, she sighs and looks away. "Sesh tells me that capturing live humans is not as easy as it would appear. That opportunities to do so without drawing notice are rare." Her eyes flick up at me. "But I suspect otherwise."

"It is just like Sesh to keep the important humans for himself and leave the dregs for his rivals," I tell her. "You should not accept a lesser human, Science Master. You should insist on a leader. If I may say so."

Her fetid breath fills the corner of the room, sickening me as she turns the thought over in her mind. Then:

"You may not," she says haughtily. "I need no advice from a dream warden." She slaps the bottom of the mural—the sleep chamber—with her tail as she turns to leave. "Your place is there, with the dreamers. Vacate these chambers. I want them ready for me when I return from the surface."

She slinks across the floor, sending the little metal fork skittering. The carrier follows her out.

I sink down in the corner, utterly dejected. Reading my father's research and imagining the surface were the only things that made my life bearable; now they are gone, and my future with them. I stare at the ancient sleep chamber depicted in the mural. My new home: oblivion.

Then I see it. Oblivion has three small, neatly bored holes in it.

Recognition strikes like the blood of the Mother. I rush across the floor, seize the fork, and bring it to the mural. The prongs align perfectly with the holes. I insert it, twist, and pull the sleep chamber out of the mural, laying the heavy stone carefully on the floor.

There, in the cavity, is a journal that I have never seen. Atop it is a small jar.

Father left me something after all.

CHAPTER

4

A CALLING

Horace Jennings

Influenza had taken Mary in 1918, the same as it did 50 million other souls. God offered me no explanation, and if he had, I wouldn't have accepted it.

In time, I learned to do for myself all the little things she had done for me: taking in the milk bottles, paying the bills, reminding myself to visit the barber. Slowly, painfully, I became a bachelor again—a boring, orderly one. With no children, no pets, and eventually not even the orchids which she had so deftly cared for, our lovely, sunlit home became an unbearably lonely place. That was when I began spending more time at the university.

Now, ten years later, upon arriving home in the wake of my sudden sabbatical, I felt lonely to the point of sickness. I had no plans for a journey of discovery, no itinerary for travel, learning, and new experiences. How would I spend my time now, without classes, students, and faculty discourse? I realized I hadn't spent more time at the university to become absorbed in work; I had done it to engage with students and faculty. Apparently, Horace Jennings was not quite the strong-willed, independent misanthrope I imagined myself to be; I needed companionship after all. Only a half hour into my sabbatical, and already I had looked inward and made a discovery. My department chair would be pleased.

I spent the next few days puttering aimlessly about the silent house: the parlor, the attic, the basement; Mary's little conservatory, now empty and imprisoned by snow; the kitchen, where Isis, her cat statuette, judged me from a high shelf. Eventually I settled, shamefully, on reviewing research topics I had suggested to some of my students over the years. Many of them had turned out to be dead ends, and none of them sparked my interest. It soon became apparent that I didn't know what my interests were. In fact, I didn't know myself at all. Unconsciously, over the course of a decade or more, I had lost myself. It was a pathetic, sobering realization.

The telephone rang through the silence, startling me. It had been so long since I'd heard it, I'd forgotten I had one. I ran to the parlor to pick it up.

My department chair.

"Hello, Jennings. How is the sabbatical so far?"

"Oh, you know how it is," I said, picking up a vase filled with dust. "A journey of discovery and all that." I hesitated. "But your advice was valuable."

"Advice?"

"Never mind. To what do I owe this very welcome interruption?"

"It's the Martinez boy. His mother, I mean. She's been trying to reach you. Sent a telegram that sat on your desk for two days, then decided to call me. She sounded very upset. Wouldn't tell me what it's about, but I can guess. I have her phone number in San Francisco. Would you mind returning her call?"

I had no news for her, but that was beside the point. "Of course. I'll call her immediately."

"There's a good man. Then back to your sabbatical with you. And take your time—don't rush into anything."

After hearing that sage advice, I took a deep breath. Then I called the number he'd provided.

"Hello?" said a little girl's voice.

"Is this—may I speak to Mrs. Martinez?" After a moment of confusion, I recalled that Mateo had a little sister. While she went to find her mother, I ran through the list of comforting things I would say to calm her down.

None of them applied. The family car had been used in a theft at a museum in Los Angeles, she told me—a theft of some kind of rock.

And a man matching Mateo's description had been seen driving away from the scene. "Why would he do something like this?" she wailed. "No lo creo! He is a good boy, a good boy!" She began to sob.

It must be a mistake. The police have confused him with another boy. Mateo could be boneheaded, but he was no criminal. Of that, I felt certain.

"You must have Mr. Martinez go to Los Angeles," I told her. "He can meet with the police. I'm sure he can straighten them out."

More sobbing, mixed with Spanish. I caught the word "muerto" and realized she was telling me that her husband had died. She had no one else who could help, nowhere else to turn. She sounded desperate.

I listened to her cry. What could be done for her? Who could possibly help? I thought furiously. And then something broke inside me. There was only one answer. Damn it all.

"It's alright, Mrs. Martinez. I will come to San Francisco. I will meet with you, then I will go to Los Angeles and find Mateo."

Her sobs relented, turning from anguish to gratitude as we exchanged dates and plans for my arrival. She thanked me more times than I could count.

I hung up the phone, dazed. I felt proud, stupid, and a little sick. What had I just done? Only then did I recall my department chair's final piece of advice: "Don't rush into anything."

So I was going to San Francisco. But I wouldn't be going alone. I knew I would need help. And I knew just who to call.

The next afternoon, there was a knock at my door. I opened it, admitting a blast of frigid air, to find Helen Parker beaming at me in a wool coat, boots, and a round, dowdy hat pulled so low it nearly covered her eyes. She still managed to look wiry and stylish. She gave me a hug and darted inside.

I led her to the parlor, with its club chairs, tasteful oriental carpet, grandfather clock, and many flowerless vases. When she was free of her coat, boots, and hat, hot tea in hand, we discussed where Mateo could have gone.

I had assumed we would review the facts at length, carefully, over the course of several hours; but in minutes her teacup was empty, her fingers drumming on her armrest. Helen, a geologist like Mateo, had many gifts; patience was not among them.

"I don't understand why we're discussing this. We know where Mateo went. He's in Los Angeles."

"The car is in Los Angeles, yes," I said. "How can you be sure Mateo is there as well?"

"Logic, Professor. The police report says that someone matching Mateo's description was driving the car away from the museum. Rocks were taken from the museum. Mateo is a geologist."

"You think he stole them?"

"I think we can't ignore the obvious, no matter how much we'd like to," she said.

Silence returned to the parlor, but for the ever-present ticking of the grandfather clock and the occasional gust of wind rattling the flue chain in the fireplace. "Miss Parker, if you think it's possible he stole from the museum, we'll consider it. What else can you tell me about him—his interests, his frame of mind?"

"He's fascinated by theories about the structure of the earth and phenomena in the earth's crust. He's fluent in Latin—he uses it to study ancient history, and he correlates human and geological events to learn more about slow geological processes."

"We know all that. What about his tastes, predilections, vices?" I leaned forward in the club chair. "Do you of anything that could shed light on why he would abandon a career opportunity to do something else? Something illicit?"

Her brow furrowed, but she didn't hesitate. Helen rarely did. "No," she said.

"An addiction, then? Opium? Alcohol? Gambling?"

"No. Not unless you count his weakness for Clark Bars. He's a Boy

Scout. You know Mateo, Professor."

Time to swim out further than I preferred. "Not as well as you. You two were close." I waited for a reaction, but her gray eyes were impassive, the corners of her mouth unchanged. I pressed on. "Is it possible that he met a woman, and that she has somehow…led him astray?"

She looked down at her empty teacup for a moment, then back at me with far-seeing, intelligent eyes that I had learned to trust. "Possible, but I would say unlikely."

"What, then?" I asked in frustration. "What could have driven him to steal rocks from a museum?"

Another gust rattled the flue chain again. I put down my tea, stomped over to the fireplace and yanked it taut. Before I knew it, I was pacing around the parlor the way I sometimes do in the classroom when I am vexed by a student's question. I felt those eyes on me.

"We need to know what kind of rocks were taken," she said.

"Yes. Of course. And we'll need to examine his home to see if he left any clues." From the mantle, I picked up the leather-bound journal Mary had given me when I retired from consulting engineering to become a professor. *This is for your next chapter, my dear professor. Please fill it with memories, not lectures.* It had been empty for many years—until yesterday, when I began using it to jot down notes for this trip. But I was determined to make it a proper journal, just as Mary had wanted.

We spent an hour completing the logistics for our journey to California. Then Helen pulled on her boots and long wool coat, and I handed her that little, round hat, now nearly dry. She pulled it on, her eyes downcast. In place of her usual confident smile, she bit her lip.

"We'll find him," I said. The words did not come easily.

She gave me another little hug, then she was gone, into the cold, darkening afternoon.

CHAPTER

5

THE ENEMY

Shila Ghiss

I am spellbound by the contents of the journal hidden behind the mural. It primarily describes how our nucleic acids set the patterns for our physiology. A part of it describes how those acids may be altered by the introduction of new genetic material: human blood. The jar contains a kind of catalyst.

My father, it seems, had prepared this for me, in anticipation of this very day.

I am about to hide the journal back inside the mural when Sesh slides into the room unannounced. He has always taken such liberties, especially where I am concerned. But now is not the time for reproval. I close the journal and slide it aside, rising from the desk.

"Have you spoken to the king?" I ask.

He regards me, his green eyes looking me up and down, his tongue flicking.

"Yes. He has taken the Science Master's side. And he wants me to take the Commander as well, whose idea of subtlety is to empty the sleep chamber and wage war. Now I need to find new humans for both of them. Leaders." He spits in disgust. "It will take time. Time we do not have." He makes a circuit of the room, examining the shelves, now empty but for a few derelict human artifacts, then makes his way to the desk.

"And?"

"And he has agreed to your request, Shila. He will let you visit the surface, so long as you do so under my supervision."

"*Your* supervision?"

"Naturally," he says, bringing his head close, his tongue flicking, sampling the air for my pheromones. "I have had more contact with the enemy than anyone. I have within me the thoughts and memories of a prominent, powerful human; that is why I was made Inquisitor. My knowledge will prevent you from exposing us."

I slip away from him, picking up the journal and retreating to the other side of the desk.

I know Sesh speaks the truth: I need him. But his true purpose is as clear to me as it was to my father. He wants to mate with me—to join his bloodline to the king's, and gain advantage. Truth and deception, as always.

"When will we depart?"

"Soon," he says. "But first you must prepare."

"The Science Master has my father's journals, but for this outdated primer," I say, tossing the journal into the trash bin as if it were not the key to all of my hopes. "There is nothing more for me to take. I am prepared."

"You are not," he counters. "In the first place, you do not understand our mission."

"Once the research is completed, we will spread a pathogen to infect the enemy," I tell him. "The journals describe—"

"That is not our mission, Shila. Your father tried that ten years ago, and he failed. But in doing so, he developed a drug that renders the enemy compliant, subservient. The Science Master will manage the production of this drug in large quantities. You will obtain the resources to support production, while I work to spread it throughout their population centers. "

Doubt prickles me from head to tail. I recall reading my father's notes on this drug years ago. It was a mere footnote in his research. I suspect the king knows nothing of it—he is expecting a pathogen, not a drug. Sesh is up to something.

He sees my doubt, and he enjoys it greatly, his pupils dilating with delight. "Research on the pathogen will take years to complete, as you well know. The drug is ready now, and it is far simpler—a matter of chemistry, not culturing. That is our path to victory." He draws back, as if to see me more clearly. "But there is more difficult preparation you must undertake."

I know what he is referring to, but I wait for him to enlighten me. He slithers around me, eyes flicking up and down as if searching me for some hidden flaw.

"To walk among the enemy, you must take their form," he says. "You know what this means."

"As well as you do."

He snorts. "I think not."

"We shall see," I tell him. "But first, I will examine this human. I would like to be certain that she is healthy."

His gaze meets mine in a silent battle of wills. We have known each other almost from birth: me, the only survivor of our brood, a daughter of scientists, niece to our childless king; and him, scion of a rival clan, bright and ambitious. He knows I am cautious, like my father, while he is cleverer and bolder than I. Perhaps that is why my father supported Sesh's many initiatives—except his advances towards me. Perhaps he, like Sesh, felt that change has come too slowly for our people. Now that I am past my prime, I am inclined to agree.

"Very well," he says at last. "Then let us do it now. There is no time to waste. Have you begun fasting?"

"Yes," I lied.

"Good. You must fast for three days. Then you will dine well."

Not if I can help it.

I am in a part of our colony I rarely see, far from my home, and many feet above it. Close to the surface. It is damper, with more sand and soil. The air here is sweeter, though I taste something foreign and earthy. The scent of the enemy, Sesh tells me. Before us is a round door of white stone. Next to it, in a circle of light from an oil lamp, a guard is curled around a long spear. His skin is tight and overdue for shedding. A very young guard, indeed.

"The ape is behind this door?"

"They are not apes," he says. "You must not think of them so. They are different. Hairless, for the most part. Not nearly as muscular. But with a highly developed brain."

"I do not need a lecture on their anatomy," I tell him. "I have read my father's notes—"

"Your father is dead, and this is not a laboratory!" he cries. I have never heard Sesh raise his voice, and it chills me. He grabs my arm and squeezes it hard. "Listen to me, Shila, and do exactly as I tell you. Do not question my instructions, and do not assume it is helpless. I bear bruises from its capture."

I bow my head. Sesh bobs his, and the guard rolls back the stone door. The earthy taste of the enemy—the human—fills the air, overpowering, unpleasant, and alarming.

I have only seen a human once, long ago, and it was dead. My father had the cadaver in his laboratory. I remember being frightened by it—especially the hair, by far the most disgusting part of mammalian anatomy.

The cell is narrow and deep. The dim green luminescence of the lichen does not reach the back wall. Something moves there, in the darkness.

My heart pounds, and I coil into myself. My instinct tells me to flee. But Sesh takes the lamp and slides into the cell. He turns toward me expectantly. I must follow.

We advance toward the rear of the cell. The human's breathing echoes off the stone walls, seeming to come from everywhere at once. Could it be lurking above us? I recall that apes are adept at climbing. I look up, but it is not there. Sesh sees me looking up, and I sense he is amused, tasting my fear. Then I hear the soft padding of the human's feet just ahead.

The lamplight finds it pressed against the back wall. It watches us with white eyes, pale, with long, loathsome hair atop its head: black with waves of gray, and cloth covering the soft, hairless flesh of its body. An adult female. Smaller than I expected.

Its mouth moves, and a rapid succession of sounds issues, tones rising and falling. A strange language, like nothing I have heard.

"Can you understand it?" I ask Sesh.

"Of course," he replies.

"Well?" I do not take my eyes from it. Not for a moment.

"It asks what we are. It realizes that we are intelligent."

I find the creature's awareness of us disturbing. "Can you converse with it?"

Sesh hisses his displeasure at my query. "Not in this form. You are not here to parlay with this human, Shila; you are here to examine it. I have already spoken with it at length. It is willful, defiant, and deceptive, like all of its species. Do not pity it."

I move closer. The human is not tied or chained. She meets my gaze. I want to look away, but I cannot. Her strange language fills the room again. Now it is directed at me. Calm. Purposeful.

"Enough," says Sesh. "I will leave it to you. It is fast, but you are faster. Catch it and make your examination. See that you do not harm it before consuming it, or its injuries will be yours when you assume its form."

"It must be alive when I consume it?"

"Of course, if you want its knowledge. And you cannot walk among them without it." His head tilts to one side as he hands me the lamp. "Has your father explained none of this to you, 'Master of Life Sciences'? Or was his spiritual tutelage as wanting as his research?"

He calls the guard, and the stone door rolls closed behind him, leaving me alone with the enemy.

To my surprise, the human emerges from the darkness. She watches me. On slender legs, she walks toward me, slowly. Her arms are longer than mine, perhaps even stronger, but they end in clawless fingers. She cannot possibly harm me...

Can she?

As she nears, I see a flash of silver on one of her wrists. A weapon? I rise to my full height, towering over her.

"Stop!" My voice echoes off the stone walls.

She does, and for a moment, I wonder if she understands me. I coil up next to her. Carefully, I bring a claw to her wrist, where I can see the source of the flash: a band of silver metal. It glows green in the lichen's luminescence.

Her eyes meet mine. I bring my head close to examine the band. Melodious rising tones issue from her mouth as she slips the band from her wrist and offers it to me. It bears symbols that might be mountains, and a bird with great wings. In its center is an oval of turquoise. This is no weapon, merely an adornment. Strange and beautiful.

I return it to her, and her eyes meet mine again, without fear. Can I push her further? *She is ready*, I think. *As am I.*

From a pouch I draw one of our probes and hold it before her: a small sphere with a covered needle extending from it.

She reaches for it, slowly and tentatively. When I do not object, she takes it from me and brings it closer to the light of the oil lamp, examining it, rotating it this way and that. More tones, rising as she taps her finger gently on the covered needle: a question. One that I cannot understand or answer.

I take the probe back from her and pull off the cover, exposing the needle. I expect her to flinch; instead, she does something with her head—not a bob, exactly, but something like it—then rolls back the fabric she wears over her arm. She places one of her slender fingers at the bend, where I can see a blood vessel.

This human is showing me where to draw her blood! It is a relief, and very fortunate; I was about to place the probe in the middle of her thorax.

I push the needle in ever so gently as she watches in fascination.

A slight squeeze of the ball activates the probe, drawing her blood. A moment later, it is done. I withdraw the needle and wipe her arm with a sterile cloth.

"I have never met an anthropologist before," I tell her. "I admire your courage."

She regards me quizzically.

I bob my head, return to the stone door, and summon the guard.

"See that she is cared for—fed, watered, and bathed. Leave the lamp in the cell, and refill it so she is not left in darkness. In three days, she is to be brought to my quarters. Have her garments washed and dried for her. Notify me or the Inquisitor of any issues. Clear?"

Coiled around his spear, his gray scales stretched tight, the young guard looked uncomfortable. But he replied with the clarity and sharpness that accompanies youths who enthusiastically follow orders.

"Clear, Royal One."

CHAPTER 6

A CHANGE OF SEASONS

Horace Jennings

The train whistled and puffed its way out of Providence, and gradually the brick and iron cityscape fell behind. I already missed the city—the familiar streets, the bookshops, and the modest public works projects I'd helped engineer: buildings, ferry landings, little bridges over the river. One by one they slipped by, a cavalcade of memories. They cheered me as we passed, offered reassurance. Then they disappeared.

My only visit to San Francisco had been in 1906, in the wake of the great earthquake. I'd hoped to be of some use performing safety inspections for the buildings left standing. Exactly the kind of naïve, idealistic idiocy that I'd come to deplore in myself. *God, the stupidity!* The entire city flattened by the quake, then the few remaining buildings engulfed in a devastating fire. Thousands dead. And me, a young fool engineer, entering the rare standing building and deeming it safe or unsafe, as if the dazed survivors, grieving over lost family, still cared for their safety. I'd examined perhaps a hundred buildings over the course of a few weeks; then, exhausted and disheartened, returned home.

The train clacked along, and the cityscape gave way to snow-covered farms and distant silos. My thoughts turned back to Mateo's desertion, and its consequences for me. I wished I were the kind of professional who cared not in the least what others thought of him: hardened, insensitive. Such were so many of the men I met in industry and academia—trailblazers in business, science, and technology. I despised them, envied them, but could never be like them. Mary had told me on more than one occasion that this was what she loved most about me; but I have long suspected that empathy is a weakness that will be my undoing. My choice of sabbaticals seemed now to be proof positive. It was a fool's errand, and no doubt.

After an hour of brooding, I chastened myself, determined to visit the lounge car and leave my misgivings behind. I shrugged on my Harris tweed, ran a comb through my thinning hair, picked up the paper, and made my way there.

We pulled into Chicago's Union Station just before noon the next day. Ellis was waiting for us on the platform, a briefcase at his side. I wasn't quite prepared for how good it felt to see him again, or to see how he had aged from a dynamic consulting engineer to a stodgy professor like me in his mid-fifties. But that impression was dispelled as soon as he greeted me.

"Horace Jennings, as I live and breathe!" he said, shaking my hand vigorously. "How are you?"

"Like you, doing my best to prepare the next generation. How are you, Charles? You must be incredibly busy. You needn't have taken the time to come to the train station, let alone take us to lunch."

"Nonsense!" he said. "We haven't seen each other in ten years. Do you think I'd miss the opportunity to see you when you're only a few miles away?"

I introduced Helen, and we weaved our way through the passengers on the narrow platform, trying not to lose each other. Only when we reached the passenger waiting area did Ellis slow to a stroll. At first I thought he was allowing us to catch our breath. Then, hearing a gasp from Helen, I looked up.

"Good Lord!" We were standing in the Great Hall, Union Station's main waiting room. Soaring more than a hundred feet overhead was a barrel-vaulted skylight more than two hundred feet long. Marble walls rose to meet it on either side, with beautiful rosettes carved along the entire length of the skylight. Enormous, fluted marble columns supported the structure on all sides, with golden Corinthian crowns. Above these stood two dramatic, hooded human figures: Night, bearing an owl; and Day, bearing a rooster.

"How do you like our new station?" Ellis asked, obviously pleased with our reaction. "It opened three years ago. It took four railroads to fund it and ten years to build, but I think the results are well worth it."

"It's…spectacular," was all I could manage.

"Did your firm design this, Professor Ellis?" Helen asked.

"Strauss Engineering? No, Strauss is not my company, it belongs to my employer, a consultant who's been working on the design of the Golden Gate Bridge for many years. He brought me on as a consultant to do the detailed structural design—which, of course, is most of the work."

"So Professor Ellis is a consultant to a consultant, if you are keeping track," I offered.

"Very funny, Horace. But no, my dear, this grand station was the work of Daniel Burnham, a native son of Chicago. A great man, Burnham. Not just an architect, but a true city planner. Pity he died before seeing this building constructed. He was 55, I believe, Horace. The same age as you, if I'm not mistaken. 'Gather ye rosebuds', eh?"

That brought a smile. "Touché, Charles. But he was 65, not 55. And you're only a few years behind me, if *I'm* not mistaken."

We exited to the street and were greeted by a cacophony of car horns, trolley bells, and rumbling overhead from Chicago's elevated train system. Providence had nothing like it. I could not help but marvel at it all.

At lunch, Ellis and I talked about some of our old projects, collaborations, colleagues, and students: which ones were brilliant, difficult, rewarding, fulfilling, etc. I lauded him for the publication of his textbook, *Essentials in the Theory of Framed Structures*, which is now a requirement for structural engineering students at Harvard and Yale and which I myself use for my classes. He, in turn, produced from his briefcase a small plaque and handed it to me. It read:

For Outstanding Achievement in Design
of the Hudson River Tunnel
The American Bridge Company Presents This Award of Honor
To Charles Alton Ellis and Horace James Jennings
December 1, 1918

"This properly belongs to you, Horace. If you hadn't helped me solve the stresses, there'd be no tunnel. I asked them to add your name to the plaque, and they were happy to do it. I intended to give it to you ten years ago, but…"

That was the year Mary had died. Ellis had traveled all the way from Chicago to attend the funeral, but that was in November. I couldn't possibly have expected him to return the following month just to hand me a plaque.

"Of course, I understand," I said. My throat caught, and I barely managed to say, "Thank you, Charles. It means a lot to me." And then, to cover the mist in my eyes: "You might have mailed it." That poked a laugh out of him, and for a moment, we were both young again.

Ellis briefed us on the Golden Gate Bridge, and eventually, the topic turned to Mateo. His role was to help direct the boring crews and help examine the soil samples. Ellis apologized again for dismissing him.

"Mateo's a remarkable young man," he said. "I've not met many students with his knowledge and drive. Do you know he is an expert in Latin? He was also interested in ancient Egyptian hieroglyphs, which, fortunately, I was able to help him with, as I have a friend in the Antiquities Department."

"He asked you to have something translated?" Helen asked excitedly. "What was it?"

"Supposedly some account of the great eruption at Santorini." He shrugged. "Not an original source, of course, just something recreated on a sheet of paper, supposedly a copy of a copy…you know how that goes."

"The eruption that wiped out the Minoan civilization?" I asked.

"Mateo was probably using the account to date the eruption," Helen said.

"Well, I wouldn't put too much stock in it, Miss Parker," said Ellis. "I think it was someone's attempt at writing a mythic poem in hieroglyphs. 'The Great Worm from Beneath the Earth' or some such nonsense. It read like something Homer's slow-witted cousin might write."

"Do you still have the translation?" she asked.

Ellis seemed confused about all the interest in something so foolish. "Well, I don't know. I gave the translation to Mateo. I recall having it typed, so I may have the draft. I'll look for it and mail it to you, if you know where you're staying. As I say, there's no ancient papyrus or tablet. He brought it to me on a few sheets of looseleaf paper, scratched in pencil. To be honest, I assumed he'd drawn the hieroglyphs himself as part of a joke."

"I see. And what did your friend in Antiquities have to say about them?" I asked.

"Well…" Ellis replied, "he said they were flawless."

CHAPTER
7

TO THE SURFACE

Shila Ghiss

Three days. To plan a life-changing leap into the unknown, three days is both absurdly short and agonizingly long.

I read my father's journal over and over. There is no need for titration or culturing or testing; no need for injections. All I need to do is imbibe the catalyst to sensitize my existing cell receptors to new genetic material, then ingest the blood—as fresh as possible—to trigger the response.

If my father is right, transformation to my human form would follow swiftly, and transformation back to my form would be possible at will, with practice, just as it is for those who consume humans, or any other prey.

If my father is wrong, then what I am about to do is not only heretical and profane, but deadly.

Hours after examining the human, I break the seal on the jar containing the catalyst. I have no way of knowing how long it has been hidden here, behind the mural, but I suspect it has been years. The liquid within is clear and viscous. I sample it with my tongue; metallic and foul-tasting. Over the course of an hour, I drink it all.

At the end of the first day, I empty the human's blood into a small vessel and drink it. It is salty—but also delicious, invigorating. I empty the vessel in seconds. I feel no different, even afterward, when I put out the lamps and lie down to rest.

By late morning on the second day, I begin to feel queasy, as if I had eaten something that disagrees with me. By evening I am ill, and in need of rest.

On the third day, the guard, the human, and Sesh appear in the study. The human, wrapped in a blanket, looks no worse for having spent days in the cell. She seems excited to be here.

Sesh's mood is foul. "Why did you insist on having this creature brought down to your chambers?" he asks. "Why not simply consume it in the cell, near the surface, as others do?"

My mood is equally foul. "Because I prefer to eat food that is clean, in a clean environment. I am not well, and I expect to be no better after gorging myself on this…creature."

The human moves to enter the study, but the guard restrains her.

"If you are not well, then we should stay and assist you," Sesh says. "You may not be capable—"

"I am more than capable, I assure you, Sesh. Please leave me to my task."

He regards me for a long moment with something that might be pity; then he bobs his head. "Very well, Shila. Remember what I have told you. Do not injure her when she struggles. Begin with the head and work toward the feet. I will be back tomorrow with a carrier to take you to the surface. You will be unable to make the climb on your own."

He gestures to the guard, who releases the woman into the study and deposits a basket with her clothes.

They leave, and chaos ensues.

The woman sees the desk, squeals with delight, and runs to it, her blanket flying behind her. Her rising tones beg answers to questions I cannot understand. She inspects every drawer, every shelf, every remaining artifact in the study, chattering all the while.

She is barely getting started when she seems to see the murals for the first time. At the first mural, she points to the great lizards, whoops and cries, and waves her arms wildly. She becomes even more animated when she examines the second mural depicting the Great Retreat. By the time she reaches the third mural, she is sorely in need of a sedative. Unfortunately, the Science Master has taken them all.

I might take one myself, were I to find one. I am nearly helpless with nausea, and my head feels as if it is splitting open. I had planned to save her—to help her escape back to the surface. At the moment, I doubted I could crawl around the desk to reach her.

"You don't understand what this means," she says. "The dinosaurs—all of human history—you've witnessed it! Have records of it! It's—it's the most important discovery of all time!"

"You must go," I tell her, laboring to breathe. "Beyond that door…in the next room, you will find the entry to my private shaft. It leads down to the Chamber of Dreamers…a great cavern. Touch nothing. At the far end there is…an old evacuation shaft…never used. It leads up to the surface…high…above the canyon. Go."

"You can speak?" I hear her say. Her feet slap the floor as she runs around the desk to find me. "Are you ill?" Her hand reaches down to touch my tail, and I see her silver bracelet. Then our eyes meet, and her face turns white. "What—what's happening to you?"

I realize then that I can understand her. What's more, I am speaking her language. I coil my tail to touch my head—but it is not my head that I feel. It is bulbous, fleshy, smooth, and misshapen; and hanging from it is a mass of horrible, disgusting human hair.

I scream, and she screams with me.

———

Fresher air. The hush of skin sliding against stone. A voice brings me to consciousness.

Someone has entered the study.

"Shila."

I can see the desk and the open door beyond. With great effort, I twist my head to see who has entered.

Sesh, come to gloat at my misery.

"I did not think you capable of this," he says, and I await the gloating and judgment he will prescribe. Death, most likely.

But he does not gloat. Instead, he speaks kindly, his tail sliding over me.

"You have done well, Shila. I expected to find the human spared. But you have proven yourself strong."

I do not feel strong. I feel bloated, weak, sick. Something alien is inside me, something that does not belong. I cannot expel it.

After a pause, Sesh continues. "I regret my words earlier. Your father was an able scientist. And though we did not always agree, I never doubted his faith and commitment."

I hear the hum of a motor drawing near. I crane my neck to see what it is: a tracked carrier, accompanied by two guards. They lift me onto it as Sesh supervises. When they are done, Sesh tries to apply a blindfold. I pull my head back, dodging it.

"Where are you taking me?" I rasp.

"To the surface," he says. "You cannot digest such a meal unless your blood is warmed. The surface above here is warm."

"And why may I not see? Is the way secret?"

He laughs—not his usual derisive cackle, but a quiet hiss of amusement.

"No, the way is not secret." He put the blindfold away. "But the surface is bright, bathed in the light of the Father. You are unaccustomed to it. You must cover your eyes, at first. And you must not try to look upon the Father. He watches over us. But we must not look upon him unless he allows it."

I have no intention of looking upon the Father. I do not believe in him. He is but a brightness in the sky, one that we do not yet understand. *What kind of father would allow his children to be banished from his sight? If he truly exists, he watches over no one but our enemies. May the worms take him!*

I accept the blindfold and let Sesh take me where he will.

The carrier crawls for a long time, smoothly and steadily. It supports my head and neck, arms and body, but I am too weak even to coil myself. Much of my body, my legs, my tail, trail behind it, sliding along the floor of whatever passages we travel.

Sesh and the two guards do not speak. I can feel them beside the carrier, subtly disturbing the surrounding air, occasionally lifting my legs and tail as we travel around some bend or corner.

Eventually we climb. We are in a gently sloped passage, and the quiet hum of the carrier grows louder, reverberating as the passage narrows. We continue for a long time.

Finally we stop. There is movement around me, then ahead of me. The rumble of a stone door as it rolls back. And then…

The freshest, sweetest, most wonderful thing I have ever tasted: the air of the surface world. It is fragrant, life-giving, exciting—everything my world is not. I flick my tongue at it, fill my lungs with it, and still I want more.

The carrier crawls forward. It jumps and bumps as we travel over rough, stony ground. Echoes tell me I am in a new cavern, warmer than any I know. Through my blindfold, I sense light. The carrier stops.

"We are here," says Sesh.

I am rolled from the carrier to a flat stone, delightfully hot. It is filled with white light that even the blindfold cannot keep out. My heart beats faster, whether from fear or excitement, I am uncertain.

"Now you must rest," Sesh says. "Your blood is cold, but the Father will soon warm it. Then you will feel your meal being digested, and the strain on your body will be relieved." He does not know that there is no meal to digest.

Let me live long enough to see the surface, even for a short time.

"I am…in the light of the Father?" I can scarcely believe it.

"Yes. Wonderful, is it not?"

My throat is suddenly dry, my tongue barely able to taste the sweet air. "Oh, yes," I hear myself say, my voice quavering, "wonderful…"

It is pure truth.

"Good. Remember this feeling in your moments of doubt, Shila. Moments when you feel your faith slipping away. Remember the Father and the Mother. The enemy cares nothing for them. In their arrogance, they defile the Mother. You will not need black lotus powder to know this; you will see it for yourself."

I hear water pouring. I move slowly towards it, and find that they have placed a stone bowl just outside the light. I put my mouth in and drink. It tastes almost as wonderful as the air.

Sesh tells me I must remain here for two days, and that a guard will remain nearby, hidden, watching for the enemy. On the third day, he will return with the human's clothing and some of the things taken by the Science Master. He will help with my transformation. Then we will depart.

Soon I am alone. I wish that he would stay with me. I do not want to be left alone here. The thought of being discovered by humans frightens me. The thought of becoming one of them now terrifies me.

Thirst. I am thirsty again. I wake in blackness, a darkness beyond my blindfold, and drink the cool water from the stone basin. A draft of cold air flows down on me from above, stirring the air of the cavern. It carries the chirping of insects and pungent scents of small animals I cannot name. I have seen very few of them in my lifetime, and these are different. Yet somehow, I can imagine them clearly, as if my mind is drawing pictures from scents and sounds.

The light of the Father is nowhere to be seen. I slide the blindfold down around my neck and look upwards. At first, there is only blackness. After a moment, I see it: a hole in the cavern ceiling through which the dimmest of light shines—light so dim it would be overwhelmed by the lichen light.

But there is no lichen here, and I need very little light to see. Through the hole in the ceiling I can see tiny points of light within the darkness. I hiss with a joy I have never felt, a wave of energy racing from eyes to tail. These must be stars! I am seeing the night!

Thirst comes again, and white heat on my eyes. I push up the blindfold. Sleep takes me before long.

When next I wake, I am again in the white light of the Father, the light of day. Something is different, however. My nausea is gone. A smell fills my nostrils—an earthy, pungent smell.

The smell of humans.

Instinctively I coil and slide the blindfold from my head.

I am blind, the light stabbing my eyes, the smell of humans filling my nostrils. I hear their noises, voices rising and falling. I coil as tightly as possible, tighter than ever, prepared to strike blindly at the next sound.

"Shila Ghiss, calm yourself."

Sesh.

"You are safe," he says, working the blindfold back over my eyes.

"Humans! I smell humans!"

"They are just the guards. They have transformed, as you and I must now do. If you do this correctly, you will be able change back to your true form at will, though the change is painful and tiring. If you do it incorrectly, you may be stranded in some intermediate state which you may not survive. I will guide you, and your instincts will help. Are you prepared?"

But I have not eaten anyone! What will happen to me?

"Yes," I say. Never in my life have I been less prepared for anything.

"Good. Listen carefully. In consuming the human alive, you have consumed her thoughts, her memories, her fears, desires, and will. You must reveal these slowly, over days, weeks, even years, or they will overwhelm you. Take them singly, and you can master them, add them to your knowledge, and exploit them. Take too many at once, and you will lose yourself—perhaps forever."

His voice rattles through the stillness of the cave, echoing off the walls. Finally, the echoes die, leaving me to tremble at the finality of his words.

"You must first clear your mind. Listen for a thought that is not your own—one that feels quiet and calm. Find that thought and reject all others. I will use a ritual to help you start the transformation and manage the pace of it. It may be long. Once started, it cannot be stopped. Are you ready to begin?"

"Yes," I say. "Please don't leave me."

"I am here, Shila. I won't leave you. Let us begin."

He begins to chant slowly, quietly. Some fable about the Father, the Mother, the king. Watching over us, protecting us. But they didn't protect us from the great lizards or the apes. They didn't protect my siblings in their eggs, my mother from disease, or my father from whatever killed him. Will they protect me from the humans?

Something clings to my wrist. I grope until I find it: the silver bracelet! The woman must have put it on me before she fled. I grasp it, pull it free, and peel back the blindfold enough to peek at it: a beautiful blue stone; a bird with great, flat wings; and four mountains. A gift from the human I set free.

Suddenly my claws retract and burn with pain. My arms and legs swell, and I watch as my skin tightens, my scales distort. White hot pain flashes down my neck and back, as if something is crushing my spine. I cannot speak or breathe or think. My skull rings, my vision blurs, and my tongue swells.

This is my end. I regret not loving my father, lying to the king, my contempt for the gods, for Sesh. I am a fool…

CHAPTER
8

GOLDEN GATE

Horace Jennings

We pulled into San Francisco two nights later, a cool, moist fog greeting us as we exited the train. After many weeks of New England winter, it felt wonderful.

There was no trace of the devastated San Francisco I had visited more than 20 years ago. It had been reborn. Before us was a beautiful, vibrant city: lovely hills, cable cars, stately public buildings, quaint houses and, when our cable car crested a hill, a beautiful bay. People hopped on, conversed briefly with acquaintances, then wished each other good morning and hopped off. And it was a good morning, after all: sunshine, a light breeze, and a cool but tolerable temperature. It was a strange, wonderful place, a bright, airy gem of a city. All of Providence seemed cold, dark, and stuffy by comparison.

The Martinez family home was a second-floor apartment over a corner market that was the family business—closed, locked, and boarded. Mrs. Martinez was frail and wizened beyond what I'd expected, with wispy gray hair and a careworn face older than mine. Her quiet demeanor made her previous outbursts on the telephone all the more heart-wrenching.

The sister that I had ascribed to Mateo was actually his niece, Juanita, perhaps nine years old, the daughter of Mateo's older brother, who died in the war. No one else lived there, and no one was coming to help Mrs. Martinez anytime soon.

She seated us at the kitchen table, and we began to elicit the facts.

She last saw Mateo at the end of July. By then he had already been spending less time at the bridge site and more in the spare bedroom that they had converted into an office for him. He didn't discuss his work or bring any visitors home. He hadn't met with anyone as far as she knew, nor had he received phone calls at home. He spent most of his time in his office, reading. She thought he might have tried his hand at baking something—a dessert, maybe.

We exchanged glances. "A dessert? Helen, did Mateo bake things?"

"Never. He could barely boil water."

"Well, was he baking something for himself, or was he making a lot of dessert for, say, several people?"

Helen, after an exchange in Spanish with Mrs. Martinez, shook her head. "She didn't see anything. She only smelled a lingering odor of something sweet. There were no empty pans or traces of food."

"Alright, let's put that aside for now," I suggested, and pressed on.

In the days before he disappeared, did he leave the house? Yes. For work or for something else? She had no way of knowing. Did he take the car on these occasions? No. Either he was picked up, or wherever he was going was accessible by trolley.

"That leaves out the bridge site," I said.

"Yes, but it leaves *in* a good portion of the city," Helen replied.

"Alright. It's time to visit his office."

Mrs. Martinez led the way down a hallway, past several bedrooms, and around a corner, Juanita tagging along behind us. She opened a door and gave some explanation in Spanish. Helen translated: apart from dusting, nothing in Mateo's office had been disturbed since he was last here.

The room was set up like a study. To the left, a floor to ceiling bookshelf lined with books and the occasional photo; in the center, a desk with multiple drawers and trays full of papers, all as neat as a pin; and curiously, against the back wall, a table with a Bunsen burner, a couple of empty beakers, and a few test tubes in a rack.

"I didn't expect he'd set up a lab," I said.

"Hardly a lab," said Helen. "He was probably just doing an occasional test of minerals for his own interest." She sat down at his desk and began going through the drawers.

I began with the bookshelf, browsing the many books and photos. One photo brought a smile—one that I was too slow and too stupid to hide from Helen.

"What?" she asked.

"Nothing—just some personal photos."

Helen had learned to read me like a book. "Out with it," she said, rising from the chair.

I put my back to the bookcase and faced her. "It's nothing. Let's focus on his work, shall we?"

She looked up at me for a moment—then snatched the photo from behind me before I could say another word. She stared at it for a moment.

"Oh God," she whispered.

It was a photo of Mateo and Helen, taken at a field site somewhere. They stood against a rock wall, Mateo in neat, pressed khaki shorts and shirt, Helen in work pants and hiking boots, a belt with field tools around her waist. Arms over each other's shoulders. Whoever took the photo had caught them laughing. They looked very happy.

"It's alright," I said quietly. "We'll find him. I promise." I steered her back to the desk. "Let's carry on."

The books were mostly geology and history texts, with a few Latin texts as well. Nothing Egyptian or Greek. The lab table held litmus paper, forceps, and a few other supplies. One of the test tubes had a fine black powder residue in it. Nothing of interest. I turned on the gas supply and lit the Bunsen burner to see if it worked. It did.

"The desk has his notes about the borings, bridge design, and site rules," Helen said. "There's a printed site map. It looks like he also traced a copy of the boring location plan, probably so he could help plan the work from home."

"Any chance there's a journal?" I asked, walking over.

"Afraid not."

On the desktop was a pad of writing tablet. I began flipping through it. The first half of it was filled with notes from the project.

"I went through that," Helen said. "Just notes on the project and boring plan."

"What's this?" In the margins of the last few pages, there were some doodles: a crescent moon on its side, cup up; and a series of snakes, finely drawn, complete with scales. "He's something of an artist, isn't he?"

"Yes," she said, "he's quite good. He even did a portrait of me once. I hope we don't find that here."

Then she looked down. "What's this?" There was a small trash bin behind the desk, all but empty. She reached into it and pulled out some wrappers—Clark bar wrappers. She held them up triumphantly.

"Congratulations," I said. Then: "Wait a minute." In the bin, under the wrappers and now revealed, was a crumpled piece of paper. I put it on the desktop and smoothed it out. In Mateo's neat handwriting was a list entitled "SFPL Reading List." There were seven items on the list. "SFPL?"

"Must be San Francisco Public Library," said Helen.

"What's our boy been reading?"

Helen scanned the list. "Let's see…Oh, Arthur Holmes! 'Mantle Convection and Continental Drift', *Proceedings of the Royal Geological Society*…ah, that's a classic."

I saw she was serious. "I'll take your word for it. What else?"

"This one's in German…" She handed it to me.

My German was poor, but good enough to read the title. "*The Origin of Continents and Oceans.* Alfred Wegener."

"Yes, of course," she said. "Wegener's theory of continental drift was the forerunner for which Holmes later provided a sound basis."

I'd thought it impossible to feel more ignorant, but once again, I was mistaken. "Oh yes, of course. See if any of those books are on the bookshelf. I'd like to know when he visited the library last."

"Right. Professor, you'd better not leave that Bunsen burner on."

"Oh my, yes." I moved to the table to shut it off—and then a thought struck me. I picked up the test tube with the residue in it and tapped it lightly against the table so that the powder would collect at the bottom of the tube. Then, using the forceps, I ran it slowly over the flame.

"What are you doing?" Helen asked.

"Just following a hunch."

After a few minutes, she turned from the bookshelf. "None of those books are here. He must have read them and returned them to the library. I suppose we could go to the library, check them out, and see when he returned them. What do you think, Professor? Professor?"

Helen's voice receded as the sweet smoke from the test tube brings a memory—or is it a daydream?

I am in my childhood home in Providence, beneath the old pear tree, a ripe brown pear in my hand. I bring it to my lips and inhale the familiar fragrance of a lazy summer day. I close my eyes and bite almost to the core. The soft, sweet fruit fills my mouth, sticky nectar runs down my chin, my throat. It tastes like picnics and pie and Mother and fireworks and recess. Like home.

I open my eyes to take another bite. Worms. Tiny white worms wiggle slowly in the pear. Half bitten. I drop the pear, sickened. I feel them inside me. I am filled with them. My skin is too tight. It crawls. Too tight. It tears, bursts, and I slither out of it. My new skin is soft and scaly and supple. I am alive, relieved. Grown up. I have done what I must. My duty. The buildings and the little bridges I designed cheer me. The gates and the citadel I have saved cheer me. The king cheers me, and the yellow crescent on his forehead, cup up, seems to smile. Mother and Mary and Ellis and Helen and Mrs. Martinez cheer me, sliding and coiling and bobbing their heads. I have saved them all.

But where the pear has fallen, the brown earth trembles. Deep, impossibly deep below, behemoths swim through the blood of the Earth like great parasites, white, twisting, burning. I have summoned them. *No.* The ground shakes and lifts beneath me. My home collapses. The buildings and bridges fall. Mary and Mother and Helen and Ellis fall. The wide world wracks and cracks open. Towers of white flesh slide upward. *No!* Mouths ringed with tentacles tear our limbs and heads from us. I scream.

CHAPTER

9

STRANGERS IN A STRANGE LAND

Shila Ghiss

Sesh throws a blanket over me, his chanting stopped as if he has forgotten the words.

I stand on wobbly legs, naked beneath the blanket, hot-blooded, yet cold. My sense of smell is blunted. I stick out my tongue, but I taste nothing. I remove the blindfold entirely, and though the light is still very bright, I can see.

Something is wrong with my vision. There are so many colors, so vibrant, like the maps in the Kings Hall. Can this be how humans see?

Sesh steps back in amazement as two strong young human males look on in amusement. "You have transformed in seconds! How have you done this?"

I try to answer him, but my tongue is thick in my mouth. "Ssssssh-sssss-gh-sssss…" The young men snicker. Then I find the words—human words. "I do not know. I followed your guidance. I found a thought."

He bids me dress in the woman's raiment, a confusing array of garments, black and white, that seem to serve no purpose. I retreat behind a rock because, for someone reason, I don't want anyone to see me naked.

I select a small garment and try putting an arm through it, but it does not seem to fit.

"Are you certain these are the correct garments?" I ask Sesh. From the other side of the rock, the guards resume their snickering.

Moments later, I have dressed without thinking, my muscles

knowing what I do not.

I march over to the guards. "Have you nothing better to do? Perhaps I should speak to the king. I am certain that he can find tasks suitable for you."

They blanch and bow from the neck. Then they step backward and turn away. A rush of satisfaction fills me; but a voice inside cautions me against pride and vengeance.

It is not my voice.

I watch with fascination as Sesh transforms. His arms and legs grow as his body shrinks. His head squashes into an oval, and gray hair sprouts from it. His transformation complete, he dresses in garments from his own satchel.

I find myself admiring him. "You seem…the same, Sesh. Yet better, in some ways. This body suits you."

He smiles at me with a small mouth and tiny teeth. "I am glad you like it. You and I wear older skins. Though our bodies are weaker, you will find that older humans have often amassed knowledge, power, and respect. The guards are younger. They will need speed and strength for their tasks." He looks me up and down. "Your human form is also pleasing." He hesitates. "I am glad you could subdue it without injuring it." He signals the guards, and they collect our things.

Along the cavern wall, a wide rock ledge rises like a ramp and winds around a bend where the cavern seems to turn back. There I can see light. We climb this ramp until we reach the mouth of the cave. The warm, delicious, sweet air washes over me like a steady current. We step outside, and…

…I must cover my eyes. It is bright—so dazzling that I fear I will never be able to see in this world. But after a minute, my eyes adjust, and I can see near and far with perfect clarity. Through the human's remarkable eyes, I can see the sandy floor of a canyon and a rushing river, green plants at its banks. Rocky walls run high above us, one bathed in the light of the Father—in sunlight: red and pink and tan; the other deep in shade: brown and gray and black.

Above us is an endless ocean of blue light, of nothingness, islands of soft white drifting slowly across. I grow dizzy looking at it, looking into infinity, and for an instant I feel as if I will fall up, forever. Instead, I fall down.

Sesh takes my arm and helps me to my feet. "Are you alright, Shila?"

"Yes…it is just…I never imagined that the surface could be so…." Something in me—something human—completes my thought. My eyes blur with wetness.

"Yes," Sesh says. "It is our heritage. That is why we must reclaim it."

—ɷɷ—

The human building stands alone near the side of the canyon. It is squat, square, and ugly, yet a part of me admires its straight lines and symmetry. Three large pipes run down the canyon wall, disappearing behind it. From its roof, wires stretch to a tall steel tower, then out of sight. We have walked over an hour to get here, and we now stand beneath a tree.

"What is this place?" I ask, kneeling to run my fingers along the course, live wood of the trunk and down over the tops of its roots. A rustle overhead tells me a small animal is moving among the branches.

"The power plant I spoke of," Sesh replies.

I have seen our colony's power plant, which captures heat from deep within the Earth to generate electricity. This plant looks nothing like ours.

"This plant conducts heat from deep with the Mother? How so? Those pipes lead up the canyon wall, not down."

"Power generation is different on the surface," Sesh says. "Humans don't use the Mother's heat; they create their own heat by burning ancient organic materials."

I stuck out my tongue, but could taste nothing. I inhaled through my nose and smelled a wondrous mixture of earth and plants—but nothing burning. I told Sesh as much.

He turned his face slowly, left, then right, then left again, as if tracking a rodent for a meal. "No," he said. "This plant is different. It converts the power of running water to electricity."

It sounds like a story for younglings. "How could it possibly do that?"

He looks down at me, and the gray hairs above his eyes draw together. "Shila Ghiss, if you wish to understand human technology, you must either consume an engineer or do your own research. For discretion's sake, I suggest the latter. Their codices are kept in libraries, and anyone may review them. That is how I have learned. But I suggest you confine yourself to studying life sciences, else you will be here for many years." He nods to the guards, and the three of them begin walking toward the building.

"Sesh!" I hiss. "You will be seen!"

He waves for me to join them. "Come. No need to fear."

We walk around the side of the building to a wide, flat area with a variety of metal machines in neat rows. All of them have wheels. Sesh opens a door on one of them and sits inside, waving impatiently for me to join him. As I get in, a sharp sound issues from the machine, then the loud thrum of a motor. It startles me so, I hit my head on the ceiling.

"What is this contraption?" Even as I ask, I know the answer.

"A conveyance. It will carry us far from here, to a large human settlement. That is where you will carry out your work." He is about to move a lever when he pauses. "Does your human know how to drive?"

"I don't think so," I say uncertainly.

"Just as well," he says. "Fortunately, I do." He moves the lever, and the vehicle rolls forward and sweeps around to a road. The guards raise their hands in what I recognize as a parting gesture.

"Are they not coming with us?" I ask.

"Of course not," he says. "They work here."

47

CHAPTER
10

NAME AND ADDRESS

Horace Jennings

I opened my eyes to find anxious faces staring down at me: Mrs. Martinez and Helen. Her hand was over mine.

"Please tell me you're alright," she said.

I was lying on the floor of Mateo's study. Someone had put a pillow under my head and a blanket over me. There was a faint smell of burnt caramel. My forehead hurt.

"I'm fine," I said hoarsely. "What happened?"

"I think you inhaled fumes from whatever you were burning in that test tube," said Helen. "You fainted. Hit your head on the way down. I thought you were going into shock."

"Damned stupid of me. Lucky it wasn't arsenic I was inhaling."

Mrs. Martinez began putting a second pillow under my head—then stopped, sniffed the air and cried, "El postre de Mateo! El postre!" For an awful moment, I thought she might be sharing the delusion I had.

Helen read my quizzical expression. "She says that odor—it's Mateo's pastry."

Relief. Little Juanita stepped over shyly with a glass of water. She handed it to Helen, who helped me sit up. "Well, that's one puzzle piece down."

I sipped some of the water. "I may have found another."

I described my vision to Helen. It was not lost on us that it seemed to fit with Ellis's description of the text Mateo had asked him to translate, and the doodles as well, though they seemed small and innocuous. We didn't know what to make of it. We were professionals—scientists—and not given to flights of fancy. Or so we believed.

My hands trembled, my voice quavered, and though I tried to hide behind the towel and ice they had me hold to my forehead, it was apparent to them. They wouldn't hear of me visiting the library. Helen would investigate the dates of the books on Mateo's reading list. If we were fortunate, one date might be recent enough to coincide with the museum theft and help prove Mateo's innocence. I reminded her that she needn't check out the books or obtain a library card; she need only examine the inside of the back covers for the dates that they were checked out.

"Hmmph." Helen slipped a jacket over her sweater and donned a maroon beret. "I'm a trained researcher, Professor. I think I can date a few library books. Honestly, sometimes I think you have no confidence in me at all." She grabbed her gloves and handbag and headed for the door.

"I have every confidence in you, my dear," I called after her. And then quietly, after the door had closed: "It is the librarian I fear for."

I was commanded to rest in Mateo's bedroom, where a soft bed awaited me, along with the police report. I gladly accepted both.

But the LAPD report was not particularly helpful. It only mentioned that a car with matching description and license plate may have been involved in a crime. The location given was a museum, the investigating officer one Harry Raymond. I tossed it aside, put my head back, and closed my eyes.

I awoke to the sound of voices. Helen had returned from the library. The results were mixed.

"All of those of books were checked out over the first three months of Mateo's time here," she reported. "Before there were any issues with his attendance at work."

"Then it's a dead end," I said, deflated.

49

"Not entirely," she said.

I was in no mood for riddles. "Well? Are you going to make me guess?"

"Mateo's was not the last name on the pocket. One more person had signed out the first three publications—the same name each time: S. Smith." She drew a folded paper out of her handbag and handed it to me. Her list had the names, library card numbers, and dates; Smith had signed out the first three books about three weeks after Mateo.

"Were you able to find out anything more about Smith? What about his card number? Couldn't the librarian give you his full name and address?"

"I asked, but…"

Helen's uncharacteristic hesitation was highly suspect. "Miss Parker, would you care to elaborate?"

"I got thrown out," she said miserably. "The librarian wasn't being very helpful. I tried to explain why the information is so important, but she wouldn't hear it. I'm afraid we got into a bit of a shouting match. Then they escorted me out."

"A shouting match."

"Yes."

"In a library."

She shrugged.

Smith. Why couldn't the name have been something less common, like Dostoevsky or Schmeckpepper? Well, one plays the cards one is dealt.

"Cheer up, Miss Parker. Even a 'trained researcher' can have a bad day. It's not the end of the world."

We said our goodbyes and were about to leave when Juanita ran up to Helen. "Miss Parker! Nana says you should take this with you." It was the photo from the Mateo's office.

"Oh—no, I couldn't."

"Please," Mrs. Martinez said. "You take it. You need it. To show to police and other people so you find him. Please."

Helen hesitated, then to my relief, she nodded, slipping the photo into her handbag. We needed that photo for many reasons—perhaps mainly to remind us not to give up.

The bridge site was our last stop in San Francisco before heading south to see the police in Los Angeles. A taxi dropped us off on a dirt road near the shore, outside a gated area. It was a cold, windy, muddy place. A guard checked our names against the visitor's list and complained that Helen was not on the list; to which I replied that I would be happy to phone Mr. Ellis and have him sort it out. A minute later, we were entering our names and addresses into the visitor's register. I looked at the sign-in sheet. The site hadn't received many visitors. I flipped back a few pages, then a few more.

It was there, at the bottom of the last sheet for June 1927. A signature: Samuel Smith. There was also an address: 46 Navy Street, Los Angeles, California.

CHAPTER
11

SOUTHBOUND

Shila Ghiss

The human carrier moves at an alarmingly high speed over the smooth road. As we crest the mountains and begin our descent, I understand the enormity of my task. I see more than isolated settlements; I see vast cultivated fields, villages, and then, in the distance, a great city, with a building taller than any we have ever built. The maps of the King's Hall are misleading; humans are everywhere. They appear to dominate the entire surface world.

We cannot possibly produce enough of any substance to drug this many humans. Sesh must know this. He must have an alternate plan. I must find out what it is.

In any event, I am grateful that my task is merely to drug them, for eradicating them would require death on an apocalyptic scale. *How could any of us even have considered such a thing?* I think of the woman in my father's study, her curiosity and intelligence, and I feel sick inside.

As we reach a lower altitude, the car becomes warm. Sesh cranks down his window, and I do likewise. The rush of air through the open windows is a wonderful sensation, like a spray of water that is not wet; but it tosses my hair about my head and in front of my eyes. I find it annoying.

"As soon as we reach a place of safety, I intend to cut off all of this hair," I tell Sesh. I have to shout above the wind.

"You cannot," he shouts back.

"Of course I can." His lack of understanding of basic human anatomy surprises me. From my father's research, I know that the hair is nothing more than dead tissue, evolved to protect the humans' epidermis, much like our scales. I find it disgusting nonetheless.

"It has no blood or nerve endings," I explain. "I can do it with a simple set of shears."

He starts to reply, but evidently does not wish to shout over the wind. Instead, he cranks his window closed again. I do the same.

"I mean you must not," he says. "Humans value their hair. Particularly females, who have more of it atop their heads. Indeed, shaping it and caring for it is important to them."

It occurs to me that Sesh may be fabricating this tale to vex me and amuse himself. "Caring for *dead* tissue is important to them?" I repeat skeptically.

"It is. Humans give more attention to this dead tissue than to their vital organs. And we must be mindful of their concerns—even the foolish ones—to avoid exposing ourselves. You would do well to set aside time for quiet reflection to examine the memories of the human you have consumed. Carefully, as I have instructed."

"Very well," I tell him. "I will keep the hair, and I will probe the memories of the woman."

I am not looking forward to this. *How did these foolish apes become the dominant species?*

Eventually we veer west of the great city and turn south, passing through a smaller settlement along the coast. Endless square wooden buildings crowd both sides of the road, each with an ugly sign and an array of windows. All of them look the same to me. Overhead is a tangle of wires stretching everywhere.

"They don't seem to have a sense of aesthetics, do they? Apart from their hair, I mean."

Sesh smiles and says nothing.

We leave the settlement and come to a stretch of road with few buildings. To the west is a vast, flat expanse of blue that shimmers in the light of the Father: the ocean. Sesh pulls the car to the side of the road, and we walk to the shore. White gulls scream overhead, and the breeze becomes a strong wind laden with salt and water.

The sea is beautiful beyond words. I have known it only as a line on a map, beyond which there is nothing. Now, though, the shimmering blue extends all the way to the horizon, where the line between the Mother and the sky is far and wide, blurred in a blue haze. I believe that, if I look carefully enough, I can see the curvature of the Earth. Endless and deadly, it fills me with awe. I feel at any moment it may rise and wash me away. Yet still I am drawn to it.

It draws Sesh as well, I can see. His gaze and his thoughts seem far away. And then, to my utter shock, he begins to sing:

"Oh the wind was foul and sea ran high.
Leave her, Johnny, leave her!
She shipped it green and none went by,
And it's time for us to leave her...

Leave her, Johnny, leave her!
Oh, leave her, Johnny, leave her!
For the voyage is long and the winds don't blow
And it's time for us to leave her..."

For a long moment, I stand beside him in stunned silence, not knowing what to say. Finally I speak. "The sea holds meaning for you, Sesh."

He never takes his eyes from the horizon, but I can see they are wet. "Yes," he says absently. "She and I are well acquainted. She taught me for many years and helped me become the man I am today. But she is fickle and quick to anger. She nearly killed me on more than one occasion. Yet I love her nonetheless."

I am shocked at this bizarre fable; it is not the Sesh I know. *"What?"*

Sesh tears his gaze from the water to regard me. His eyes dart to the sky, then back to me. "I speak of my human counterpart, of course," he says. "Sam Smith."

We walk along the shore and stop before a solitary building that is to be my laboratory, at least until the Science Master arrives. To my surprise and delight, it fronts on the land but extends on a pier over the water. We walk to the front, where there are windows covered inside by cloth, and a sign overhead that I cannot read. I find it confusing and frustrating.

"Meditate," Sesh advises me. "You cannot gather knowledge effectively without reading. Spend time with the memories of your human, and you will read their writing easily. She is a learned woman."

"So I gathered. What is her name?"

Now it is Sesh who seems confused and frustrated. "Do you know…I never asked her! But her some of her possessions are in a bag inside this building. I am certain her identification card is among them."

Inside is a large room of human furniture with purposes obvious and mysterious. Sesh explains that this first room is a ruse to conceal the laboratory.

He unlocks the next door with a small piece of metal, presses a switch, and overhead electric lights illuminate a cavernous room, many times the size of my father's own laboratory. Tables, equipment, shelves, and supplies fill the entire space, more than ever I have seen. There is little human equipment here, however. While human technology has surpassed ours in energy and transport, they are still relatively ignorant in life sciences.

But even with this well-furnished laboratory, we could not possibly produce this drug in sufficient quantities to subdue even a fraction of the nearest settlement, let alone the entire human population.

When I am done inspecting the room, Sesh bids me join him in a sitting area where the lighting is dimmer. On a wide piece of furniture with cushions and a soft yellow fabric, I remove my uncomfortable footwear and curl up next to him. It is warm and comfortable.

"Shila, I must speak to you about our work here, and our goal." His lips fold into his mouth in what might be concern, but I do not yet understand human faces.

"Yes?" I say. In the dim light of the sitting area, his eyes reflect the brighter light from the rest of the laboratory. There is something different in them. Something like desire.

"As you have seen, the human population far exceeds our ability to produce your father's drug."

"Yes," I say. "I have reached this same conclusion."

He bobs his head in a way that seems right for Sesh but strange for a human. "Nor could we consume them all. But if we focus on their leadership and key scientists, the humans themselves can help us subdue their population."

Humans subduing humans. From what I know of them, Sesh's logic is sound. "Go on," I tell him.

"If we are to engage their leadership and scientists, we need support from our own experts to direct them. That task will fall to the Commander and the Science Master."

I lean away from him, my hand sinking into the cushion. "I confess, it surprised me that the king dispatched them to the surface after a decade of limiting observation to only a few operatives." The eternally awaited conflict with humanity now seems about to break.

Sesh fixes me with his eyes. "He does not know."

"*What?*" I leap to my feet.

"He does not know. He still believes we are going to spread a pathogen. But the Commander and Science Master tell me it is hopeless. Ten thousand of us—against two billion humans? Even if we were to develop a pathogen that is 99 percent fatal—and your father was nowhere near such an achievement—that still leaves twenty million humans. We cannot win such a war."

"Then you must tell the king, Sesh. Make him understand."

He folds his arms across his chest and sinks back on the sofa. "You know better than anyone that it will do no good. Not unless we can prove we have a better solution. Once the Commander and Science Master join us, they will verify our proposition: that we can make enough humans compliant to turn the ship of humanity to our desired destination."

I am not sure who is speaking. The ideas seem like Sesh's, but the words belong to someone else.

"He must not know," he says. "Not until we can prove our plan workable."

I sink back down beside him, into the forgiving softness of the sofa. "I don't wish to deceive the king," I say, "but you are right. We must make him see. I will help you."

"Thank you, Shila," he says, and he slips his arm around my shoulders. Without thinking, I embrace him and crush him toward me. The smallest of cries comes from his throat, and when I look at him again, I see that his eyes are wet. He brings his lips toward mine…

Something within me screams a warning. I push him away and wrap my arms around a cushion.

"Forgive me, Sesh. The transformation…it confuses me."

Sesh, too, seems confused. "There is no need to apologize. Human emotions are primitive and unpredictable." He stands and straightens his jacket. "Take today and tomorrow to collect yourself and assess your human's knowledge. If you need to travel, use their streetcar system. Then I will show you the place where we distribute the drug. It is a short distance south of here. The process is already underway."

I nod, and Sesh exits swiftly through the door to the ruse room, leaving me alone with the woman inside of me. We have much to discuss.

CHAPTER
12

CITY OF ANGELS

Horace Jennings

During the day-long train ride to Los Angeles, the potential futility of our endeavor weighed on us. The police report might amount to nothing more than a stolen car, the Smith character a mere coincidence. It was entirely possible that Mateo had come to some sad, evil end. It was a sobering thought.

As we rushed through the gathering darkness, we made out many features of Southern California that were completely alien to New Englanders: deserts, canyons, palm trees, orange groves, oil rigs, and airfields, all juxtaposed in ways that seemed to make little sense, as if the ground were fickle and couldn't decide what new thing to sprout, natural or man-made. And at its center, a growing city that I thought was likely to become a great metropolis: Los Angeles.

What promise or threat had drawn Mateo here, if indeed he were here?

Our hotel, the newly completed Los Angeles Biltmore, was said to be the largest hotel west of Chicago. The interiors evoked the Italian Renaissance: hand-painted frescoes; carved marble fountains; embroidered tapestries; oak-paneled walls and crystal chandeliers. After a light meal, I retired, leaving Helen to explore the rest of the hotel amenities.

The next morning, I admired the view. Our rooms overlooked Pershing Square, at the center of which was a lovely wooded park. People strolled the lanes among the trees or sat on benches reading the newspaper. I opened a window and was greeted by a delightful breeze. The weather was quite warm for early March—but then, this wasn't Providence.

At half past ten, we met in the lobby: Helen in a floral dress and brimmed hat, me in a white linen suit and bowler. We admired each other, tossed in a few barbs for good measure, then set off for the police department.

Los Angeles had an excellent trolley system that netted the entire city. As we hopped off the yellow streetcar, we were afforded a beautiful sight. Across a park, rising more than 400 feet above the city's Civic Center was its latest wonder, the new City Hall. A stately tower some 32 stories tall, it stood like a sentinel watching over the city. On either side of the tower, the building's base extended in wings of perhaps ten stories, like the epaulets of a soldier. At its top, a great ziggurat reached toward heaven. Never had I seen a building whose architectural statement so matched its purpose: a center of government, and a hall of leadership.

But we were not heading for City Hall. Our destination was the smaller, meaner, more ordinary brick building immediately before us: police headquarters.

In the lobby, we were greeted at the tall front desk by a corpulent, mustached officer whose placard read "Sgt. Hickey" and whose uniform read one size too small. But he was courteous enough and offered us seats while he rang for Harry Raymond. The latter eventually appeared: a muscular man, not much taller than Helen, with thinning hair, perhaps 40 years old. He was not wearing a uniform, which I took as an indication that he was a detective and not merely an officer.

Raymond led us through a door and into a large, chaotic room with a low ceiling and innumerable columns, desks, and telephones. Where there should have been windows, there were instead offices with closed doors, so that there was no telling day from night. Stacks of papers were piled on every desk and filing cabinet.

To my disappointment, Raymond led us to a desk, not an office. He began taking down information: our names, addresses, and occupations. How long had we lived in Providence? I had to explain where I taught, how long I'd been teaching, and worst of all, exactly what I taught: physics, mechanics of solids, material properties, fluid dynamics. It was clear he didn't understand any of it. And if that weren't excruciating enough, he began asking Helen the same questions about geology.

Through it all, Harry Raymond chicken-scratched notes at random intervals, sometimes writing nothing at all—I suspect, when he didn't understand or couldn't spell the words we were using. Brows knitted and lips pulled aside, he may have felt a bit of the same consternation that I did at his ignorance.

Finally, he got around to discussing the theft at the museum.

"So, Mr. Jennings, why are you here?" He began tapping his pencil on his pad of chicken scratch.

What? "Why, we're looking for the owner of the car, Mateo Martinez."

"Well, sir, we don't have any information on the individuals leaving the scene. We're looking for them, of course."

"Individuals?" said Helen. "You mean there was more than one person in the car?"

"Were there any eyewitnesses who could—"

"Let me stop you right there, Mr. Jennings. You don't know what happened in that museum, do you?"

"Of course I do." I couldn't keep the irritation out of my voice. "A rock—a mineral specimen of some kind—was stolen."

He must have noted my tone. He folded his arms and held my gaze for an uncomfortable moment. I realized then that I wasn't dealing with one of my students. "Mr. Jennings, this wasn't a typical burglary. A man walked casually into a museum, past visitors and staff, took a Louisville Slugger to a glass case, and casually walked out with the rocks as if he didn't have a care in the world."

"A Louisville—what?"

Now it was Raymond's turn to be irritated. "A baseball bat, Mr. Jennings. Jesus, don't they have baseball in Providence? He smashed the cases with a baseball bat, picked up the rocks, and walked out. He didn't say anything, he didn't threaten anyone. Then he got into the car—Mateo Martinez's car—and it sped away from the scene. Now do you understand why we believe this man is dangerous?"

Helen took out the photo of her and Mateo. "Is this the driver, Detective?"

Raymond took the photo and studied it. "It might be." He eyed Helen in her slinky floral dress. Then he looked me up and down. "Look, Mr. Jennings, Miss Parker. You seem like nice people. Let me give you some advice. Go home. Let the police handle this. That's their job, and sometimes it's dangerous work—"

"Wait," Helen said. "Aren't you the police?"

"Me? No, I'm just a consultant. The Department brings me in to help track down stolen cars." He gave us a crooked smile. "I guess I'm pretty good at it. I run a small detective agency."

"Well then, we'll hire you," said Helen. "We'll pay you to help us find Mateo."

"The police are already doing that, Miss Parker, so there's no need. Besides, they don't appreciate competition in their cases. It's out of the question. You both should head back to Providence." He closed the notebook next to the photo of Mateo and Helen, then opened a drawer to put them away.

"Please, Detective," Helen said. She began to cry. I had never seen Helen shed a tear in the five years I'd known her. She cried silently at first; then, as she tried to speak, she shuddered and sobbed. Officers at other desks looked up to see what was going on. "Please. We've come all this way. We've come so very far. Please don't send us home with nothing. We've got to find him. Won't you please help us?"

I couldn't bear it.

And strangely, as I watched, Detective Harry Raymond broke, just as I had broken when Mrs. Martinez called me. "Please, Miss Parker. There's no need to be upset." He yanked a handkerchief from his pocket and handed it to her. "I'll take the case. Please. It'll be alright. Let me see what I can do." He produced a card from his jacket pocket and handed it to me: "Electric Torch Investigations", complete with a little flashlight symbol. "Come to my office tomorrow morning, 9am. The address is on the card."

"Thank you, sir," I began. "I appreciate—"

"Now let me tell you something, Mr. Jennings—both of you. This is not a game. This is not a classroom exercise or a field trip. This is Los Angeles. There are hucksters, whores, and gangsters here who would just as soon kill you as look at you. I've seen it firsthand. It can be a dangerous place, especially for bystanders like professors and students. So go ahead and ride the yellow cars and see the sights, but don't go looking for trouble. Don't go wandering around at night, and for God's sake, don't go investigating this museum robbery on your own. Are we square?"

Helen and I nodded without a word.

"Alright, then. Tomorrow morning at 9am."

We left in silence, and I felt glad to be out of that awful room and back in the sunshine. Helen was still dabbing her eyes with Raymond's handkerchief, composing herself. "I'm sorry about that— what happened back there. I don't know what came over me. It just seemed so hopeless. I'm sorry, Professor, I had no right to hire the detective with your money."

"Nonsense. I'd been thinking about hiring a detective, anyway. When you want something done right, hire a professional, I always say."

"I agree," she said. "He could work out well. I like him. I trust him."

"I wouldn't go that far," I said.

The next step for us was to find out what we could about this Smith character. We had an address, and City Hall was just across the street.

If the outside of the building was stately, the interior was magnificent. A great hall led through the building from front to back, walls and floor of marble, high arched entries admitting sunlight to either end. At its center was a soaring rotunda supported by smooth pillars of brown marble veined with white. Here, the floor was inlaid with geometric patterns, and the domed ceiling featured murals depicting Earth, Wind, Water, and Fire, as well as mythological figures symbolizing courage, perseverance, and progressiveness.

To my amazement and delight, prominent murals depicted the angels of technology: Civil Engineering, Science, Mechanical Power, and more. It was a veritable cathedral dedicated to man's achievements, and to my life's work as well. I'd have knelt and prayed there, if I could have done so without making a spectacle of myself.

A small free-standing sign with an arrow directed us to the Hall of Records. We followed it down a long corridor and found a set of double doors, a worker literally painting "Hall of Records" on one of them. I hoped the records were complete and recent.

I expected it would take us less than a half hour, with no assistance, to find the tax map for 46 Navy Street. Instead, it took us from late morning to mid-afternoon. Working against us were the byzantine tax system, the common name, and the location itself, which had only recently been incorporated into Los Angeles: a waterfront community known as Venice.

Forty-six Navy Street was a warehouse on a pier, owned by a company called Maple Leaf Imports. Maple Leaf Imports was owned by an individual named Samuel Smith. Samuel Smith had a home address listed in Vancouver. Mr. Smith, apparently, was a Canadian.

We debated briefly, right there in the file room, whether these facts made it more or less likely that the mysterious Mr. Smith—geologist, importer, and Canadian—was somehow involved in Mateo's disappearance. The entire thing seemed inane.

We left the building, squinting in the bright sunshine, and we made our way back to the streetcar stop. There was a newspaper stand nearby that sold maps of the streetcar system. I picked up a map and a newspaper.

While we waited for the next streetcar, Helen reviewed the map.

"You know…if instead of taking the streetcar back down East First Street to the hotel, we were to take the North Spring Streetcar toward Glendale…it would take us…" She stopped.

"Where?" I asked.

She pointed to a spot on the map.

"No. Absolutely not."

"Why not?" Helen demanded.

"Must I spell it out for you?"

A motorist leaned on his horn, prompting a pedestrian to dash out of the street and onto the sidewalk between us. He mumbled an apology, then continued on his way.

"The detective said not to go wandering around at night," she said. "And as you can see, it's still broad daylight."

I scowled at her. "He specifically warned us against investigating the museum robbery on our own."

"We wouldn't be investigating," she said. "We'd be visiting, just like any other tourist. If the museum is still open to the public, where's the harm?"

Something about this didn't sit right with me. But I was curious about the museum and exactly what had taken place there.

Helen saw my hesitation and pressed her advantage. "It's so close. I'll bet we could be there in less than a half hour."

CHAPTER
13

THE DEPARTED

Shila Ghiss

She does not have much to say, this woman, which seems odd, because she spoke to me so excitedly when she saw the murals. My meditations do not help. Her thoughts and memories lie beneath sand and stone. They will not rise to the surface unless I am in duress. I decide to be more forceful in prompting her.

On a small table in the sitting area of the laboratory is her... handbag. I bring it to one of the examination tables, where the light is better. I open it and empty its contents onto the table.

It is a curious assortment of personal effects: a small purse of coins and paper currency, which humans use to regulate their activities and resources; colored paint and powder, to adorn her face; a brush for the endless maintenance of the dead hairs streaming from her head; a writing implement; and mysteriously thin sheets of soft paper and fabric whose purpose I cannot discern. All of it is a waste of time.

I push a wastebasket beneath the edge of the table, intent on sweeping most of these things into it—beginning with the hairbrush. Instead, I pick it up and sweep it across my head. I feel my hair, unruly from the car ride here, beginning to obey. It is a pleasant sensation, and somehow, it makes me more confident. It is not at all what I expect from dead hair cells.

I may have been hasty.

Among the detritus are some clearly useful things. A map of the public transportation system; a badge bearing an image of a building. Perhaps her workplace?

Finally, I find a card with a photo on it. I have not seen myself since

I have transformed, yet I know the photo is me, just as I know the name that appears next to it: Susan River. The face is both alien and familiar, the hair black and gray, the photo unflattering yet somehow precious. I care for Susan River. I care what happens to her.

In the next instant, I remember: I sent her off, alone, through the Chamber of Dreamers, and on a long climb to the surface. She may have been caught, perhaps eaten. She may have fallen, been injured, died alone, in the shaft or on the surface.

I am brought low by these thoughts—sickened, sorrowful, regretful. My eyes become wet again, and my vision blurs. What little concern I had for her, saving her to spare myself the ordeal of eating her. *How could I have been ready to kill so many of them? Am I a monster?*

My eyes drip onto the table, and I feel my nose becoming wet as well. I reach for the thin, soft paper, and it feels familiar, comforting. Instinctively, I reach for the small round case with the colored powder in it. There is a mirror inside.

I hold her face in my hands. She looks back at me, sad, but strong and resolved.

Then I hear her—the same voice that spoke to me in my father's study, excited for the future, as if she is standing behind me, leaning close. For a moment, the hairs on the back of my neck rise. I feel her hand on my shoulder, reassuring me.

She sees some larger purpose in me—in all of my people—a purpose that I myself do not see. She wants me to know her. I want that as well.

I will visit her room and her workplace. I will collect her clothes and possessions. I will come to know her, to know everything about her. I will prove to her that I am not a monster.

—⁂—

The room where Susan River lived is small. Its windows look out upon other buildings and rarely see the light of the Father.

Humans, I learn, require furniture. In this small room there is a bed, a chest of drawers, a desk, a mirror, and a bookshelf. The desk provides a smooth surface for writing; the shelf stores books. Everything else is a waste of precious wood.

I examine the chest. Its drawers are filled with clothing. If humans shed their skins as we do, they would have no need of clothing. Instead, they wear a bewildering range of clothing in endless colors and fabrics. Susan River has relatively few garments: blouses, skirts, sweaters, and undergarments, all neatly folded. I select a new set of clothes: a high-collared black blouse, a pleated skirt, and a green sweater with buttons. They carry a pleasing scent—a mixture of flowers and pheromones. I take it in and feel her presence all around me.

I stretch out on the bed, on a green blanket made of coarse, woolen cloth. I lay my cheek against it, and it itches my face, so I push it away, like an old skin to be shed. I look up, and for a moment I see familiar faces from long ago smiling down at me. They are wrinkled, toothless. I can barely remember them, but I remember their kindness.

The desk has small drawers. In them are papers with writing—Susan River's writing. I know the words from her memory of writing them. I learn that her true name is Sudden River. She was born many years ago, during a rainstorm in a place called New Mexico. She came here, to Los Angeles, to study other human cultures, and her studies led her to travel the wide world. Finally, she returned to Los Angeles, to share what she has learned. Here she uses the name "Susan".

There are also pictures—photographs of people who look like her, young and old. In one, a man and woman sit in chairs as she stands before them, a child. They raised her, taught her, cared for her, and she for them as they grew older.

There is a small wooden box, empty but for a photograph of her mother. I know what this box held: the silver bracelet that I now wear, a gift passed down from mother to daughter.

So many memories. They are happy and sad, like the light of the

Father slowly dying at day's end.

I did not know that a family could feel like this. I wish they were my family. In a strange way, they are.

On the bookshelf are many texts, old and new. I can read them! And after only a few words, I remember the contents of all of them. Many are stories of people who lived long ago. Some are stories of people across the oceans. Humans have different histories and beliefs. Susan River knows a great deal about them.

In some ways, she and I are alike. We study our people: she studies their spirits and beliefs; I study their bodies. Many of the people she studies have been dispossessed, just as mine have been. But instead of hiding and plotting, they have adapted and become a special part of the usurper's society.

We both revere Mother Earth. And just as I was overcome by the light of the Father in the entry cavern, each morning, Susan River is moved by that same light.

I stand before her mirror and look at her. I know her: courageous, compassionate, reverent. She cared for her father, even in his old age. She is all the things I am not. I long to be like her: a pathfinder, a teacher, not a monster.

There is still time.

Suddenly I desire to walk in her footsteps—to spend a day as she would spend it.

I leave her room and walk downstairs to the street. I have the identification badge with her workplace name. The yellow streetcar will take me there. My spirits rise as I board it.

CHAPTER
14

THE DOCENT

Horace Jennings

Helen was right. Twenty minutes later, after leaving City Hall, we stood before a Spanish mission perched on a hilltop above an arroyo. White walls, terracotta roofs, and a great square tower looked down on us. A shuttle took us up a long drive that twisted around to the museum entrance. I couldn't help but imagine Mateo racing down this hill recklessly, his thieving passenger screaming at him while clutching the stolen rocks. I kept that image to myself.

At the entrance, a museum staff member in a tan jacket accepted our donations, provided us with a printed guide sheet, and admitted us to the museum. It was dark and cool inside.

We had a little over an hour before the museum closed, which at first seemed like plenty of time. According to the literature, the museum housed one of the world's finest collections of Native American artifacts. The holdings were divided into four areas: Pre-Hispanic, Spanish Colonial, Latino, and Western Art and Artifacts. I quickly realized that there was no way to know which area was the one from which the mineral specimens were stolen; and I wasn't about to become conspicuous by asking.

I started with Western Art and Artifacts and was immediately rewarded with displays featuring large mineral specimens: turquoise. The theft had been a week ago; if these were the specimens, they'd been replaced and their display cases repaired rather quickly. *Too quickly.* We moved on.

As an academic, it was impossible for me not to become engrossed with the displays of Navajo art and artifacts from New Mexico:

pottery, sand paintings, and jewelry. I stood before a case containing a flat tray of sand in blue, white, yellow, black, and red: a great bird soaring over a mountain range in glory, like an angel.

"A thunderbird, isn't it?" I asked Helen, who had her nose a few inches from the placard describing how the painting was made.

"Yes," she said absently. "A protector of humanity and a symbol of great power. It brings thunder and lightning and wind, but also the rain needed to grow crops. A common belief in Native American tribes—the Crow, the Sioux, the Cheyenne…"

"I didn't realize you were an expert."

She looked up from the placard. "I'm not. Remember that mining jaunt in Montana you sent me on three years ago?"

"Ah. That explains it." Which, of course, it did not. "The Navajo seem like a peaceful people."

"Naturally," she said. "It's a matriarchal society."

"Naturally," I said quietly.

But she heard me, judging by her scrunched nose. "*Anyway*, I'm glad we got to see this. It's going to be destroyed next week, replaced by another sand painting."

"What! Why?" I stared at the case, the painting within, and all the work that went into it.

"Sand paintings are temporary. That's the whole point. You really should read the placards, Professor."

"Yes. But that's why I have graduate students."

I moved on to the Pre-Hispanic collection. Soon I was in a long room with glass wall cases containing pottery, tools, and art objects. This collection included artifacts of early Native Americans and Aztecs in what is now Southern California and Mexico. A dozen or more visitors wandered the gallery along with us, including teachers and school children. Several of the children paused before one case, laughing, whooping, and making mock sounds of fright. When they had moved along, I saw it contained a rather chilling statue: a thin, skeletal figure with crossed arms and an oversized skull rendered in white stone. His large round eyes—pupilless—stared out at us from beneath what looked like a bishop's mitre.

"Who is this friendly fellow?" I whispered.

"Mictlantecuhtli, the Aztec god of the dead," Helen read from the placard. "He ruled Mictlan, the underworld." He must have been revered, as there were many statuettes of him in various shapes and sizes.

I drifted into another gallery, this one with various mosaics and paintings of a creature that was part bird and part serpent, including a sculpted figure that erupted from carved wall stones. The placard beneath each was marked with the name "Quetzalcoatl," along with the date and location where it was found. Most were found in northern Mexico and Southern California, the dates ranging from the turn of the century to 1923.

Looking up, I saw something that stopped me in my tracks. Here was a painting of Quetzalcoatl in vivid colors and sharp detail. A god many stories tall, he floated above a city of Aztec ziggurats, his rainbow wings spread, his gaze harsh and judgmental.

Helen's hand touched my arm. "Look familiar?" she asked, a smile playing on her lips.

I realized that I had stopped breathing, and I let out a shuddered breath. "Not particularly. But I've had enough of snakes and worms."

She read the name of the artist. "Guillermo Meza," she said. "Nine years old. The boy, not the painting."

The same age as Juanita. "A precocious lad. I'd say he has a future in the art world."

We passed into a third gallery. Here there were jewelry, weapons, and ceremonial objects fashioned in turquoise, lapis lazuli, and other semiprecious stones. One of the cases was boarded up.

"May I help you?" asked a polite voice. It belonged to a slight, distinguished-looking woman only a few years younger than me: high cheekbones, dark eyes, and dark hair with streaks of gray, parted in the middle. On her wrist was a silver and turquoise bracelet. She wore an elegant green sweater over a high-collared black blouse, and a long, pleated skirt. Her badge marked her as a docent. "Let me know if you have any questions."

I thought quickly. "Can you tell me about Quetzalcoatl?"

"Ah, yes, Quetzalcoatl, the Aztec and Mayan creator god. He was also the patron of rain, science, agriculture, and much more. His name means 'Feathered Serpent' in Nahuatl, the Aztec language. We usually find him depicted as a combination of the green quetzal bird and a serpent."

"Is he good or evil?" Helen asked.

The docent smiled. "Contrary to the way he is often depicted in Western culture, Quetzalcoatl is known as a kind and benevolent god, a friend to mankind. He is respected and appreciated for his empathy toward all forms of life, especially humans, whom he had a role in creating."

"That's a relief," I mumbled to myself.

"This painting is fascinating," Helen said. "It seems filled with meaning and purpose. Can you tell us anything about the artist?"

"Guillermo Meza Álvarez. He is extremely talented, is he not? And only nine years old! Even at this young age, he is becoming known for his oils depicting fantastic backgrounds and often distorted human figures." She smiled mischievously. "Many seem to be denunciations of human society."

"Almost as if he is passing judgment," Helen observed. "Unusual for a boy of nine."

At that moment, as if to underscore the point, a group of schoolboys from the other gallery ran through us, whooping and shouting. Their chaperone arrived a moment later, red-faced and panting.

"I'm sorry, Miss," he said to the docent. "They're being especially awful today." He hurried past, calling out names and issuing threats.

If the docent was perturbed, she didn't show it.

"I have a rather odd question," I said. "Can you tell me anything about worms in these cultures? Were they part of the belief system?"

"Certainly," she said. "For the Aztecs in particular, worms played a symbolic role in creating humanity. It is said that Quetzalcoatl descended to the Mictlan, the underworld, to retrieve bones that would become humanity's forbearers. Mictlantecuhtli, the Aztec god of the dead, agreed to give the bones to Quetzalcoatl only if he could blow a conch-shell horn with no holes in it. It was then that Quetzalcoatl tricked Mictlantecuhtli. He had worms drill holes in the conch shell to have it make a sound when he blew upon it. So you see, without worms, humanity wouldn't be here."

I was about to ask her exactly how big theses worms were, but Helen interrupted me.

"We were sorry to learn about the theft from the museum," she said, gesturing toward the boarded case. "I assume they were mineral specimens. I see that the specimens and semiprecious stones in the other cases were made into jewelry and other objects, but I gather that was not the case with the minerals that were stolen."

"Stolen?" For the first time, the docent appeared stumped. Evidently, her store of cultural knowledge did not include current events. There was an awkward pause as she stared blankly at the boarded case. Then she seemed to remember, and her face darkened.

"Yes. That is correct. The stolen minerals were cobalt specimens. Ancient cultures prized them for their striking blue color. It was thought they had magical properties."

"Cobalt?" I said, looking to Helen.

"A ferromagnetic metal with strong magnetic properties..."

"Were you here at the time of the theft? Did you see what happened?"

"I'm afraid that's a question best answered by the police." She paused, lost in thought; then voices sounded from the next gallery. "Excuse me," she said. "Duty calls. I see that it's almost closing time. I hope you have enjoyed your visit to the museum."

After she left, Helen asked the question that had plagued us since we first learned of the theft. "Why in the world would someone walk into a museum and smash an exhibit case in front of visitors just to steal a few cobalt specimens? It doesn't make sense."

I pondered this in silence, but had no answers. We turned to leave the gallery, now empty except for an older woman in a tan jacket and badge—another docent. "I'm sorry," she said, "the museum is about to close."

We had managed to get through this without drawing attention; now was not the time to overstay our welcome. "Yes, of course," I said. "The other docent reminded us. We were just on our way out."

She cocked her head to the side. "Sir," she said, "I'm the only docent here."

CHAPTER
15

INQUIRY TO THE INQUISITOR

Shila Ghiss

The yellow streetcar clacks along the track that runs from Los Angeles west to Santa Monica. There I will change to a red car that will take me south to the warehouse laboratory. But I will ride the car further south to our distribution center in the town called Venice. People seek this town for its beaches and for amusement.

I do not seek amusement. I seek answers.

I enjoyed returning to the museum earlier. It was strange, at first. The guard asked me where I had been for the past weeks. I was not wearing my uniform. He asked me if I was "still on vacation". I did not understand, so I smiled and nodded, as I often see humans do. But he admitted me, so I was unconcerned.

I went first to the Navajo collection, then to the Aztec collection to see the work of Susan River's favorite artist, a young boy whose fantastical paintings seem to take humanity to task. My spirits rose, and my heart lightened.

Soon after, I met a man and a young woman whom I found engaging. From their earlier conversation, which I'd overheard, I knew they were once teacher and student. They seemed to respect, admire, even amuse each other. The young woman is fortunate to have such a teacher.

A bell rings, and the streetcar slows to a stop beside a wooden shelter with a bench. A young couple climbs on and takes a nearby seat, chatting and laughing.

I recall the questions about the theft of the stones. I did not know they were stolen, but I remember the stones themselves: large, blazing blue.

And another memory comes to me as I remember the questions: Sesh—or rather, Sam Smith, the gray-haired man that is Sesh's human form—asking Susan River about the stones. Telling her that he had a collection of them. Offering to donate them to the museum, if she thought the museum would be interested. Leading her to his car to see them. And then…

…I understand now why I fended off his advance. Susan River was trying to warn me.

What I do not understand is his interest in the cobalt stones. But I intend to find out.

The building that houses our distribution facility is deceptively large—a ruse, like the front rooms of the warehouse. Sesh shows me the hidden entrances and exits that lead to the areas below it, where it is warm, damp, and dimly lit. In my true form, I would have found it comfortable, but as a human, I find it abhorrent. Mildew, mold, rust, and wood rot are everywhere. The basement is decaying like a corpse.

The Commander and the Science Master are behind a door across the corridor from Sesh's office. Sesh has told them to expect me. But when we reach the door, Sesh puts an arm before me, barring my entry.

"They have not yet changed," he says. "They await the human subjects I have chosen for them. Before entering this room, you should return to your true form. The Commander will look down on a human."

"He will look down on the king's niece? Nonsense."

"You don't understand." He puts a finger in the collar of his suit, perspiring. The humidity, no doubt. "We must project strength if we are to work with him."

Whatever intrigue he is playing at, I refuse to let it entangle me. "I will return to my true form to meet them, as you suggest. But we are all subjects of the king. We work as one. I will remind them if they have forgotten."

"As you wish," he says. "Meet me upstairs afterward."

I wait until Sesh leaves before removing my clothes. I look down at my skin—Susan River's skin—tawny, scaleless, and soft. I feel vulnerable and exposed without my clothing. The floor is hard beneath my soft feet, the odor of the basement offensive. Yet I am reluctant to transform back to what I once was.

I force myself to remember the clench and stretch of my back muscles, alternating with the clench and stretch of my belly as I slide along; the hardness of my scales; the strength of my body, the power of my jaws.

Then it begins. My tawny skin greens, my skull aches and flattens, my vision distorts, then becomes clearer in the dim light. A fiery pain runs down my spine and intensifies in my tailbone as my back is slowly pulled apart. My arms and legs burn and shrivel. I become more powerful, but I already miss walking. And as my skin hardens, my temperament hardens as well. My thoughts grow cold, callous, and impatient as Susan River drifts away.

I smash my head at the door and nearly break it down. "Science Master!" I hiss. "Commander! In the name of the king, open this door!"

It wasn't much of a confrontation. The Commander was deferential, though his body is larger and more powerful even than mine. The Science Master was far less condescending than she had been in my father's study.

The humans they were to consume are city leaders, they said. Perhaps, once they were situated, they could help find a more worthy human for me.

Evidently, they both still feared the king, and by extension, me. It felt good and alarming at once, like the thrill just before a fight to the death.

When I return upstairs in human form, Sesh seems happy to see me.

The feeling is not mutual.

"Something is troubling you," he says, putting aside a bottle of amber liquid. It bears a label confirming that it is forbidden for human consumption. There are countless others similar to it on shelves behind the long wooden bar; yet there are also innumerable seats and drinking glasses, suggesting that humans will imbibe the contents of these bottles nonetheless. Like so many things in this world, it makes no sense.

Sesh picks up another bottle. "I thought you found the use of a drug to pacify humanity preferable to a pathogen that would exterminate them."

"I do," I say. "I am not troubled, merely curious. How many of us are there?"

"Here? Only a handful, to borrow a human expression," he says, smiling. "We will leverage those we have already bent to our will."

"And how many in total from our colony are now on the surface?"

"Never enough," he says, examining the bottle. He shakes his head in disgust. He has internalized human body movements more than he realizes. "Parish!"

A tall, muscular man in a business vest and tie swaggers out from behind the bar. To my alarm, he wears a weapon strapped to his shoulder, one that could easily kill any of us.

"Keep your shirt on, Sammy," the man says. "I'm right here. What seems to be the problem?"

"Why is this bottle not sealed?" Sesh demands.

"How the fuck should I know? You're not paying me to be a bartender. Ask McAfee. He's supposed to be checking them." The man turns his back on Sesh and begins to saunter away.

Sesh puts a hand on the man's shoulder—reaching up to do so—and wrenches him around to face him. "I'm asking *you*," he hisses, shaking him.

Incredibly, the man is neither angry nor frightened. He shrugs. "I'll find out," he says. He walks away.

Never have I heard anyone speak so to Sesh, ever. Even the king has more respect for him than this surly ape.

"Why do you employ such dangerous humans?" I ask him. "And to let them keep their weapons—it's madness."

Sesh waves his hand. "He has his uses. And your father's drug is highly effective, especially taken in regular doses, as Parish does. There is no danger." Then he remembers my question. "Why do you wish to know how many of us are on the surface?"

"Here is a better question: why are you reluctant to tell me?"

"I see a change in you, Shila. And not a welcome one."

"If I am changed, it is because I am enlightened. Why did you steal mineral specimens from the museum?"

He regards me with one eye, as if he were looking at something through a microscope. "You have been communing with your human woman, I see."

"Answer my question."

"I am the king's Inquisitor, Shila. I ask questions; I needn't answer them."

"And I am the king's heir. You will answer me, or you will answer to the king. Choose."

His face suddenly grows red. He hurls the bottle he'd been examining. It flashes over the tables and across the room, smashing against the far wall. When he finally speaks, white spittle fills the corners of his mouth.

"The stones are part of an alternate plan. In the event we cannot subjugate the humans."

"And what of Susan River?"

"I don't know who—"

"The woman you took from the museum. Why her?"

He throws his head back and cries out—a mockery of the small cry he gave when I embraced him two days ago. That cry, I feel, came from love; this cry comes from utter contempt.

"So, this is the answer to the riddle. You let that thing corrupt you, exactly as I counseled you against. You take her side—the side of a human woman—over your own kind and the king's Inquisitor."

He waits for an explanation, an expression, any kind of response from me. I give him none.

"You stupid, insolent girl! You walk the surface for a few days, yet you have the temerity to question me—*me!*—when I have been here for *years!* Has it not occurred to you that her knowledge of humanity may be of value to us?"

"What occurs to me is that you are keeping secrets, from me and from the king. I won't have it. And neither will he."

He shrieks with rage and hurls another bottle against the far wall. Then he storms out of the room and through a door leading to the lower level.

Another human walks over to me quickly. He is tall, gangly, with big ears and a sneer. "McAfee, ma'am," he says. "Can I help you?"

I point to the far wall. "Clean that up."

Sesh

Investiture, convocation, commencement.

At his desk in the cramped basement office of the speakeasy, Sesh stared at the paper on which he had written these three words in the human language. He had done it unconsciously, he knew; or rather, Sam Smith had done it.

A good man, Smith. Devoted to his family, his crew, and his purpose, just as Sesh was. A leader. But Smith's compassion for others and tolerance of their mistakes was infuriating. It had enabled Shila to rattle Sesh with her arrogant, childish behavior. Gods! Sesh needed to spend more time in his true form, to collect himself, if he was to lead his people to the surface, and to ultimate victory. But that must wait.

The old guard stood before him, awaiting permission to speak, eyes cast at the floor. So respectful! Shila could learn from him.

He'd been with Sesh for many years—far longer than the juveniles who helped bring Shila to the surface. Strange to see him as an old man in stained farmer's overalls; a servant as guileful and loyal as he deserved grander attire. Sesh waved his hand, and the guard began.

"Investiture will be in Owens Valley, a few hours north of the colony by car. That there's a place with a history of violence, so's any disturbance ain't a-like to 'rouse suspicion. I know this'n is the last bunch of rocks, and if'n it ain't enough, well, things could go sideways right quick. I done found a suitable spot. I reckon it's remote enough not to rile the locals, and anyways, them hayseeds ain't a-like to raise a fuss." He smiled. "I know, 'cause I'm one of 'em."

"Well done," said Sesh. His servant's new vernacular brought a smile to his lips. "And you, my friend—how do you plan to give this gift without becoming a stain upon the ground?"

The old guard smiled. "I got that all worked out, Inquisitor. Don't you trouble your head about me."

"I am glad. And the convocation?"

"Entry cavern's ready. Our boys from the power station got them added power cables placed. They're routed to the chamber from below, so's the power cain't be interrupted. They'll be plugged in soon, then we'll fire up that there machine and shake out the bugs." Then, with great effort and concentration, he said solemnly, "All will be ready for you when you arrive, Inquisitor."

Sesh was pleased. The old guard was thorough and left nothing to chance. He was entitled to his older human form; he'd earned it.

"Very well," he said. "Commencement will take place as soon as the convocation is completed. There is no way to stop it, so be sure to be in a safe area if you value your life." He rose from his chair and clapped him on the shoulder. "I certainly do."

The old guard bowed from the neck and left.

CHAPTER 16

THE PROFESSIONAL

Horace Jennings

The next morning, the streetcar left us two blocks from Harry Raymond's office. We walked past it twice before seeing the little electric torch drawing from his business card in the window. A black open-top Model A was parked in front.

When I knocked on the door to Suite A, Harry greeted us with his crooked smile. "Welcome to my office. C'mon in and have a seat."

"It's a bit of a secret, isn't it?" I remarked.

"Yeah, well, my business is mostly word of mouth." He seated me in a wingback chair, Helen on a sofa next to a table with some very questionable-looking nuts. He sat on the edge of his desk. The rest of the office was worn carpet and filing cabinets.

We talked for a bit about the Biltmore—he wanted to know what the rooms were like, what the service was like, etc. Then we got down to business. We reviewed everything we knew about Mateo and his disappearance, including his field work and our visit to the bridge site. We told him about the reading list and Smith's name in the library books and in the visitor's log at the construction shack. Finally, we told him about our research at City Hall, and Maple Leaf Imports. We left out the museum visit and the mysterious docent—no sense telling him that we ignored his advice.

Harry made few notes.

"What do you think?" I asked.

"I think I underestimated you two," he said. "Good work."

I'm not sure why the praise of a small-time detective meant anything to me, but it did—a great deal, in fact. A glance at Helen told me she felt the same way.

She picked up a few nuts, but immediately put them back down. "But…isn't it unusual for a geologist to be in business as an importer?" she asked.

Harry gave a short, scornful laugh. "Not in L.A."

"But… what would a geologist know about the import business?" I asked.

"Not a damn thing," he said. And then, reading our confusion: "Don't you two get it? He might enjoy being a geologist, but he makes his money with his other business."

"He makes money as a Canadian importer?" Helen asked skeptically.

"No, as a bootlegger, goddammit, as a bootlegger! You know, whiskey? Jesus, how do you people live 200 miles from Canada and not know about bootleggers?" He shook his head. "This Smith guy's a bootlegger for sure. He may not have anything to do with your friend."

"Well, how can we find out?" I asked. "Should I call his office in Vancouver?"

He laughed again, holding his head and kicking the front of his desk with his short legs. I felt my temper rise. The same part of me that enjoyed his praise found his disdain unbearable. "What the hell is so funny?"

"Jennings, there is no office."

"But the tax records say—"

"Forget the tax records. If this guy's Canadian, I'm Calvin Coolidge."

"Hmmph." The tone in Helen's voice told me her impatience was growing, a situation that rarely ended well. "So where does that leave us, Mr. Raymond?"

Harry held up his hand. "Tell you what. I'll make some calls. Why don't you and the professor here do a little more research on Sam Smith this afternoon? Call me with the results. Then tonight, I'll go check out this warehouse."

But Helen's tone only got worse. "You're just giving us busy work. The tax records are a waste of time—you just said so yourself."

"Who said anything about tax records?" He hopped off his desk and sat in the chair behind it, producing a business card and scrawling something on the back of it. He handed it to her. "I want you to go downtown to the LA Times office. Research Department. Ask for Myrtle, and show her this card. Call me when you're done, and let me know what you find out."

She looked at the back of the card. Whatever was written there, it barely seemed to placate her. "Fine," she said. "But we're coming with you this evening to investigate the warehouse."

"Nothing doing," he said. "I work alone."

"Really? Because we've provided you with a name and address, and so far all we've gotten in return is a useless police report and some moldy nuts."

It's a pity Helen never heard the saying about flies, honey, and vinegar.

Harry didn't miss a beat. "Door's right there, Miss Parker. Best use it before you turn on the waterworks again."

She went red, and Harry lit a cigarette like he was in a cabaret and they just turned the lights down. *So damned stubborn, both of them.*

I stood and held the brim of my bowler with both hands. "Harry, couldn't we just…wait in the car? Out of the way?"

He turned his head aside to blow a puff of smoke, and I took the opportunity to shoot Helen the iciest glance I could muster.

The office was silent as we waited for Harry Raymond to deliver his judgment. When he did, all he said was: "Don't get out of the car."

Harry had written four words on the back of his business card: "I need that favor."

It was enough. Myrtle spent more than an hour in the dusty basement file rooms of the *LA Times,* rounding up old copies of the paper, and Helen and I spent another hour reading them and taking notes. By early afternoon, we knew a great deal about Samuel Smith: sailor, husband, father, shipping magnate, philanthropist—and yes, Canadian. His was a sad story.

He was a modest man from modest roots, leaving his family's Canadian farm to become a sailor on an American schooner in the 1880s. After learning the ropes and saving his money for years, he bought his own small ship, and in the 1890s, he built a series of shipping lines that rewarded him with ever-increasing wealth. The society pages of the *Times* reported that Smith married an LA socialite in 1898, and they raised a son here. His philanthropy—primarily the funding of schools and hospitals—brought his wife to the pinnacle of LA's social circles.

Then came 1918. Smith's son, Albert, was a war hero; he died in the Meuse-Argonne Offensive, days before the armistice. His wife died the following year of influenza, like Mary. By all accounts, Smith was a broken man afterward, selling most of his shipping lines. He taught at UCLA for a few years, then lived as a recluse.

Ere but for the grace of God go I.

The business section of the *Times* carried a minor news article about him three years ago. He'd restarted one of his old businesses, importing furniture from Vancouver. The article included a photograph. Smith looked older than me—distinguished, with gray hair. Somehow the photo didn't fit with the broken man of ten years ago. With Myrtle's permission, I kept the article.

In none of the papers was there any mention of Smith being interested in geology, nor any clue as to how he might be connected with Mateo's disappearance.

We recounted all of this to Harry that evening on our way to the warehouse in Venice.

"Huh. Well, call me Calvin." That was all he had to say.

We drove through the darkness, past bean fields and oil rigs. When we reached Santa Monica, we turned south on Pacific Avenue. Soon after, the road became bumpy and treacherous, and Harry had to slow to a crawl to avoid potholes. To our right were shanties and little shops, all closed; but up ahead I could see a large shadow: a long building with a pier extending into the water behind it. Harry stopped the car a few hundred feet from it and turned off the engine, then the headlights.

We were plunged into darkness. It was so quiet we could hear waves breaking on the beach.

Harry reached under the seat and pulled out a small case. A moment later, he was studying the building with field glasses.

"No lights, and nobody home, I'd say. Jennings, there's an electric torch in the glove box. Don't turn it on, just hand it to me."

I did so.

"Alright. I'm going to have a look. This will probably take ten, maybe fifteen minutes. Don't get out of the car. If I come running out, feel free to pick me up. Otherwise, no movement, no noise, and no lights."

He got out, pressed the door closed silently, and began stalking down the road toward the building.

I watched as he disappeared into the shadows. I listened to Helen breathing in the back seat. Then I heard her window being rolled down, felt a cold wind, and smelled salt air.

"What are you doing?" I whispered.

"Nothing," she whispered back. "I just want to see. Pass me the field glasses."

"This isn't a matinee at the Bijou. Just sit tight."

A huff of exasperation. Then a cluck of impatience.

"Problem, Miss Parker?"

"Yes, problem," she whispered sharply. "What if he needs help?"

"Let's worry about that when the time comes."

The time came about 20 minutes later. A figure came creeping towards us from the warehouse, and my heart began beating in my throat. Fortunately, it was Harry.

He opened the door and waved us out. "C'mon."

"What?" I whispered. "You want us to get out of the car? Are you sure?"

"Yes, goddammit. I need you."

I never expected those words from Harry. I couldn't imagine why he would need us, and I wasn't sure I wanted to know. But we got out of the car all the same and followed him to the building.

It was chilly and dark. The wind whipped my suit and made a mockery of what little hair I had. Twice I stepped in potholes filled with water up to my ankles.

The building was a large, single story wood structure with a broad sign across the top: Maple Leaf Import Company. There was a front door, a couple of windows, and a driveway leading to a loading bay with a large roll-up door.

Harry led us through the front door like he owned the place, turning on the electric torch with his hand over the front the to keep light to a minimum. We crept through the deep shadows of two rooms: an office that looked abandoned, then a large room filled with tables, chairs, wardrobes, and other furniture. In the back was yet another door. Harry opened it, and once we'd gone through it and were well away from the street, he removed his hand from the front of the torch and shined the light all around.

The rest of the building was one big room with rows of tall, long tables. On each was an assortment of unusual glassware, tubing, bladders, and strange-looking equipment. There were no windows.

"Alright," he said, "what in hell is all this stuff?"

"It must be a distillery for making spirits," I said. "I suppose you're right about this fellow Smith being a bootlegger. Looks like he also makes moonshine. Although…." I looked around the shadows outside the torch beam. "I don't see a still, or copper tubing, or a vat of mash, or burners. It's strange. I've never seen equipment like this before."

"Maybe they make moonshine differently in Canada," Harry said. I couldn't tell if he was serious.

"There are kegs and bottles," Helen said. She was already far down the room, toward the roll-up door. "Wait, there's a desk over here, and a sitting area. Harry, bring that torch over here."

Harry obliged, and I joined him and Helen in examining the desk. In square cubbies were bound sheafs of heavy parchment. I pulled one out and flipped through it.

"What the devil...?"

It was filled with loops, whorls, and squiggles—pages and pages of it. There was not a straight line in the entire sheaf, except for a few diagrams and schematics, which were unintelligible.

"Do you recognize it? Could it be shorthand?" I asked Helen.

She shot me a look that for anyone else might have been accompanied by an obscene gesture.

"Merely a question, Miss Parker. I'm not suggesting you take dictation."

"Maybe it's Canadian," she replied dryly, glancing at Harry. He was not amused.

"What's this?" Something on the desk caught my eye: a cup. Not a measuring cup or a piece of laboratory equipment, but a brown ceramic cup with three painted images: a red circle, a blue circle, and between them, a yellow crescent—cup up.

I handed it to Helen, and she examined it. The light of Harry's torch shadowed her eyes and mouth like a theater mask. In them, I saw hope and fear.

A motor sounded outside. A truck was pulling up to the roll-up door. I pocketed the cup. We looked around for a place to hide. There was none.

From the front of the building came a voice filled with aggravation.

"Who the fuck left the front door unlocked?"

CHAPTER
17

A NIGHT TO REMEMBER

Horace Jennings

The overhead lights snapped on. We crouched in the shadow behind the last row of tables as someone strode into the room. To my left, Harry reached into his jacket and drew out a revolver. I looked at him, and he looked back at me with a cold, dead expression. All business. I began to perspire.

A clank followed by a long rattle, and we heard a truck engine running beyond the now-open roll-up door.

"McAfee, you asshole, you're supposed to be responsible for security. How come the front door was unlocked?"

"She must have left it that way," came another voice. "Dumb bitch."

"I'll tell her you said so, you fucking janitor. C'mon, let's get those cases and get back to the bakery."

The two men walked to the back wall and began loading bottles of hooch into the back of the truck. I got a look at them as they passed us: two tall men, one muscular, with a vest, rolled-up shirtsleeves, and a shoulder holster; the other gangly, with big ears. Harry's gun followed the man with the shoulder holster everywhere he went. I held my breath, expecting gunshots at any moment.

But the two men never noticed us. A few minutes later, the muscular man closed and locked the roll-up door, then shut off the lights and left the room.

Once the truck motor faded away, Harry stood, turned on the torch, holstered his pistol. I showed him the cup.

"Detective, the symbol on this cup matches the drawings Mateo made back in San Francisco," Helen said.

We waited as Harry shone the light on the cup. I was expecting him to dismiss it, as he'd dismissed the other information we'd offered. Instead, he nodded.

"Okay. Jennings, Miss Parker, I've got good news and bad news for you. The bad news is that the guy with the ears is former LAPD. Guy McAfee."

Lord. "How about the other guy?" I asked. "The one with the gun. You know him?"

"Yeah. That's Johnny Parish. He's *current* LAPD. Detective, senior grade. Homicide." He shook his head and made for the front door, waving us to follow.

Helen ran past me and grabbed Harry's arm, bringing him to a stop. "And what's the good news, Detective?"

The crooked grin reappeared. "I know where they're going."

Harry drove past a long pier with an amusement park while I pulled off wet socks and put my shoes on without them. At least I wouldn't squish. A few minutes later, we were pulling up to 52 Windward Avenue.

It was a bakery: Menotti's Bakery, according to the sign. A closed bakery, at night, with about thirty cars parked nearby: Studebakers, Mercedes, even a couple of Pierce-Arrows, as well as many Model As. Harry drove past the building and parked on the south side, away from the other cars. He turned off the engine and put his gun and shoulder holster in the glove box.

"Wait," I said. "Are you joking? You're ready to gun down a homicide detective in a warehouse, but now that we're walking into what is likely their hideout, you're putting your gun away?"

"I can't come in with you," he said.

"What? Why not?"

"Parish knows me. His office is twenty feet from my desk. Seeing me would only make him suspicious."

"I see," I said, swallowing hard. "Shouldn't I take the gun, then?"

He laughed. But then, seeing my distress, his expression grew serious. "Jennings, have you ever been to a speakeasy?"

"No, I have not. I prefer my sherry in the comfort of my own parlor."

"Good for you. But out here in the world, when you walk into a speakeasy with a gun, it usually gets taken away from you at the door."

The car went quiet. None of us moved. After a moment, Harry said, "You want to find your boy? The answers are in there. Are you in or out?"

No choice, and no doubt. "In," I said. Helen opened her door and got out.

I turned back to Harry, who silenced my protest.

"Take her with you," he said. "She'll help, believe me. You'll both do fine. Just nose around and see what you can find out. I'll be right here waiting for you."

I got out and closed the passenger door, leaning into the open window. "If we come running out, feel free to pick us up," I said.

We walked over to the building. A few dim lights partly illuminated each side of it, leaving most of it in shadow. Through the front windows, the bakery appeared dark and deserted. Around the north side of the building there was a Coke machine; around the south, where Harry was parked, were cellar doors. I tried them; locked from the inside. Finally, we walked around to the back. A young man in blue overalls sat on a stool next to a large service door, evidently trying to read a newspaper in the dim light. He looked up at us through a small haystack of blond hair. His gaze lingered on Helen for a moment before he went back to reading his newspaper.

"I do declare," she said in an Alabama drawl, "I'm as dry as a graham cracker, aren't you?" She looked at me and inclined her head toward the newspaper.

I didn't know what to say. I was very thirsty, in fact. But I don't do dialects.

After rolling her eyes at me, Helen checked her makeup in a compact, then brought her face to the newspaper and slowly peeled it down, exposing the young man's face and the funny pages.

He gaped at her.

"I beg your pardon," she drawled, "would you kindly tell me where a girl could quench her thirst?"

He dropped the paper. "Uh… ah… try the Coke machine, miss. It's… ah… around the side."

We walked back around to the Coke machine, out of earshot. "Well, that didn't work," Helen said miserably.

"No, it didn't," I said. "But that drawl that would have made Huey Long proud."

"What do we do now? How are we going to get through that door?"

"First things first. I'm parched." I put a nickel in the machine. Only then did I see the sign on the side of it: out of order. "Damn. Figures."

"He must have known it was out of order," Helen said. "Why wouldn't he tell me that?"

We looked at each other; then I pressed the button under the coin slot.

There was an audible click, and the entire machine swung out a few inches, like a door. We entered, and I closed the machine behind us, impressed with its movement and balance.

That should have been enough, but it wasn't. Inside was a storage room. A second man, this one in a dark suit, awaited us before a narrow door. From somewhere below, I heard faint music.

"Welcome to the Del Monte." He opened the door, revealing a room the size of a phone booth, and the music got momentarily louder. "Our elevator only accommodates two people at a time." I poked my head in, hoping to find some evidence that it was safe. I didn't.

"Step in," the man encouraged. "You, too, Miss, don't be shy. It's easiest if you face each other." We did so, and I doubted you could slip a sheet of paper between us. The man smiled at me and mouthed, "You're welcome."

Jazz music, the clink of glasses, the low roar of conversation, cigarette smoke, and perfume assaulted my senses as soon as the elevator door opened. We stepped out of a nook and into a long room with an equally long bar lined with people sitting on countless leather padded stools: young, old, men, women, and every one of them well-dressed people of means. Behind the bar were five levels of lighted shelves stocked with every imaginable alcoholic concoction and mixer, and a half dozen bartenders pouring drinks. Opposite the bar were booths, barrels, crates, and anything else that might pass as a table. We took a pair of seats next to a barrel.

"Rather crowded, isn't it?"

Helen scanned the room. "Yes. We need to reconnoiter. We're looking at the public space; we need to find a way into the private space."

"Agreed," I said. "Let's split up. We'll do a sweep along both walls and see what we can find. Maybe talk to some of the patrons. But don't ask too many questions and don't go through any doors without me. We'll meet at the far end of this place."

She nodded and headed for the left wall near the elevator; I followed the bar on the right wall, weaving my way through the crowd. The music got louder as I approached until I felt I must be right on top of it. As I turned the corner, I found myself nearly on stage. On a low platform an ensemble of brass, strings, and drums beat out a jazz tune; to my left was a parquet floor with dozens of revelers jumping and spinning. The air was stale and smoky; the space limited. The music ended to laughter, applause, whistling, and cheering at the band. Many people took the opportunity to leave the dance floor, giving me a view of the far side: more barrels and tables. I pressed on toward them.

I sat down at an empty table and surveyed the room, noting the doors and trying to determine the functions of the rooms beyond. One door, I noted, was locked. I thought it might be a restroom, but those were clearly marked. Another door was marked "Staff Only". From that door emerged servers carrying trays of drinks. One of them, a rather provocatively dressed young woman, came over to my table.

"Sir, would ya like a drink?"

"No, thank you, I just had one." An idiotic thing to say, when there were no empty glasses on the table.

She seemed unperturbed. "Are ya sure?" She set her tray down and took a seat at my table. "Why ya sittin' here all alone, anyhow?"

I assured her I was here with friends, to no avail. She made it her duty to befriend and encourage me, telling me that everyone here was from some place else, as if her New York accent wasn't a clue. I confessed I was from Rhode Island.

"Huh! How about that? I never met anyone from Rhode Island. Well listen, honey, you'll make friends here. I did. It may take a little time, but—"

"Young lady, I assure you, I am not alone here."

She huffed, annoyed, reminding me of Helen. "Okay, Mister. If you say so. But if ya change your mind about that drink, just wave at me. I'll be around."

She walked away quickly with her tray, leaving me alone at the table—more alone than I'd felt since my sabbatical started. I wished I had ordered that drink. I looked out at the sea of faces…and one of them looked back. High cheekbones, black hair streaked with gray. Dressed elegantly. Regally.

The docent from the Southwest Museum! I got up and marched straight toward her. As I did, the band began playing again—this time, something slow. I knew then what I had to do.

"I beg your pardon. Would you care to dance?" I extended a hand.

She stood and smiled. "There is no need to beg," she said. She took it.

The last time I danced was with Mary, before the Great War; so I thought myself quite courageous, asking this beautiful woman to dance with me, sockless, my hair no doubt unkempt.

I would soon learn that I knew nothing about courage.

Shila Ghiss

My curiosity drives me. The man takes my hand, and we begin the dance.

"Allow me to introduce myself," he says. "I'm Horace Jennings. I'm a professor at Brown University."

"A pleasure to meet you again, Professor Jennings." I cannot tell him my name. Not yet.

But if this perturbs him, he does not show it. He dips me gently. "Why were you at the museum?" he asks.

Such a silly question! He must know that I belong there. I laugh at this silly man with his untended hair and his wet shoes—and for a moment it feels as if all of my cares have fled. "Is that really what you want to ask me right now?" I reply. My head, of its own accord, sinks to his shoulder.

"…It was…" he says. "Now I'm not so sure."

"There are many things we cannot be sure of," I tell him, as Susan River's mother once told her. "And some that deserve all our trust."

"That may be true," he says. "But it's not particularly helpful."

The music shifts, and we spin round each other slowly. I realize that, like me, he does not know who or what he can trust.

"You seemed not to know about the robbery," he says. "At least at first."

"I had forgotten." Until her memories reminded me. "Why is the robbery of interest to you?"

He tells me of a student missing for six months. He needs to know if he should still hope.

Sesh. It must be. I feel sick as I realize there is little hope for the boy. But I must not show this to Horace Jennings.

"We must always hope," I say. "But we must also act. Please, let me ask you a question. Why did you ask about worms at the museum?"

"I had a dream about them," he says. "More of a vision, really."

A vision. "Tell me about your vision."

"I was home, my home from long ago. But I was changed, somehow. I became something else. Not human. There was an earthquake. It destroyed everything and everyone I knew. Then things emerged from the ground. White worms rising into the sky. It was horrible. Apocalyptic."

Why would this man, who cannot possibly know of the ancient things deep in Mother Earth, see the great worms? It cannot be a coincidence.

I choose my next words carefully. "Some would say that nature can be violent or beautiful, harmful or healing. Nature is in balance, neither good nor evil; but we are not. It is we who bring good or evil into the world." *Humanity brings evil,* or so I have been raised to believe. Now I am not so certain.

The music ends, and the crowd applauds. I bow my head. "I have enjoyed dancing with you, Professor Jennings." I turn to leave.

"Wait! Wait!" he pleads. "You seem to know what's going on. You seem to understand. Can't you tell me something useful? Just one useful thing?"

I hesitate for a moment; then I decide. "Don't drink any of the alcohol here."

"What? Why not?"

A smile comes to me as I give him my answer. "Don't you know? It's illegal."

CHAPTER

18

A NIGHT TO FORGET

Horace Jennings

I watched as she walked away, past the band and around the corner. Gone. More than a little confused, I wandered back to my table and turned to sit. Helen saw me and practically trotted over.

"Were you—was that—?"

"Yes," was all I said. I plopped down. She pulled out a chair and sat. The band began playing a jazz number.

"Well?" she asked.

"Well, what?"

"Who is she? Why was she pretending to be a docent?"

"I don't know," I said. "She's something of a mystery."

Helen was about to say something when the New York waitress descended upon me like the Red Baron.

"Hey! Rhode Island!" Her drink tray refilled, she set it on the table and patted me on the cheek. "See that? What'd I tell ya? You're gonna do just fine here!" She removed two drinks and slid them over to Helen and me, looking left and right as she did so. "On the house." Then to Helen: "This is a swell guy ya got here. Take it from me. Bottoms up!" She took to the air again, scouting for other lonely souls.

Helen raised an eyebrow, then pressed on. "Did you get her name?"

"The waitress?"

Her eyes narrowed, and I held up my hands. "No."

"Well, is she a docent, or isn't she?"

"I don't know. She does seem to be an expert on indigenous

peoples, and I'm certain she knows more than she's telling. Beyond that—a mystery."

Her brow furrowed. "Professor, this woman may have been part of the museum theft. She may even have followed us here. Or if not, she may have useful information, but we may never see her again. Didn't she tell you anything?"

"Just a warning not to drink here."

She cocked her head to the side. "Really? My mother could have told us that."

"Yes, well, next time we'll invite her along."

I gave Helen my assessment of the nearby doors. We focused on the one that was locked, watching to see if anyone went in or came out.

We didn't have to wait long. A tall, lean man with big ears in a suit with even bigger lapels had been going from table to table, whistling as he did so. He now stopped at our table.

"Evening, folks. Just checking to see if everything is to your satisfaction."

Helen and I gave him a medley of responses. "Indeed." "Oh, yes." "A fine establishment." "Excellent."

He nodded and walked off toward the locked door, whistling.

We both recognized the voice and the ears from the warehouse: Guy McAfee. He pulled a key chain from his pocket.

"Helen—get to that door before it closes behind him!"

McAfee unlocked the door and walked through it. The door swung slowly closed. Helen bounded toward it, narrowly missing servers and patrons. She caught the handle just as it closed…then opened it a few inches. I arrived a moment later, and she looked back to ask whether she should pursue. I held up a hand.

"Let's give him a lead," I said quietly, "otherwise, he may hear the music and know the door's been opened."

Half a minute later, I opened the door and stepped onto a metal grate. Helen stepped in behind me. She closed the door quickly and carefully, without so much as a click. Absolute darkness closed in around me; I could see nothing. But the hiss of my leather soles against the grate reverberated into a yawning space below. I drew a lighter from my pocket and struck a flame. Helen stood frozen beside me, holding her breath. Metal stairs wound down into a moist, inky blackness that swallowed my light. I crept down, step by step, sliding my hand along the metal railing, Helen's breathing barely audible behind me.

When there were no more stairs, I flicked on my lighter again. We were at the bottom: a door. I glanced at Helen, her face tense and shadowy in the light of the flame. She nodded, ready. I opened the door.

A steam tunnel ran left and right in either direction, sparsely placed lightbulbs casting a feeble glow on the floor. It was warm and humid, with a smell of mildew and rotting wood. Rusted pipes ran along the ceiling.

"This way," I whispered, moving to the right.

Whistling echoed from the corridor ahead of us. It sounded like "Listen to the Mockingbird." The whistler stepped into the corridor and turned to face us. Big ears and big lapels. McAfee.

"I'm sorry, friends. This area's not open to the public."

Helen stepped forward. "Excuse us, please. We're looking for Sam Smith. He may know where—"

"Sweetheart, I don't care if he knows Al Jolson. Get back up those stairs."

Nuts to that. I didn't care for his tone with Helen, and I was getting pretty damned tired of hiding, apologizing, and asking nicely.

I stepped in front of her. "We're not going anywhere until we get some answers."

"Oh my," he said. "Are you going to teach me some manners, mister? That should be fun." He waved me towards him.

I obliged and strode towards him. When I was within five feet, a stiletto appeared in McAfee's hand, a broad smile on his face.

I hesitated just a moment; then I smiled back at him and thrust my hands into my pockets. The fingers of my right hand closed on

99

the ceramic cup. "I've taught stupid young men before, but none as stupid as you. What do you think you're going to do with that knife? Kill me? Your boss wouldn't like that. Neither would your pals at LAPD. I'm happy to call them, if you like. Or maybe you'd prefer to do it, McAfee."

That got his attention. "You know me? I'm flattered. Sure, I'll call them," he said. "Right after I carve you like a Thanksgiving turkey. I'll tell them where to find the body."

I circled him slowly. As I did so, McAfee began feinting, his long arm thrusting the stiletto first at my face, then at my midsection. He was laughing all the while.

"Helen," I said without taking my eyes from him, "go back upstairs. Find a phone. Call the LAPD and ask for the Chief's office. Tell him all about this speakeasy and Maple Leaf Imports and their rat-faced ex-employee here. And be sure to tell them Parish is in on it."

McAfee went beet red. He ran right at me, knife in the air, whether to kill me or stop Helen, I couldn't say. I grabbed his arm with my left hand while my right swung the cup down on his head. It connected with a sharp *crack*, and McAfee dropped like a sack of dirty laundry. The knife clattered to the floor.

It's amazing what you can do when you stop giving a damn.

I knelt beside him and felt for a pulse. He was fine. "You were right," I said into his ear, "that was fun." I stuffed the cup back into my pocket, picked up the stiletto, and left him there, ignoring Helen's shocked expression. "Let's go."

I turned the corner. The corridor went about thirty feet more. Two doors across from each other, and one at the end. I tried the left door; locked. I leaned back and stamped it with my foot, smashing it open and taking part of the door frame with it. Satisfying.

It was a small room—an office of some kind. A curved wooden desk was strewn with papers. Against the wall stood a wooden rack with square cubbies holding various papers and ceramics. A quick perusal revealed many of the same scribbles we'd seen at the warehouse.

I found an empty satchel and filled it with all the papers, ceramics, and unusual objects we could find.

I moved to the door on the other side of the corridor, also locked. A sour smell came from it, and the wood was crumbling. I kicked in this one as well. Hot, steamy air with a dead animal smell greeted us. In the dim light from the corridor, I could make out shapes: a long table and chairs. A dining room? But there were shapes on the table—two long, strange shapes…

Helen found the switch and clicked on the lights.

I tried to make sense of what I saw—but I couldn't. On the table stretched two grotesque reptiles: heads, fangs, and serpentine bodies like snakes; short arms and legs like mutant salamanders. One had an enormous, muscular body of black and gold; the other, smaller, was solid black. They lay sprawled and motionless on the table as if gorged after some awful feast.

And they were. For as impossible, as loathsome as the things were, what brought me near to retching was what protruded from their mouths: the pallid legs of a woman from the smaller one; the shoulders and head of a man, face down on the table, from the larger one. The things were still digesting them.

"Christ…" I heard myself say. "Lord Jesus Christ, save us!"

"Oh, God," said Helen. "Oh, God…Professor, is there any chance that they're still…"

"What?…No, the woman…she must have at least suffocated by now…Help me turn the man over."

"Wh—what?…" She began to come apart.

"The man! Helen, he may still be alive! We have to roll the creature and turn him over."

We gathered what shreds of courage remained to us and heaved the thing by its arms and legs. It twitched and rippled slightly, but offered no resistance. With great effort, we managed to turn it on its back. I gripped the man by the shoulders, the back of his head between my arms so I wouldn't twist his neck. I turned him over…

His face was a yellow death mask, his eyes closed.

"No, Professor…he's—he's dead."

But he was not dead. He opened his eyes.

Helen screamed. My blood froze. I uttered a strangled cry, and then his eyes fixed on me. In them I saw horror, pain, fear, regret… and pleading—pleading for an end to his suffering. I shall never forget those eyes for as long as I live.

Helen staggered backward and looked away. I grabbed the stiletto from my jacket and plunged it into that poor man's chest, twisting the blade to make sure he was dead. Then I pulled it out and plunged into the throat of the serpent. Great gouts of blood spurted and ran, some green, some red. The serpent began to twitch and spasm. I tried to carve it, as a butcher would carve a pig, but the stiletto was useless for carving and the scaly hide all but impossible to cut.

"Professor!" Helen cried. "Professor! Leave it! We've got to get out of here."

I yanked the knife out of the thing, blood running, and ran out of the room. We fled around the corner with the satchel, back the way we had come.

I heard a door close from somewhere up the corridor. We slowed, then stopped. Someone was bent over McAfee. No—some *thing*. It stood upright like a man, head extended forward on a long neck, a thick tail balancing its other end. A great serpent it was, like the ones we had just seen—but this one was neither gorged nor dazed. It turned toward us.

"Wh-what—what is it?" Helen said.

"I don't know. But we've got to get past it."

Sesh

Sesh checked the human called McAfee. It was alive, but unconscious. Something had clearly attacked it. A moment later, he saw what it was.

Humans. Two of them, creeping toward him, one with a blade—and was that the satchel from his office? Had they broken in and stolen his papers?

He uncoiled and slid towards them.

Humans. The impudence, the arrogance! Their ape brains, ever deceitful, always bent towards violence, cruelty, and destruction. They defile the land, kill for sport, slaughter each other, just as they'd killed Albert in the Great War, poor, sweet young Albert, his son and heir, never to marry and raise children and inherit his wealth.

Sesh hated them, was sick of them: their smell, their petty squabbling, and their pointless machines and edifices. Soon enough, he would wipe them all away. But these two—they would die right now.

They attempted to move past him, but he slid his tail across the corridor, blocking their way.

"I have mouths to feed. Mark me, I'll make good use of you," he hissed. They couldn't possibly understand him, he knew; but he understood every word they said.

"Wait," said the one carrying the blade—a male. "It's wearing something, isn't it? It looks like a vest."

"Clothing?" said the smaller one, a female. "Do you think it could be intelligent?"

Father and Mother, their stupidity!

"Possibly. Perhaps we can reason with it." The male human put the blade away and put down the satchel. "Helen, take the bag," it said. "Follow me when I tell you." It held up its hands and walked slowly toward Sesh.

"Professor, no!" said the female. "These things are killers! What more proof do you need?"

Killers? Perhaps. But better stewards of this precious world than these witless apes.

The male continued toward Sesh. Stupid indeed. This would be easy, and most enjoyable.

Hands in the air, the human put its back against the wall of the corridor. "We are not here to harm you," it said. "We just want to leave. Do you understand?"

"Oh, yes," Sesh hissed. "I understand very well. And so will you, when my fangs are in your neck." He drew back and coiled against the opposite wall, raised his head, then bobbed it once.

The male extended its hand towards the female and slid along the wall, never taking its eyes from Sesh. "Helen, come—"

"Look out!" the female screamed.

Something hit Sesh hard. Scales and muscle and an unmistakable scent.

Shila. She coiled round him and held his neck in her jaws.

"You—how dare you—"

He felt a pinprick further down his neck.

"Sleep," she said.

He felt himself growing groggy. He watched helplessly as the humans ran past. But the male stopped and drew the blade.

"Professor, no!" cried the smaller human.

"This one's intelligent," the man said. "We can't just let the other one kill it." He plunged the blade into Shila. She released him. The last thing Sesh heard was the humans' footsteps echoing as they ran down the corridor.

Horace Jennings

The thing's blood soaked my sleeve. We were halfway up the stairwell when we heard Parish's voice through the door above.

"McAfee, you fucking stock boy, you're supposed to be watching the customers. If I have to come down there, so help me, I'll put that knife up your ass."

We ran back down and looked to our right. The creature in the vest was still lying in a heap down the corridor; but the one I had stabbed was nowhere in sight.

We went left, moving cautiously in the dim light. At the end of the corridor, on the left wall, was an opening. As we crept toward it, we heard heavy breathing. Something was waiting for us.

I drew the stiletto, my heart in my throat. Then I put one eye around the corner and peeked into the opening.

Steps leading up. And on them, the docent, her white sweater and black blouse stained with blood. She flinched when she saw me.

"Good Lord, what are you doing down here? What's happened to you?"

She looked up at me, confused.

A heartbeat later, Helen appeared. "She's been attacked by one of those things. Probably by the one you stuck with the knife." She began examining her.

"We must leave," the docent said, her breathing labored. She pointed up. "Stairs."

Helen and I helped her up the stairway as best we could. It was narrow and steep, ending in a set of cellar doors. At the top, I slid back the bar, opened them to the cold night air, and found myself on the south side of the building. Harry's Model A was parked nearby, the red glow of a cigarette the only sign he was there. I waved him over.

"Go at once," she said when we were all outside, the doors closed behind us.

"Not without you," I said.

"I will arrange my own transportation."

"Excuse me," said Helen, setting down the bag. "Would you mind telling us who you are?"

"I am a friend," the docent said. "Isn't that obvious?"

But Helen would not be put off. "Not particularly. And friends generally know each other's names. Mine is Helen Parker."

"My name is Susan River. Now please, go."

Harry pulled up beside us and got out of the car. He was none too pleased.

"Christ, Jennings, what the hell?" He flicked his cigarette to the ground. "I told you to snoop around, not go shopping and get into a fight. Who's the broad?"

"A friend," I told him. "She needs a doctor. Help me get her into the car."

CHAPTER
19
LEADS
Shila Ghiss

I awake in a strange bed, in a strange room. Everything is white: the bedding, the walls, the floor, even the clothing of the people who enter and leave the room. But bright yellow flowers spring from a vase beside my bed, and the orange light of the Father slants through a window. The day is just beginning, and the air is fresh, though the room carries a faint chemical odor. Antiseptics, I think.

This must be a hospital, where humans care for their sick and injured.

I was injured...

Beyond the flowers are three chairs, and in them are Horace Jennings and Helen Parker, both of whom appear drawn and weak; and the man who drove us last night, short and strong-looking. He sees me looking at him and nudges Horace Jennings, who was asleep. "She's awake," the man says.

"What? Oh. Yes, so she is." He stands and comes to my bedside. "Good morning, Miss River. How are you feeling?"

"I am well," I tell him. "There is no need for concern."

He tilts his head to the side, which I take as doubt. "You lost a lot of blood," he says. "Fortunately, we were able to give you a transfusion."

I do not know what a transfusion is, and Horace Jennings can discern this from my face. It never ceases to amaze me how many muscles there are in human faces, and how the slightest contortion, conscious or otherwise, enables communication.

"We supplemented your blood with our own. Well, not me. Your blood is type O, and I am type A, so I couldn't help. But Harry

Raymond and Miss Parker are both type O, and they gave you some of their blood."

I find this alarming, but I try not to let my face show it.

"You're welcome," says Harry Raymond, though I did not thank him. I realize that thanking them is appropriate.

"Thank you both. I am grateful for your help."

"Of course," says Horace Jennings. "Do you have any family that we should call to let them know you are here?"

My only family now is the king, and he will not leave the colony to visit me in a human hospital. Susan River's family is far away, and it would not be wise to involve them.

"I have no family."

They look at each other.

"Any friends?" Helen Parker asks.

"You are my friends."

Again they exchange looks. Helen Parker says, "Yes. We are."

Afterwards, a Master of Life Sciences—or what passes for one here on the surface—comes in and examines my wound. It has been closed with thread, and he replaces the soft white fabric that covers it. He tells me I may be able to leave the hospital tomorrow or the day after, and recover at home.

Helen Parker offers to bring clothes and other things from my room. She tells me to rest, and that they will have many questions for me once I am discharged.

I am glad that I will have at least a day to consider my answers.

Horace Jennings

Back in my room at the Biltmore, I asked Harry for the third time if we shouldn't report the creatures and their human victims to the police. He didn't entirely believe us, of course—who would? But he told us that Parish would likely be the detective assigned to investigate, so there was no point.

"The best thing you can do now is collect evidence to go with your testimony," he said. He inspected my dining table, with its fresh-cut flowers and fine china, and the marvelous view of Pershing Square. "Jesus. If I'd known you were this rich, I'd have charged you more than fifteen dollars a day."

"Yes. And with no contract, we're just lucky you're a man of your word."

That seemed to irritate him, so I stopped talking.

Helen brought in the bag we took from the basement of the speakeasy. The contents proved enigmatic. There was no shortage of paper, but the writing on it was indecipherable: endless squiggles, whorls, and circles run together, an insane cursive. In my youth I used to play at codes and cyphers, using math to break simple replacement codes; that was useless here, as the letters or characters, if indeed characters they were, could not be distinguished from one another. Without a parallel copy in a known language, it was hopeless.

One sheet of paper had three words written in English: investiture, convocation, commencement.

"What the hell does that mean?" Harry asked.

"Nothing," Helen said, "unless they're planning on opening a university."

"Even if they were," I said, "the words are in the wrong order. The convocation—the call to gather—comes first; then the investment of honors; then the actual commencement ceremony. It doesn't make sense."

"Really?" Helen asked. "*That's* what doesn't make sense to you?"

I saw her point. But those words bothered me. They didn't fit. I folded the paper and stuffed it in my pocket.

There were four small ceramic jars that looked like something Mary had once used for makeup. I examined one closely. When the top wouldn't pull off, I tried unscrewing it. That didn't work, either—until I tried turning it in the wrong direction. I carefully unscrewed the top and brought the jar to my face. I nearly dropped it before frantically screwing the top back on. It was filled with black powder. I didn't open any more jars.

Finally, there was a narrow metal cylinder. It appeared to be made of silver, and it looked for all the world like an ancient scroll case, and in remarkably good condition. At one end was a flat cap, and engraved upon it was the word "Stabiae" and beneath that, the letters "PCT".

"Latin?" Helen suggested.

I was reasonably proficient in Latin, having learned it as a student and read Virgil, Cicero, and a few others many years ago. I'd always felt that a good education began with the classics. But "Stabiae" had no translation. Perhaps a proper name. And "PCT"—I doubted it was an abbreviation for percentage.

"I don't know," I said. "Hopefully, there's a scroll inside that will prove more useful."

I turned the case over in my hands and inspected the opposite end. I wanted to be sure that this end was not the cap.

"C'mon, Jennings, just open it already."

"Harry, I don't come across treasures of antiquity every day. If you don't mind, I preferred not to destroy this one." He rolled his eyes and muttered. I'll confess to feeling briefly satisfied at having my expertise come into play for once.

The cap came off remarkably easily, and I realized with consternation at that, of course, it had already been opened. There was indeed a scroll inside. I slipped it out, and with the utmost care, unrolled it across the table: a single piece of parchment with text written in Latin.

I read through it, growing more and more astonished as I penned each line in English on some writing tablet. Helen paced and Harry smoked a cigarette at the window. When I was through, my hands trembled and my stomach churned. I called them over in a hoarse whisper.

"Good heavens, Professor, you're as white as a sheet. What on earth could possibly be worse than what we saw last night?"

I handed her the writing tablet. She began to read aloud.

"*Of the account of that the survivors of Stabiae provided to him, Gaius Plinius Caecilius Secundus adds this brief but exceedingly strange tale. I shall not include it in my writings and ask that if it be later found, it be destroyed, as I do not wish it to taint the accuracy of my other histories.*

"*Pliny writes that several of the survivors claim to have seen a thing emerge from the melted rock at Herculaneum. A great worm, they say it was, the exposed portion of which measured at least 30 cubits and whose maw exceeded 6 cubits. About the maw were tentacles, as a squid may have, and these it used to tear the limbs and heads from hapless victims crawling away from the heat.*

"*One of the survivors claims to have heard the creature's thoughts, as cold as the flowing red rock was hot, and with no more malice. It came from deep below the earth, he said, where all the world was red rock flowing; and it could make the earth tremble and split at will, and this it did to fetch a few baubles of rock from the surface, though in doing so it brought about the ruin of Pompei and Herculaneum. And having retrieved its baubles, it sank again into the scalding rock.*

"*Pliny believes that it is these creatures who cause the earth to tremble, and he would add these Vermis Terrae, as he calls them, to the knowledge of Man, that we may come to understand them and perhaps even use their knowledge of the earth for our betterment. But I say that Man should not have such knowledge, nor such teachers. It is most like that the Stabiae survivors were overcome by the same vapors that killed Pliny the Elder, and that these Vermis Terrae are a fancy; and if not, we should never speak nor write of them again.*

"*Upon my death, let this account be put to the fire.*

"*Publius Cornelius Tacitus.*"

Helen gasped. "Tacitus...the Roman historian?"

I nodded.

Harry was not impressed. "I don't get it."

"This is a record by Tacitus, a renowned Roman historian!" Helen said. "It's an account told to Pliny the Younger by survivors of the volcanic eruption that destroyed Pompei and Herculaneum in 79 AD! Even if the content is utter nonsense, it's still an incredible, invaluable archeological find."

"Which you stole," Harry said.

"From creatures that were eating people," Helen countered. "Or from the people that were harboring these creatures, take your pick."

"What if it's true?" I whispered.

"What? Professor, don't be—"

"Absurd? After what we've just seen? It sounds very much like the text Charles Ellis translated for Mateo—the Santorini eruption. Two different volcanic events, more than 1,600 years apart, with the same description of giant 'earth worms' emerging from the lava? That can't be a coincidence."

Harry crushed out his cigarette. "So, first giant snakes, and now giant earth worms?"

I knew how it sounded. "Harry, if this is true, then the serpents are a mild aberration by comparison. And in my vision—"

He threw his hands in the air. "Oh, now we're bringing visions into this? Well, why didn't you say so? I'm sure the LAPD chief can convince the DA to admit those as evidence. Right after he has the two of you locked up in the looney bin."

Helen ignored him. "True or not, I agree, it sounds like the text Mateo asked Ellis to translate."

"I'll call Ellis and give him the hotel address," I said. "He can mail us his translation as soon as he—"

"Christ!" Harry yelled. We both shut up. "I can't believe this horseshit. We need *hard evidence!*" He smacked his hands together. "*Hard!* Not Roman history, not visions. What about Sam Smith? Your dance partner was in the basement of his club. What did she say about him?"

"I—we didn't ask her." There just hadn't been time…

Harry smacked himself on the forehead so hard it left a handprint. "I can't believe I sent you two geniuses into that speakeasy. I should have known better. Jennings, here's what's going to happen. I'm going to start asking questions, and you're going to write them down. Then tomorrow we're going to ask your friend every one of those questions and see what she says. After that, we're going to pay a visit to Sam Smith."

"Not back to the speakeasy, surely?" Helen asked, blanching.

"No, at his home."

"His home?" I asked. "How in the world do you know where he lives?"

He smacked himself again. "The phone book, Jennings! Jesus! Ever hear of that? The phone book and a few calls to make sure I got the right Sam Smith."

It probably wasn't a good time to tell Harry that we'd been to the museum where Susan River posed as a docent and Mateo fled a crime scene. I was afraid he'd give himself a concussion. But I didn't see that we had much choice.

He turned out to be quite calm about it. A moment later, I understood why.

"You got her home address and room key from the hospital?" he asked Helen. She nodded. "Good. Let's go."

The address was in Chinatown, an impoverished area with a modest commercial center. Harry drove us past one- and two-story brick buildings lining narrow streets, with various signs in English and Chinese: Dragon's Den, Lotus Garden, and so forth. Paper lanterns had been strung across the main street in celebration, and there was even a theater that noted its next production in Chinese; but many of the stores and shops carried smaller signs that read "Vacant" or "To Let." The neighborhood was like an old man in denial of a terminal disease.

"You know this area, Detective?" Helen asked from the back seat.

"Sure, I know it. The wife and I used to come here all the time when we were first married—yes, I'm married." He looked in the rear-view mirror. "Wipe that smirk off your face, Miss Parker. You, too, Jennings. You think detectives can't have families?"

"Well, Harry," I began, "you never—it's just that—"

"Yeah, you can stop digging that hole. And before anyone asks, yes, I have children, a boy and a girl, and no, I don't have any pictures."

"This seems like a hard place to live," Helen said as we passed a dance hall and a bawdy-looking flophouse.

"Used to be a lively place before the Great War. Then the state passed a law barring Chinese from owning land. So other people came in and owned it for them—not nice people. They turned a lot of properties into brothels and gambling halls. And that just brought in more people—the wrong kind. Then comes Prohibition, and the bootleggers moved in."

"That's…awful," said Helen.

"Sure," Harry continued. "But you know who was the worst of the lot? Not a gangster or a bootlegger. It was an engineer." He looked at me.

I laughed—until I saw by his expression that he wasn't joking. "A civil engineer?"

"That's right. Working for the railroads. He decided this neighborhood would be the ideal place for a new train station. Once they clear away all the buildings, that is."

I thought back to the magnificent Union Station in Chicago, and I felt a little queasy.

"But weren't the people in the neighborhood given any choice?" Helen asked. "This is America, after all."

"Sure, it's America. They were given a choice. In fact, the entire population of Los Angeles got to vote on it two years ago. The choice was either an elevated railway or a train station." He looked back at her through the mirror. "They chose the train station. It's in the planning stages now, but it'll be built in a few years. They're going to call it Union Station."

"Isn't that the same name as…" Helen began. She stopped when she saw me rubbing my temples. "That's why so many of the buildings are vacant," she said. "The neighborhood is on borrowed time."

"The price of progress," Harry said. It cut deeply.

We pulled up to the address, a dingy two-story building with alleys on both sides. No one stopped us as we walked through the front door and climbed the stairs to Susan River's room.

It was clean, but small and sad, especially compared to our palatial accommodations at the Biltmore. The furniture was shabby, and the few windows admitted very little light from the alley.

"I suppose this is all she can afford," said Helen, gripping her elbows as if the room were chilly. "Let me see if I can find a change of clothes for her."

I busied myself examining a small bookshelf. I found many titles on Native American and Mesoamerican culture and lore, and other indigenous peoples around the world. There were books on art, history, and geography as well. Exactly what I would expect from a docent at a cultural museum.

Harry found an envelope on her bureau with photos and letters. He held a few of them up for us. "No family, huh?" He went through them one by one, every word and every picture, while Helen and I waited.

"Well?" I asked him as he put them all away. "Satisfied?"

"That she's a docent? Maybe, or else some kind of scholar. But she lied about not having a family, and she lied about working at the museum that day. Trust me, this broad's hiding something."

"Is that so?" Helen said, stuffing the clothing she'd collected into a paper bag. "Well, *this* broad thinks you're a neanderthal."

Harry just grinned at her. "It's only been a few days, doll face. The wife tells me I'm an acquired taste. Give it time."

CHAPTER 20

MAGNATE

Sesh

Sesh sat in the sunroom of Sam Smith's hilltop mansion, its broad window overlooking the ocean. There were many comfortable chairs in this room, and Smith had spent many hours here—in this same chair, he knew—seeking tranquility.

Sesh had yet to find it.

It had taken years of planning, moving slowly and cautiously among humans, to infiltrate their organizations with the handful of guards he had trained. But the guards were too few, the infiltration too slow. And there were some who succumbed to the temptations and pleasures of humanity, who forgot who they were. He had arranged imaginative deaths for them, purportedly at the hands of humans. His most loyal servants needed human counterparts who were equally loyal to him—to Sam Smith. And so Sesh began to seek out Smith's old shipmates for them to consume. It worked beautifully, enabling him to build a strong, unified crew.

For humanity's destruction, the king had decided on a plague. It would spread throughout the world and kill them all, leaving their infrastructure and devices intact, for examination and use when his subjects emerged from the depths to reclaim the surface. Shila's father, tasked with delivering this plague, had failed in his first attempt ten years ago. It had killed only fifty million—a tiny fraction of them.

There would not be a second attempt, Sesh had decided. For in the aftermath of what humans called the Spanish Flu, in the endless reformulations and testing on human subjects, the great Master of Life Sciences had stumbled upon something he hadn't recognized as valuable: an undetectable liquid which, administered in regular doses, made humans compliant.

It was then that Sesh saw the path to victory: the mass production of the serum; a magnate to provide resources and a distribution network; and a great cataclysm to create chaos and the opportunity to seize control of the western half of this continent. With care and discretion, the rest of the continent would follow, and eventually, the world.

It was unfortunate that Shila's father did not agree. But then, he had never cared for Sesh, despite supporting his advancement. He was a myopic scientist; poisoning him had not been difficult. Sesh knew it would also be necessary for the king to die if the surface was to be reclaimed. Shila's uncle was too cautious, rigid, and unimaginative to thwart humanity's accelerating progress.

Sesh had hoped Shila would be different. She had certainly seemed different when she was a young adult. He'd hoped she might join with him and become the mother of a new dynasty. Instead, she'd been corrupted by the human she'd consumed. She sympathized with them, betrayed him. She would have to die as well.

"Mr. Smith?"

"Hmm?" The young man stood by in his khaki slacks and buttoned-down white shirt. *So much like Albert.* Sesh hadn't noticed him standing there. "Yes, my boy?"

"I've rechecked all the locations and numbers, sir, based on the information you've provided. I've transferred them from Dr. Lawson's map of the fault line to your map of Southern California. It's upstairs if you'd like to review it."

"Thank you, my boy. And the total of all the numbers?"

The boy smiled broadly. "Twelve, sir."

"Outstanding!" The boy was a magician. A dozen locations along hundreds of miles of fault line, and only twelve worms required. Sesh thought it easily manageable.

He rose from his chair and clasped Mateo on the shoulder. "I'm proud of you, son. You've done very well. And in recognition of your work, I'd like you to join me at the convocation."

Mateo stood speechless for a moment.

Sesh laughed. "Of course, if you have other plans…"

Mateo embraced him. "Thank you, sir! I'd be honored!"

"Nonsense. You deserve to see the fruits of your labor. We are family, you and I. And together we have a fine future before us."

For a while at least, tranquility came to Sesh.

CHAPTER
21

SECRETS REVEALED

Shila Ghiss

The hotel where Horace Jennings and Helen Parker are staying is the most beautiful, comfortable, luxurious place I have ever been. The ground floor is filled with frescoes, fountains, statuary, and beautifully carved marble and wood. The ceiling is remote, the floor covered with shining stone and soft carpets. Humans walk through this magnificence in every direction; yet many seem unaware that it exists. I can barely take my eyes from it.

An elevator whisks us to the fifth floor, where we enter Professor Jenning's room. It is airy, sun-drenched, and filled with soft chairs and fine furnishings. I am shown a paper with an endless list of foods that delights and confuses me. I select something that Susan River would enjoy—a meal with corn, lamb, and leafy vegetables—and I am told it will be brought to the room shortly.

The detective begins questioning me. He asks me about a young man called Mateo Martinez. I know nothing about him.

Then Sam Smith. I cannot tell them who and what he is or what he has done. Instead, I mix truth and lie together. I say he is a patron of the Southwest Museum, where I work as a docent. He collects art, and I helped him when he visited by explaining the origins and meaning of some art. But on his last visit, he seemed interested in me personally, so I avoided him and took time away from work. I know nothing about the theft of stones from the museum, and it seems unlikely that Mr. Smith would be involved in such a thing. *Why does Sesh want these stones?*

Why was I at the speakeasy, and what was I doing in the

basement? I had overheard museum guests talking about this place, and I was curious, so I went there. When I met Professor Jennings, I remembered him from the museum. I advised him not to drink the alcohol there because I'd heard it was tainted. I was in the basement because I followed him there. He seemed troubled, and I was concerned about him.

The detective sat down at the table next to me and spread his thick fingers on the tabletop before him. "You were concerned about a man you only met once, briefly?"

"Yes. He and Miss Parker seemed ill prepared to explore the prohibited areas of an illegal establishment. I thought they might be in danger."

The detective looks at Jennings. "Well, you're not wrong about that," he says.

The professor grins at me, his hair almost as unkempt as it was that evening. It is…endearing.

"Let's talk about what happened in the basement," the detective says. "You saw one of these…creatures. Is that right?"

"Yes."

"And it bit you?"

I remember Professor Jennings stabbing me with cold steel as I struggled to keep Sesh from harming him—the shock, the pain. It felt like…betrayal. My eyes become wet.

"Yes," I tell him.

"With its fangs."

"Yes, of course, with its fangs." Susan River would have kept the irritation out of her voice. But I feel myself becoming upset.

The detective leans forward in his chair. "How did this creature—a serpent of some kind, if I understand correctly—bite you with only one fang?"

I study him intensely, the way I do when I am about to strike: his brown eyes searching mine, his slightly bulbous nose and crooked bottom teeth. I would very much like to strike him.

"I don't know, Detective. I only know it hurt me very much."

Helen Parker rescues me. "Maybe she bit herself," she says dryly. "Show the detective your teeth, honey. He may need some convincing."

They begin to argue, but they stop when someone knocks at the door. A man pushes a cart into the room. He spreads a white linen cloth over the table, sets silverware and glasses, and uncovers a dish that makes my mouth water. There is also a small cake and a carafe of coffee. He shuffles some of the fine china cups to the table, bows, and leaves.

I thank our Mother, the Earth, for giving us life and sustaining us. I cannot tell if the words are mine or Susan River's. I am hungry, but I force myself to eat slowly, with dignity and solemnity. The room is silent.

There are no more questions. After I finish my meal, Professor Jennings removes my empty plate and replaces it with things that he and Helen Parker have taken from the basement of the speakeasy: documents, medical jars, and an ancient human scroll. I begin reviewing the documents, hissing quietly as I do. *Sesh's alternate plan! These pages hold some clues to it.*

"Can you actually read this?" Helen Parker asks. "How?"

Only then do I realize that I have become absorbed in it, and they are all watching me. *I am a fool.*

"No," I say at first. Then, seeing the objection forming on their faces: "Some of it, perhaps."

Now they are excited. As the detective looks on in amusement, the two of them begin chattering away at each other, theorizing and speculating wildly about my kind. Absurd. But I envy their rapport.

"There's one other thing," Professor Jennings says. "This was in Sam Smith's warehouse."

From a drawer, he produces my father's cup.

I find myself gaping as this man, this human, dangles before me something I once touched daily with reverence: a personal possession of my father, who spent his life trying to destroy all of them. I picture him at his desk, paying me no mind as I pour water into his cup.

Perhaps I loved him after all…

"This ceramic seems unbreakable," Jennings remarks.

Indeed, our ceramics are far stronger than any I have yet seen here on the surface. This cup has always seemed everlasting to me; but it reminds me that we are not. I acknowledge his comment absently as I consider what to do…

I must create a myth—one that will enable me to work with them to uncover Sesh's plans without divulging what I am. I must command their respect while maintaining my independence.

In a flash, I see it before me, fashioned from Susan River's knowledge of ancient cultures and Sesh's mastery of lies. *Each step I take down this path leads me closer to becoming a traitor, a monster—or both.*

―⁂―

Horace Jennings

"Alright," I said. "You can read their writing—at least some of it. So what can you tell us about these creatures? Where do they come from? And for that matter, how do you know so much about them? If I may ask, that is."

"That's four questions, Professor," said Helen. "Save some for me."

"These are fair questions," said Susan. "Let me try to answer them one at a time. At different times, and in different places around the world, fossil records and archaeological explorations have uncovered anomalies—evidence that does not fit with the world as we understand it to have been. For example, advanced alloys found in stone age sites; written languages predating human writing—in fact, some predating humankind. Some of these anomalies have simple explanations, and some have been revealed as hoaxes. But there are several that we cannot explain, except by the existence of another civilization—here, on the Earth, before humans."

"That's impossible," Helen said flatly. "The geological record doesn't lie. And there is no record anywhere of a civilization predating humans."

"I am sorry, but there is," said Susan. "It simply has not been shared. There are records in China, dating back thousands of years, of anomalies found during excavations for buildings and canals. They point to a civilization whose writing is comprised of curves and waves, with no straight lines. Even here, in North America, native peoples pass down stories of these creatures through their oral traditions. Some even create a mythos around it, as you have seen with Quetzalcoatl. And on very rare occasions, an artifact is found—a metal box, for example, enclosing a polyhedron with strange properties; or a phial containing a powder that produces an altered state of consciousness or perception beyond the physical world."

"Good Lord," I heard myself say. "Mateo's powder…"

"The elders of these ancient peoples recognized that such things, in the wrong hands, could bring about disaster. And so, they created an order of wise men and women to safeguard such knowledge, to learn more about those who created it—and to keep it secret from the rest of the world."

"You," I said. It was a statement, not a question. "You are one of the wise."

"No. I am but a student."

"Impossible," said Helen. "I don't believe it."

"You have already seen the proof, Miss Parker," Susan said. "In fact, you have seen more than artifacts; you have seen the creatures who employ them. Do you really doubt your own eyes?"

For a few minutes, we sat in silence. Harry poured some coffee into the one of the exquisite cups that had been placed on the table, and sampled the cake. Eventually, he cleared his throat and asked a few more questions.

"Miss River, what brought you to the Del Monte speakeasy?"

"As I said, I overheard museum guests talking about it, and I was curious."

"Yes, of course. But you somehow got through a locked door and into the basement. You admit to knowing Sam Smith, who appears to be supplying this place with liquor. And you seemed to know the way out of the basement."

"All true," she said. "Your question, Mr. Raymond?"

"Well, Miss River, don't you see how suspicious that might seem? A woman, clearly an outsider, in a den of criminals, operating with impunity?"

She smiled. "Yes. I can see how that might seem suspicious to a man like you. A detective. Do you suspect me of working with these criminals?"

They locked eyes for a tense moment. Then Harry said, "No. I don't think you are working with them. And it's clear that you saved my clients from…well, something. We are all grateful for that. But you are not telling us everything, are you?"

"No," she said. "I am not. But I have already told you more than I should."

"Really?" he said skeptically. "And why is that?"

She said nothing; she merely stared back at him impassively. Neither one of them was prepared to back down. Harry, though, had a limited supply of patience.

"Miss River, I don't like it when people withhold information from me. Particularly when it's information that my clients desperately need. Now perhaps we're not entitled to know whatever secrets you are keeping from us. Fair enough. But I believe we're at least entitled to know *why* you won't tell us. Wouldn't you agree?"

Another tense moment, and I expected harsh words between them. Instead, she replied cooly, "Very well. You wish to know why I will not disclose all that I know, and I give you this answer: Because the elders forbid it. Because this knowledge is dangerous; it will put your lives at risk. And because, should you share it with others, they will be equally at risk."

"I see," Harry said, and it was clear he was having none of it. "I won't debate this with you, because I can see that your mind is made up." He pushed out his chair and stood. "Jennings, Miss Parker, I think we've taken up enough of Miss River's time. I've arranged for us to meet with Sam Smith at his home tomorrow morning. Miss River, I'll call a cab to take you home."

"Wait!" she said. "Detective, you must not meet with Sam Smith. He is a dangerous man."

"Why?" Harry asked. "Because he made a pass at you?"

She went silent. Smoldering.

Harry dialed the concierge and asked for a cab to Chinatown. Then he swept the papers, scroll case, jars, and cup into my briefcase, pulled two dollars out of his pocket and placed it in front of her.

"Miss River, there are two things I'd like you to consider. First, I think you should let us decide what risks we are willing to take for ourselves. And second, you are not the only one in possession of forbidden knowledge. My clients have just showed you a trove of documents and artifacts that I'm sure you'd like to review. It's a pity we can't help each other." He tossed his business card on top of the bills. "If you change your mind, call my office."

He opened the door for her, and before she left, she looked at us with a mixture of disapproval, concern, and regret. Helen and I rose to follow her out the door.

Harry blocked our way. "Try not to lose any more blood, Miss River. Next time we may not be there to help you." He pushed the door closed.

The mood in the hotel room was somber after Susan River left. Harry took a small notebook out of his pocket, jotted down some notes, then put it away. The conversation left a bad taste in my mouth.

"We were making progress, Harry. She was telling us the facts. Until you insulted her and walked her out. I hope you know what you're doing."

"Look, I know you hold this—Susan—in high regard. But if you let her call the shots, you'll never really know what's going on, and you'll never find Martinez. She should have leveled with you when she met you at the speakeasy. So if she wants anything more from us, she'd better pony up the facts—all the facts."

His detective slang was grating on me. "Is that all you've got? A mixed bag of clichés?"

The feeling was mutual. "No, smart guy. I'll tell you what I got. I got blood on my car seat from saving her sorry ass. I got a bruise on my arm from giving her *my* blood, and I got LAPD asking where I've been for the past two days. You know what else I got? I got us a meeting tomorrow with a rich guy who's actually going to lead us to your boy, not some mystery broad telling us stories about snakes."

He grabbed his hat. "I'll meet you both in the lobby tomorrow morning at nine. And don't bring that briefcase with you."

CHAPTER
22

CITIZEN KANE

Horace Jennings

Helen and I had dinner together, then went for a walk in the park outside the hotel. After our time in the basement speakeasy, the hospital, and our rooms, nice though they were, it felt good to be outside on a cool, clear evening. Here it was, early March, and yet it felt like late spring. I could see the appeal of Southern California.

We reminisced about Mateo. She told me about the time he'd visited her at the mining camp in Montana in the dead of winter; she'd taught him how to ice skate. I told her about the time I took on him to an Army Corps of Engineers dinner in Boston; I'd taught him how to tie his necktie. We exchanged stories about his legendary naivete: the time he loaned his watch to a complete stranger and watched him walk away with it; the time he gave her an all-too-honest opinion on her new hairstyle; and the time the crew team tricked him into single-handedly trying to rebuild the college boathouse, which had burned down 50 years ago. I suspected Helen could add more personal stories.

The last time I spoke to Mateo, I told her, he'd called me from San Francisco to tell me about meeting Andrew Lawson, who was leading the geotechnical investigation for the new bridge. I'd met Lawson back in 1906 in the aftermath of the terrible earthquake, and Mateo was just as much in awe of him as I was back then. (Helen: "Oh, yes! I'm in awe of him, too!")

Lawson, one of the best known geologists in the world, had just been made professor emeritus at Berkely. Compared to him, I was a kindergarten teacher. But Mateo looked up to me nonetheless.

127

By half-past eight, Helen was tired, so we took the elevator back to our rooms. I was restless, unsettled. I tried reading the evening paper, but it was one-third city intrigue, one-third help wanted ads, and one-third real estate ads. Between the ticking of the desk clock, the conversational arrangement of the furniture, and the vases of flowers, I felt as if I were in a waiting room. I cast the newspaper aside and went back down to the hotel restaurant for some tea.

Sitting alone at the table next to me was a big man in a stylish blue suit, white shirt, and a green silk necktie.

"I beg your pardon," he said. "I didn't intend to eavesdrop, but I overheard part of your conversation in the park with the young lady. Did I hear that you are a professor? May I ask what you teach?"

"Civil engineering," I said. "Though I'm currently on sabbatical."

"It's wonderful to meet you," he said. "This city is growing so fast, it can't get out of its own way. We need people like you, Professor…"

"Jennings," I said. "Horace Jennings. Brown University."

"It's a pleasure to meet you, Professor Jennings." He rose, stepped over to my table. He had a firm handshake and an easy smile. "My name is Kent Kane Parrot."

I read about him not ten minutes ago. He was a friend of the mayor and involved himself deeply in city politics. My surprise must have been clear and amusing.

"I see you heard of me."

"Only what I read in the papers, Mr. Parrot. This is my first time in Los Angeles."

Parrot's eyes lit up. "First time in LA? Well then, you've got to come up to my rooms! I'm in the penthouse, and it has a spectacular view, especially at night." Before I could protest, he'd walked me to the elevator, where the young, uniformed operator greeted him by name.

"Penthouse, sir?"

"Yes, Eddie. Mister—I mean, Professor—Jennings is going to join me for a nightcap."

"Yes, sir."

"I—well, thank you, Mr. Parrot."

"I go by 'Kane,'" he said. "I've always hated the family name. Got teased mercilessly when I was a kid. Still happens from time to time."

Kane, I judged, was at least six feet tall, but in the elevator he seemed a titan. He had rugged good looks and a commanding presence. I couldn't imagine anyone teasing him.

"Kind of you to show me your rooms. I hope it's not an inconvenience."

"Not at all," he said. The elevator stopped, and we stepped out into a long corridor with a plush carpet and very few doors. Kane led me to the door across from the elevator.

Inside was a large foyer, tastefully decorated with chairs, urns, a mirror, and watercolors of cityscapes and landscapes I'd seen in Los Angeles. A wide corridor led away from the door, rooms on either side of it revealing a study, bedrooms, and a kitchen. Each was spacious, windowed, and well furnished.

My own study had always felt comfortable and complete—Mary had seen to that. Compared to Kane's study, however, it was tiny, shabby, and childish. Where there were not windows, there was expensive wood paneling; where there was not paneling, there were bookshelves in sections: history, literature, science, and technology, and the widest section on nature and earth science. There were even a few rare books under glass, though I couldn't identify them. A massive, ornate desk dominated one end of the room; a long table with a city map, the other.

We walked through an archway at the end of the corridor and into a great room with windows on three sides. Here were two levels: on the first, a long dining table and various cupboards and sideboards; two steps down were windows and wing-backed leather chairs, a sofa, bar, radio, and victrola.

While I was still marveling at the furniture, Kane slid open a glass door, admitting the fresh night air, and led me outside, down a final step to the terrace. We faced east, but we could see to the north and south as well. All of Los Angeles lay at our feet, a sea of shimmering lights and monuments to man's ingenuity and audaciousness, while in the distance, the mountains and forests beckoned. In the cloudless sky, stars and the faintest sliver of a new moon struggled to compete with the lights below. Kane had not one but two telescopes: a refractor, aimed at the city below; and a reflector aimed skyward.

"Kane, this place—it's overwhelming. Truly wonderful. You are a fortunate man."

"Thank you," he said. He stood between the two telescopes, master of heaven and earth, hands in his pockets, eyes cast at his feet. "I know it's a bit much. But I've always wanted a place like this. A place where I could retreat from the world, but still see it, study it. I've always admired men like you, Jennings. Scientists, engineers, academics. People who spend their lives studying the world so they can better understand it and make it a better place." He paused. "Come. Let's go inside and get something to drink."

Kane's bar was nearly as well stocked as the Del Monte: liquors and mixers, liqueurs and garnishes. "What can I get for you?" he asked, stepping behind it, rubbing his hands together.

"Nothing, really," I said, though I was truly in the mood for a drink.

"Come now," he said, splaying his fingers across the polished wood. "If you're concerned about the law of the land, it doesn't apply here. I can assure you, no one will know."

"Well…" I said, weakening.

"Wait!" he said. "Let me guess." He sized me up, as if examining my clothing could tell him my preference in alcoholic beverages. "Vermouth? No, that's not it. But something sweet and smooth. Here, I have just the thing." He pulled out a beautiful crystal decanter filled with a golden brown liquid, then produced two wine glasses. He led me to the wing-backs, set the glasses on a side table, and poured one for each of us.

I took a small sip. Sweet, smooth, and a wonderful finish. "Sherry! And an excellent one at that. Kane, how on earth did you know?"

"One of my many hidden talents," he said, "scarcely used these days, now that alcohol is verboten." He sipped his own and smiled broadly. "Tell me about your work."

And so I told him about my long and varied engineering career, and the many projects I'd worked on: railways and stations; bridges and highways; hospitals and schools; and so many more. He seemed genuinely interested, even impressed. I sipped my sherry, and reflected from below in the open glass door, the sea of glittering lights winked at me. I found myself having a very enjoyable evening.

When I finished, he said, "There you are. This is what I'd like to discuss with you."

"Oh?"

"Yes. You see, Jennings, civil engineering talent is especially critical in a growing city. As I said, we need people like you."

"You're joking. You already have men like me. Better, in fact." I recounted my impression of the beautiful new City Hall tower, the trolley system that ran through the city and out to the coast, and the magnificent dams, power stations, and aqueduct system that I'd only read about.

But Kane had already made up his mind. He was the kind of man who, unlike me, always knew exactly what he wanted. And what he wanted now was for me to accept some job or position. I waited to find out what it was.

He dismissed the great public works I'd mentioned with a wave of his wine glass, nearly spilling his sherry. "That's all very well," he said. "But soon we'll be building a new train station and a new airfield—one with lighted runways and illuminated navigational aids, so that planes can land even at night. And there are myriad new buildings needed: schools, hospitals, post offices, and all manner of government buildings. You don't expect a bunch of water engineers to manage such a diverse range of projects, do you?"

"Well, I—"

"You have the education and diversity of experience we need. And you bring perspective, Jennings. The broader perspective that engineers so often lack."

A gust blew in from the open door to the balcony, and Kane's silky green tie undulated as he spoke. "You know what happened in Owens Valley when they built that aqueduct, don't you? It destroyed the valley. They took a hundred-mile swath of fertile farmland, drained its water, and turned it into a desert. The only thing that grows there now is sagebrush."

"No," I said. "That can't be true."

"Of course it's true! Why do you think the farmers and landowners there hate the city? It's because an engineer made the decision, with no real input from elected officials. And surely you've heard about the plan for the new train station in Chinatown? You know it's doomed the entire neighborhood."

"Yes," I said, remembering the conversation with Harry, "but I'm an engineer, too, not a politician."

"But you have the breadth of experience to know when an engineering decision needs a broader review. That sets you apart from the others. That's why we need you." He drained the last of his sherry, and rose to get more.

"Need me for what, exactly?"

"City Engineer," he said. "Head of the Bureau of Engineering for the City of Los Angeles."

I inhaled sherry down my windpipe and had a small coughing fit. Kane, with a bemused look, slapped me on the back several times.

"Kane, that's absurd. I'm an outsider. I couldn't find my way to City Hall without a streetcar map."

"That's exactly what we need," he said, sitting back down, his sherry refilled. "An outsider. Someone with the credentials, but untainted by partisanship and local factions."

"But you already have a City Engineer. I read about him—Major Shaw, isn't it? A war hero. Habor Engineer, and a member of the County Flood Control Board."

"Bah!" Kane waved him away. "Another water engineer, master of projects already completed. Exactly what we *don't* need."

"But he built the city's streets. The highway over the Santa Monica

Mountains. Bridges, grade separations, tunnels. A thousand miles of storm and sanitary sewers. *City Hall*, Kane! The man saw it done. And he lobbied Congress to build a massive dam to bring water and power from the Colorado River. How could you possibly let a man like that go?"

"Me? I'm not letting anyone go. I don't hold any office. But I know the people who do, and they want to be sure we are looking forward, not backward."

"It just seems…"

"Don't be coy, Jennings. This is the capstone of an illustrious career. All you have to do is say yes. Now, are you interested or not?"

"Well…yes, of course I'm interested."

"Fine," he said, rising. "Think it over. But don't take too long. The city is a machine with a lot of moving parts, and it never slows down. I'm meeting one of the City Council members for lunch in a private dining room downstairs at 1pm tomorrow. You're welcome to join us—I'll give the hotel staff your name. If you'd like, we can discuss the details then. If you're not ready…well, there might be a little more time. But not much."

I rose and thanked him, and he showed me to the door, where he gave me a firm handshake.

"I enjoyed having you here tonight, Jennings. Whatever you decide, I want you to know that you have my respect and admiration—two things I don't give lightly. Goodnight."

CHAPTER

23

MEETING OF THE MINDS

Horace Jennings

"Remember," Harry said as we neared our destination. "Let me do the talking."

His Model A climbed a hill, rounded a sharp curve, then slowed to pass through a set of open iron gates. The driveway circled a large fountain with a statue of Aquarius at its center, the water splashing down at its feet. Behind it rose a huge mansion with a square hip roof and wrought-iron balconies. It seemed to squint at us.

Harry parked off the circle, and we climbed broad steps to a pair of heavy oak doors with iron rings. A man in black and gold livery opened one door and admitted us.

Inside, the house was dark and cool, and it smelled of cigars. It seemed to be decorated in a Mesoamerican motif, though I was no expert. Wood carvings, blankets, and innumerable works of pottery lined every table and shelf. There were paintings, as well, and my eyes landed on one that was quite strange: a man being born from a cactus—or was it a cactus transforming into a man?

"That looks like a work by Guillermo Meza," I mused aloud.

"Very good!" said a voice behind us. It belonged to a man of perhaps sixty years who looked stronger and happier than the man whose photo was in the newspaper clipping.

"Sam Smith. You must be Horace Jennings." His head bobbed up and down in an oddly familiar way as he extended a hand. "I didn't expect you to be an art expert."

I shook it. "Hardly an expert, Mr. Smith. I've just seen some of Meza's work in a museum. A pleasure to meet you, sir."

I introduced Helen and Harry. Smith greeted them. His smile seemed genuine, but his gaze lingered too long for my taste. "Come," he said. "Let's sit in the sunroom, shall we?"

He led us through one room with a massive fireplace and into another with six plush chairs arranged in a circle and a wide window overlooking the ocean. But none of us bothered with the view. Standing before the window was a slender young man in a white shirt and khaki pants, a mop of black hair obscuring the face that we had desperately hoped to see again: Mateo Martinez.

Helen was on him in a moment, sobbing, her face buried in his chest, her arms wrapped around him as if she never intended to let go. Mateo, for his part, was equal parts delight and befuddlement.

"Helen, darling, what—?" Then he saw me, and his befuddlement grew. "Professor Jennings, what are you doing here?"

Helen spared me the answer. "We're here to take you home, you idiot!"

"Ah, the follies of youth," said Smith, sighing. "They make an old man smile."

"That they do," I said, bringing a handkerchief to my eyes. I felt as if someone had removed a crushing weight from my back.

Harry said, "Mr. Smith, we can't thank you enough for agreeing to meet with us. I know you have a few concerns, but if you'll indulge us, we'll address them."

"Of course," Smith said. He gestured for us to sit.

Helen sat next to Mateo and laced her fingers through his. Harry sat on the other side of her. He leaned to her ear and whispered, but I heard him nonetheless.

"Not bad for a neanderthal, eh, Miss Parker?"

She blushed—an exceedingly rare sight—and gave him a weak smile. I sat next to Harry, and Smith next to me. The chair on the other side of him remained empty.

The servant in black and gold brought in tea and set it on a side table.

Smith explained that he'd gone to San Francisco to learn more about the bridge and its potential impacts on shipping and commerce. Andrew Lawson gave him a tour of the site. There, Smith met Mateo and soon realized that his understanding of the local geological conditions would be useful to his next business venture.

That intrigued me. "Really? What kind of venture?"

Smith smiled awkwardly. "I'm sorry, I'm afraid it has to remain a secret until I announce it. But young Mateo, here, has been extremely helpful. He's obviously learned a great deal from you, Professor Jennings."

"Yes. Everything but common sense, it seems." I didn't want to seem rude, so I returned his compliment. "I understand that you were a professor as well, Mr. Smith, and highly regarded. I seem to recall reading that you taught at UCLA."

"I did teach for a while, yes. And like you, I'm no stranger to students who sometimes lack…common sense, as you say. But Mateo is brilliant, and a fine young man. Reminds me so much of my son, Albert. I've grown quite fond of him."

Mateo beamed at this compliment. The servant brought the tea around on a tray, first to Harry, who I knew would sooner swallow motor oil.

"No, thank you. Mr. Smith, I mentioned on the phone that the LAPD has asked me to look into a potential connection between Mr. Martinez's car and the theft of mineral specimens from the Southwest Museum. I'd like to ask him a few questions about it, if you don't mind."

"Of course," Smith said. He called the servant over, who'd been about to pour tea for Helen. Smith gave him some instructions, and the servant put the tray on the side table and left.

Mateo told Harry that he'd met an old man at the museum who needed a ride. He'd given him one.

"Where to?" Harry asked.

"He said he needed to get to Lone Pine."

"Lone Pine?" Harry's face held the same expression it had when we told him about the creatures in the basement of the Del Monte.

"That's a three-hour drive. You drove a man you just met halfway up Owen's Valley?"

"Of course not," Mateo said. "I loaned him the car. I got out in Santa Monica and took a taxi back here."

Harry looked at me. I shrugged. *Welcome to Mateo's world, Harry.*

Mateo didn't understand the fuss. "He's a baseball coach. He needed to get back in time for a game."

Harry seemed to be trying to pull his face off with one hand. "Sure he did, kid. And did you get the car back?"

"Not yet," Mateo said. "But I gave him Mr. Smith's number. I'm sure I'll hear from him soon."

Harry looked at Smith, who pursed his lips and gave a subtle shake of his head. That was that.

Helen's relief at seeing Mateo had worn off, replaced by something much less pleasant. She withdrew her hand. "Six months without so much as a letter or phone call." She closed her eyes in a supreme effort to control herself, "Do you have any idea—any idea at all—how worried your family is? Your mother? Little Juanita? Did you ever stop to think of them?"

"I'm sorry," he said. "I got absorbed in this project. It's incredible—it's…well, I can't talk about it. But believe me, it's important."

"I'm sure it is," she said. "But your part in it is done. It's time to come home."

He pushed his hair back from his eyes. "I can't."

"Excuse me?" She stood, arms akimbo. I knew that pose. *Explosion imminent.*

"I can't," he repeated. "I'm needed here. Just a few more days. It's almost done."

"Have you lost your mind? Your family's store is closed! They haven't the money to pay the rent! *You gave away the family car!* And now you tell me you won't come home?"

"Mateo," I said, "Son, your father's dead. He died a few weeks ago. Your family needs you. Surely you're man enough to see that."

I watched as the news about his father sank in. He ran both hands through his mop of dark hair, his face contorted as if he were being torn in two.

"Mateo," Smith said, "fetch yourself a cup of tea and wait for us in the library, would you?"

Mateo nodded.

"There's a good lad," said Smith.

Mateo rose, poured himself a cup of tea, and left the room without another word.

"Just like my Albert," Smith said. "Impossible to change his mind once it's made up. But if Mateo's absence has strained his family's finances, I'm sure I can help. If you provide me with the account number, I can wire $5,000 today. Would that be sufficient?"

Before any of us could recover from the shock of this offer, a man entered the room. Vest, shoulder holster, badge on his belt.

Parish. He took the seat next to Smith and eyed Harry.

"Raymond," he said. "Still moonlighting, I see."

"Parish," Harry said. "Looks like I'm not the only one. I guess homicides are down."

"For now," Parish said, smiling.

Smith introduced the rest of us. "Detective Parish advises my organization on matters of security. He tells me there was a theft from one of my businesses."

"Really?" Harry said innocently. "Which business was that, Detective?"

Parish's smile disappeared, and I expected an expletive-laden tirade. But he seemed to have learned self-control. Instead, he said, "Menotti's Bakery, in Venice."

"Oh," Harry said, smirking. "Someone stole some dough?"

That set him off. "You fucking half pint! I'll wipe that smirk right off your face!"

Ah. There we are. Only Harry Raymond could get under someone's skin so quickly.

"Detective," Smith said sharply, "I'll thank you not to use such language in my home. Now tell Detective Raymond what was stolen."

Parish's glare could burn a hole through steel. "Papers," he said. "Ancient documents and artifacts. Valuable enough to put the thieves away for many years."

"I'd prefer not to get involved with a long criminal investigation," Smith said. "That's why I took your call, Detective Raymond. I'm told you're very resourceful. I'd like you to work with Detective Parish, here, and see if you can recover my artifacts. If you do, I'll see if I can talk some sense into Mateo. I certainly don't want to keep him from his family—though I'll admit, it's wonderful having him here."

"I'm sure we can help," Harry said. He stood. "If you don't mind, my clients would like to see Mateo once more before we leave."

"Of course." He nodded to Parish, who got up and left. "He's not a prisoner here, after all. He's just…well, rather dedicated."

Sesh

When his guests left, Sesh stood in the library beside the chair where Mateo sat with head in his hands. Truth be told, his heart ached for the boy.

"Did it pain you to see your friends, Mateo?" he asked softly. "You seemed happy, at least at first."

"I was. I am. I just…" His face fell, and Sesh's heart ached all the more.

"I know what it is to have divided loyalties, my boy," he said. "To feel a duty that must be preserved at all costs. Believe me, I know. And Albert knew it as well. He gave his life for it."

"But Albert was strong," Mateo said, his face lined in pain. "Brave. A hero. I'm none of those things."

"No," said Sesh. "No, you're wrong about that." He knelt beside the boy. "You're strong, brave, true. You always do what's right. That's what I admire most about you."

Sesh felt a bit nauseous. His diet, no doubt. These beastly humans and their strange variety of foods, drink, and vices. They would be the death of him. But Sesh had to be strong. For Albert. For Mateo. For his people, his mission. He would see it through.

He left Mateo in the library and found Parish, standing alone in the living room before the enormous unlit fireplace, gazing into it as if it were burning.

"Follow them," he told Parish. "Find out where they are staying. They'll lead you to Shila. Kill her first, then the rest of them."

"What about the papers, the artifacts?" Parish asked. "Don't you want me to recover them?"

"They don't matter," said Sesh. "I don't need them. In a few days, none of this will matter. Just see that Shila and the others die before they talk to anyone."

Parish nodded and left by the back door, leaving Sesh alone with the bizarre paintings of Guillermo Meza. His eyes fell on the one titled "Polyphemus": a giant, twisted creature with a singular eye, and a mouth, torso, and hands in all the wrong places. It stalked figures who fled in terror.

Even if they did talk, who would believe them?

CHAPTER

24

POST-PARTUM

Horace Jennings

We got back to the Biltmore well before noon. The lobby was humming with activity, and servers were already buzzing around the restaurant in preparation for lunch. Amid a set of club chairs, some well-placed ferns, and strong misgivings, Helen and I said our goodbyes to Harry Raymond. He assured us everything would be alright.

"I'm happy to keep taking your money, but the job's done," he said. "We found your boy. I don't know what hold Smith has on him, but all you need to do is call Smith and bring him the briefcase. It belongs to him, anyway, and we've seen enough of his businesses that he'll play it straight. The rest is up to the kid."

"What about the things at the speakeasy?" Helen asked. "What about Susan River?"

Harry shook his head. "I'd stay away from that br—that person, if I were you. She's trouble. I don't know what you two saw at the Del Monte, but my advice is to forget it. I told you the day we met, LA is a dangerous place. Don't go looking for trouble. Get your boy and go home."

We shook hands and parted company.

"It's probably time you went home, too," I told Helen as we headed for the elevator.

"Me? Why?"

"There's nothing to be gained by you staying here. I'll bring Smith the artifacts tomorrow morning."

"But—what if Mateo won't come with us?"

"We can't force him to leave, Helen. We've told him about his family, his father. The rest is up to him." I rang for the elevator.

She let out a sigh of surrender. "I suppose you're right. But can't the two of us travel back to Providence together?"

"Certainly. But I may need an additional few days here."

Her steely gray eyes flashed up at me. "What in the world for?"

"I may have a job opportunity here. One that will require that I move here.

The elevator arrived. I got on; Helen did not.

"You can't be serious," she said.

"I am."

"Going up," the operator said cheerfully.

Helen just stood there.

"Aren't you coming?" I asked.

"No, I'm not." She spun on her heel and walked back toward the lobby.

I puttered nervously around my hotel room. It had been a long time since I'd been on a job interview—for that's what this lunch with Kane and the City councilman was, really. Kane wanted me to be City Engineer; and I realized that I wanted it, too, more than anything I'd wanted in a long time. But the councilman would have to be convinced.

As I paced around the room, the sunlight, the flowers, the china, the woodwork reminded me that the stakes were higher now. The Biltmore was not some ramshackle inn on the outskirts of Providence. And this opportunity was not about a small hospital or a ferry landing or a little bridge over a river; it was about shaping America's next great metropolis.

My eyes fell on the plaque that Charles had given me in Chicago for helping with the East River Tunnel. I picked it up. What would this sad little plaque from ten years ago mean to men like Major

Shaw, who helped build Los Angeles, or William Mulholland, who built its dams, aqueducts and power stations, or Andrew Lawson, who mapped the San Andreas fault? What would it mean to men like Kent Kane and this City councilman, whoever he was, who chose these great men? I threw the plaque in the trash bin.

Here, with so many needs and such incredible growth, there was no end, no limit to what might be built. Transportation centers, towering public buildings, and the most modern infrastructure in the world: bold, soaring achievements that would stand the test of time and create the kind of legacy I'd always hoped for. I would help to plan, guide, and approve them—not an overwhelming task for a man of my experience, I thought. I could do it, if only I were given the chance.

And unlike others who seemed blind to the needs of the downtrodden, I would ensure that every improvement was implemented thoughtfully, with care and concern for the citizenry. I would be their defender, I told myself. Perhaps I, too, would become a Professor Emeritus like Lawson, or write a textbook like Ellis—or better yet, a memoir. Perhaps I could develop guidelines for Los Angeles that would become a model for other cities across the nation. Think of it!

And think I did, indulging in a succession of heroic daydreams that grew ever grander, until I realized that I needed to get downstairs if I were to meet Kane on time.

A steward directed me to the private dining room once I mentioned Kane and gave him my name. At the far end of the great dining hall was a section that jutted out from the Biltmore: a sprawling skylight, and beneath, a statue of Dionysus amid a small forest of shrubs in urns. Beyond this was a glass wall with a door, and behind it a sunny, glass-enclosed dining room looking out onto a private garden. A second steward took my name at the door, admitted me, and showed me to one of eight small tables.

Kane beamed at me as I approached. "Ah! Jennings! So glad you could make it!"

Feeling breathless, overjoyed, and fortunate, I beamed back at him. "Thank you for having me, Kane."

"Allow me to introduce a key member of our illustrious City Council."

The man with his back to me rose and turned.

He clasped my hand in a limp handshake, and I found myself looking into the living eyes of death: the head and chest protruding from a snake; the pallid face that I'd turned over; the haunted eyes that met my own, the mouth moving wordlessly, pleading silently for me to end its suffering; the shocked mask of death as I plunged the knife into his chest, then twisted it.

He looked into my eyes. He knew me, knew what I'd done. He smiled, scratching idly at a small bandage on his neck.

I ran. Kane called after me; I ran. Past the steward, knocking over guests, heedless, headlong, I ran, until I reached the elevator, where I frantically tapped the call button. Once inside, the doors closed, I cursed myself and my hubris as the operator regarded me fearfully.

When we reached the fifth floor, I shot out of the elevator and ran to Helen's door. I pounded on it to no avail; she was gone. Then to my door, where I practically broke the key off in the lock. The door opened, I fell in, then fell back against it as it closed behind me.

I cast wildly about the room, a madman looking for some earthly token to preserve his sanity. My eyes fell on the briefcase. I grabbed it.

In a flash, I knew what I had to do, where I had to go.

I dared not take the elevator—*it* might be on its way up to my room right now. I went into the bedroom, locked the door, opened the window, and climbed out onto the fire escape. I flung myself down each flight, feet pounding down the rungs of the ladders. I dropped from the last ladder to the sidewalk, picked up the briefcase, and ran.

I didn't stop until I was in a taxi, headed for Chinatown.

Shila Ghiss

There is a knock and my door, and a voice calling me.

Horace Jennings' voice. Upset. Frightened.

I open the door and find him standing in the dim light and peeling green paint of the second floor landing. He looks as if a demon has chased him. At his feet is the briefcase with the papers and artifacts.

I let him in, sit him in my only chair, and pour water from a pitcher into my only glass. I hand it to him and he drinks it rapidly. Then he tells me what has happened.

He does not understand how a human eaten by a serpent might come back to life. But I do. It is an awful truth, our transformation; but unless I explain it to him, he will remain tormented by what he has seen.

I must try.

"These creatures must eat their victims to assume their forms. They must eat them alive to possess their knowledge and memories. Once they have done this, they can assume the form at will; but the transformation taxes their bodies, their strength."

His face grows pale. "That—that's horrible. But it can't be true. I don't subscribe to all that supernatural nonsense."

"It is not supernatural. It is nature. Evolution, if you prefer. These creatures have evolved to do this over many millions of years."

"It does fit with what I've seen." He looks away, then his gaze searches my room, as if he might find an answer here. Finally, his eyes return to me. "But...how could you possibly know that?"

"As I have said, stories of these creatures have been passed down for millennia, but kept secret from all but a few."

He nods. "So you've said. I understand that many indigenous peoples have a tradition of oral history," he says, rummaging through his briefcase and pulling out parchments, "but how can you possibly understand this writing?"

I find myself admiring this man for his knowledge, as well as his skepticism. He will not accept my words at face value, even though they offer an explanation; instead, he must dig ever deeper. He would make a fine scientist.

"Let me explain the writing system and read these documents aloud. I will translate them for you, and you can record it. Perhaps then it will make sense. Have you pen and paper?"

He finally smiles, and it gladdens me to see it. "Are you really asking a university professor if he has pen and paper in his briefcase?"

"I am," I tell him. "In my experience, teachers are less than perfect."

He produces a fountain pen and a leather-bound journal. "My wife would agree with you. That's why she gave me this journal."

I find it amusing and fitting that Horace Jennings has a mate. "I would like to meet this woman, I think."

A cloud passes over him. "She died, unfortunately. Ten years ago. The Spanish Flu."

My father's work. It hits me hard. "I…didn't know. I am very sorry."

"It's alright. You couldn't have known," he says.

It is not alright. And we should have known.

For the first hour, I explain the process for writing our thoughts. We do not record words but actions and ideas, which are represented by curves in the writing. Horace Jennings does not truly understand this. Eventually I explain less and translate more. But I cannot betray my people or divulge my identity. It makes the translation trying—especially when I translate portions of Sesh's journal.

I learn that Sesh poisoned my father to remove him as an obstacle; that he planned to mate with me; that he hoped our children would one day lead our people to victory. Sickening, misguided, and very much what I expect from Sesh.

My throat grows dry and my voice hoarse as I learn of Sesh's treachery. Horace Jennings sees my distress, though he does not grasp the true cause.

And then, to my amazement, he takes my father's cup from his briefcase, fills it with water from the pitcher, and offers it to me.

My eyes blur with tears. I don't know why. I sip the water and put down the cup. Horace thinks he has offended me, or that something is wrong with the water, or that I am ill. He places his hand on my face. I place my hands on his and draw him closer. We kiss, and my heart leaps as if I am reborn in a new world.

I am.

CHAPTER
25

CHINATOWN

Sesh

In his office, Sesh gripped the telephone with one hand, choking the life out of it as he spoke into it.

"Well?"

In his other hand, Parish's voice, thin and tinny, buzzed from the speaker into his ear.

"They're staying at the Biltmore. They have two rooms on the fifth floor."

"And? Where are they? What are they doing? Have they left the hotel?"

"Jennings came running through the lobby like he was on fire. He took the elevator up to his room."

The placid seascape paintings and framed photos of Smith's many ships did nothing to comfort Sesh. "I'm not in the mood for a mystery, Parish. Keep talking, and don't stop until you've told me everything you know, or until I tell you to shut up."

A pause at the other end of the line told Sesh his words had sunk in. Good. Parish constantly needed reminding of who's in charge. Perhaps his dosage should be increased. Sesh would have to weigh that against allowing Parish initiative and a free hand.

"I showed my badge, made up a story, and got the manager to let me into his suite. The bedroom door was locked—no key for that, I had to break it down. The bedroom window was open. He went out the fire escape. No sign of the artifacts."

"So he saw you and fled?" Sesh felt himself flashing hot. He would never get used to these damn mammals and their damn warm blood.

"Not likely," said Parish. "In the lobby, he was running toward me. Something at the far end of the dining area spooked him."

"What about the other two?"

"Gone, both of them. Nothing of interest in the girl's room, and Raymond's car isn't here."

"Alright. Find out what spooked Jennings, then find out where Shila is staying. Take care of her first, then do the others."

A pause. "You want me to wait here at the hotel until they come back?"

"No, Parish. You're a detective, remember? Find out where Shila lives. Start with the Southwest Museum, for god's sake, that's where she used to work."

He hung up in disgust. No, he couldn't increase Parish's dosage. He'd already lost his edge, Sesh could tell. It seemed Sesh would have to put up with his surly demeanor a bit longer.

Horace Jennings

I'm not sure how this happened.

One moment, I was giving Susan a drink of water; the next, there were tears; and then she was kissing me.

I hadn't been kissed in ten years. I hadn't been *alive* in ten years. I'd forgotten what it felt like—love, tenderness. I'd forgotten that it was all that really mattered in this world.

You can guess the rest.

I told myself that I would never forget love again. I told myself that Mary would understand. I was sure of it.

I'm not sure how this happened. But I'm glad it did.

Shila Ghiss

Afterwards, Horace removes the bandage on my wound.

"It looks good. At some point, we'll have to get those stitches out. Does it hurt?"

"No," I tell him. The pain is a distant memory. At the moment, I feel only contentment. I wish it would never end. But I know better.

Susan River recalls something a humble priest once told her: *There is no love without sacrifice.*

I know there will be more sacrifices ahead—many of them. I will make them. Will Horace make them, when the time comes? I cannot know.

For now, I read Sesh's ramblings and examine the other writings. He has shunted more electricity from the power station—far more than what we need for the colony. He is studying the geology of California. He has stolen mineral specimens from the museum: cobalt. And he has built a machine of some kind. There is a scrap of paper with three words written in English: investiture, convocation, commencement. University terms used at a graduation ceremony, but their meaning is unclear to me.

Most disturbing of all, there is an ancient human scroll that refers to the great worms. May we never see them again.

Sesh does nothing by chance. These things are all connected, I know. And I suspect that the stolen electrical power is the key to finding out how.

There are also the three jars taken from my father's study: black lotus powder, venom antidote, and healing ointment. I may make use of the last when the thread is gone from my wound.

The daylight fades in the alleys beyond my windows, and my room becomes too dim to continue. Horace lights a lamp.

"It's getting late," he says. "How would you feel about dinner?"

I cannot resist teasing him. "Professor Jennings, are you asking me out on a date?"

He blushes a dusky pink. "I suppose I am," he says. He moves from the lamp and embraces me gently. "Sorry, my last date was in 1897. I may need a little practice." He kisses me again.

He does not need practice.

We enjoy dinner at the Long River, a restaurant Susan River could seldom afford as a docent. We stroll back along the boulevard, and spots appear on the sidewalk. My head and shoulder grow damp. I look up at the dark sky, and I realize it is raining.

What a strange, wonderful world this is, with no walls or tunnels, where I can stare into infinity, and water falls from the sky!

We pass the theater, then dance halls and clubs of ill repute. Horace apologizes for what has happened to the neighborhood, as if something is wrong and it is his fault.

We reach my building and Horace stops. He looks across the street, then looks up toward the windows of my room. He takes my arm.

"Keep walking," he says. He steers me further down the boulevard, out of the circles of light cast by the streetlamps on the wet, dirty sidewalk. "Did you turn out the light in your room before we left?"

"No, I didn't."

"Well, it's out now, and there's a Pierce-Arrow parked across the street. I think someone's in your room."

"The door is locked," I tell him. "It must be my landlord."

"Not necessarily," he says. "Stay here, out of the light, and watch the entrance. Let's see if we can find out who it is. I'll call Miss Parker. This may be an opportunity to get her out of the Biltmore without being watched. I saw a payphone at the end of the block." He walks away.

The hiss of rain grows louder, my clothing wetter. The entrance to my building is dark and distant. I need to be closer to see who enters and leaves. I cross the street and creep through the rain back toward the long, narrow shape of the car, parked in the shadows. When I reach it, I find it unlocked. I have an idea.

A few minutes later, from the back seat of the car, I see him coming down the front steps: Sesh's dangerous, unruly detective, Parish. He is carrying the briefcase.

The time has come for Shila Ghiss to act. I stretch my back as far as I can and recall the sensation of the ground sliding past my belly. I wait to feel my flesh harden to scales.

Nothing happens.

Parish crosses the street towards me.

I try to focus on myself, on Shila. I try to taste the air with my tongue, but I cannot.

He approaches the car.

Panicked, I lie on the floor in deeper shadow, hoping he will not see me.

The driver's door opens, and the hiss of the rain, the smell of wet street and wet clothes fill the car. Something heavy lands on the back seat. I hear the front seat creak beneath his weight and the driver's door thump closed. Then silence.

I curse Susan River for her weakness and vulnerability. I command my fingertips to turn to claws. Nothing.

"Where is this bitch?" I hear him mutter. A clink, a brief flash of light, then cigarette smoke.

Minutes go by. In the speakeasy, it was easy to transform back to Shila Ghiss before I met with the Commander and the Science Master. Why is it now difficult? *What if I can never go back?*

I try again. I summon my anger. I think of Sesh, of the king, of my father, but it is no use. Sesh had said that if I spend too much time with Susan River's thoughts, I could lose myself forever. Is that what has happened?

I try to recall how I transformed the first time. It happened quickly—Sesh was impressed, I remember. How had it started? The bracelet! I was looking at it when I first transformed. I try looking at it now, but it is invisible in the darkness. I raise my wrist to the backseat, where the black shadow becomes gray, and finally I see a tiny gleam of silver. I focus on it, the blue stone, the details I cannot see. But nothing happens.

If the bracelet brought me to Susan River and humanity, perhaps something else can return me to Shila Ghiss. My hand brushes whatever it was Parish tossed onto the back seat. It feels like…a briefcase.

Horace's briefcase! Parish must have collected Sesh's journal and the artifacts to return them to him.

"Let's make this a little easier," Parish mumbles.

The engine starts.

The noise creates an opportunity. I open the briefcase and feel around inside it. My fingers close on something familiar: my father's cup. My cup, now. I focus on it.

My tailbone begins to ache. Then my back, as if I am being pulled apart from head to toe. Then my scalp hurts, and my face. It is slow, not at all like the white-hot pain and wrenching of my first transformation. Something is wrong.

The car lurches forward and swings around hard as my body stretches. My tailbone feels as if it is being yanked out, and I feel my tail grow rapidly. But my arms and legs don't change, and my skull barely flattens. The car squeaks to a sudden stop. I raise my head in mid-transformation. My eyes feel strange, my vision is distorted, but we are on the other side of the street.

"Is that Jennings?" Parish says, peering through the darkness and rain. "What the fuck is he doing here?"

A flash of panic fills me.

"Well, there's a simple solution to that," he says.

The engine roars and the car lurches forward.

"Don't move, Professor…" he says, laughing.

I grip the seat with human hands while my tail emerges into the light to find his neck. I have never seen part of myself through human eyes before: vivid green with a jet black stripe.

"What the f—"

I coil my tail around his throat, squeeze as hard as I can, and yank his head backwards.

The car swings to the left, skidding. We jump the curb hard and slam into a lamppost. For a brief second it is quiet; then breaking glass and screeching metal as the lamppost crashes down on us.

Lying on the floor of the backseat, I release Parish, who is groaning and muttering, and push my half transformed body back into the shape of Susan River. There are footsteps racing toward the car.

Horace looks down at me, opens the rear door. "Good lord! Are you alright?"

"I'm fine," I tell him, covering my head with my arms. But my head, at least, is human again.

He helps me out into the rain, oblivious to the tail peeking from beneath my skirt as he grabs the briefcase. He takes my hand. Then we run through the darkness, me loping awkwardly as my tail continues to shrink.

CHAPTER
26

DAMN TOURISTS

Horace Jennings

The air was crisp and the sunlight bright as the Studebaker climbed the road into the mountains. According to Helen, we were some 50 miles northwest of downtown Los Angeles. Whatever Parish might have planned for us, I doubted he would find us up here—assuming he was well enough to search, that is.

By sheer luck, Helen had been out on a long walk while Parish was ransacking our rooms at the Biltmore, but back in her room when he was in Chinatown and I'd called from the payphone. She'd grabbed a suitcase, hailed a cab, and checked us into the Culver hotel a few blocks away. She did all of this without question or pause, a testament to her trust in me.

But this morning, after I rented the Studebaker, the questions rained down like a storm in the desert. Why wasn't I taking the City Engineer position? How could the dead man from the Del Monte possibly come back to life? Was I sure it was him? Why did I take the briefcase to Susan River? Weren't we going to give it back to Sam Smith? Why was Susan River sharing my room at the Culver? Why did Parish ransack our rooms, and why did he try to kill me? Was Mateo in danger, too? Should we try calling Harry Raymond? And why in heaven's name are we driving up into the mountains to see a dam?

I answered what questions I could. As for the dam, Susan answered that one.

"Whatever project your friend Mateo Martinez is working on, it involves electricity being stolen from the power station in these mountains. He may not be aware of that. If we can prove it, we may convince him to leave Mr. Smith voluntarily."

"It seems like our best chance," I said. "The police can't help us, and we can't exactly kidnap Mateo at gunpoint. I put in a call to the Deputy Chief Engineer of the Water Department. Told him I'm a professor of civil engineering from Brown University and I want to develop a course in hydroelectric dam operation. He's going to meet us at the powerhouse."

Helen seemed satisfied, at least.

The dam was constructed across the San Francisquito Canyon at the point where a wide plateau dropped into a deep, narrow canyon that wound its way through the mountains. Here, workers could build a dam of minimal size across the narrow canyon, creating a broad reservoir behind it at a higher elevation—an ideal condition.

There was nothing minimal about the dam, however. As the road approached the rim of the canyon and the dam finally swung into view, it was a breathtaking sight: an immense wall of concrete, gently arched inward toward the reservoir, two hundred feet high, four times as wide, thirty feet thick at its crest, and an untold thickness beneath the water. The weight of the water against the dam compressed the concrete arch, actually strengthening it and channeling the weight into the sides of the canyon itself. The downstream face of the dam was stepped in increments of five feet vertically, like a great pyramid. Truly, this was a wonder of the modern world, a marvelous testament to human ingenuity.

A road traversed the top of the dam, treating us to a view of the canyon as we drove across it: a red wall to the west, and a pale pink wall to the east.

Susan drank it in. "Mother Earth is beautiful," she said, "even more so in the light of the—sun."

"Yes," Helen said, without taking my field glasses from her eyes. "The reddish area on the west side of the canyon is almost certainly sandstone—probably a conglomerate of sandstone and gypsum. Quite strong. But that pale area on the east side looks a bit chalky to me. Might be talc or mica schist."

I smiled inwardly. *Ever the geologist, Helen.*

"Does that concern you?" Susan asked.

Helen put down the glasses. "Mica and talc are subject to delamination and slippage."

I doubted that Susan understood Helen's concern. "It's a bit late for field borings," I said. "The dam's already built. I'm sure the engineers tested this area extensively before they built a dam here."

The reservoir stretched endlessly into the distance. Try as I might, I struggled to imagine that even the booming metropolis of Los Angeles could ever use all that water.

The downstream side of the dam offered a spectacular view of the San Francisquito Canyon, as well as a two hundred foot drop to the base of the dam.

Water and power went hand in hand. The dam's primary purpose was to store drinking water for the city; but it also provided hydroelectric power. From the road across the top of the dam, I could make out Powerhouse No. 2 at the foot of the eastern wall of the canyon. Large pipes angled down that wall, carrying water that spun the enormous turbines, generating electricity. Transmission cables strung along towers carried this power all the way back to Los Angeles.

Powerhouse No. 2, far from being an industrial shed, turned out to be a beautiful building. About three stories tall, it was a two-to-one rectangle in federal style, its eight long windows, entries, and hip roof perfectly symmetrical. From a distance, I couldn't see a single brick, and I wondered if the entire building—or at least the façade—might be poured concrete. It looked more like a bank than a powerhouse. An audible hum came from the building.

An assortment of trucks and construction vehicles were parked in a paved lot to the right of the building. Standing next to a tarp-covered truck were two men in overalls and one man in a suit: H.A. Van Norman, the Deputy Chief Engineer, a square-jawed man with a rectangular face and rectangular glasses to match. He appeared agitated. I made brief introductions.

"Oh, hello," he said distractedly. A forced smile told me he was normally an amiable fellow. "I nearly forgot you were coming."

"Is it a bad time, Mr. Van Norman?" I asked.

"Not really. It's just that we seem to have misplaced a couple of cable reels."

"I'll go find the Chief," said the one of the men in overalls, ambling toward the entry. "He's probably in his office. It's by the—"

Van Norman strode past him. "I planned the building, Peterson. I think I can find it."

He led us through the front entrance to a small reception area, where a secretary stood as we breezed past. An audible, low frequency thrum filled the room. We walked through the opposite door and down a short corridor with three small offices on one side. Here, the thrum was more noticeable.

Van Norman marched to the last office, where through the window we saw a beefy, balding man sitting at his desk, drinking coffee, and reviewing a set of plans. The sign on the door read, "Stanley Dunham, Chief Construction Engineer." Van Norman threw the door open.

"Stanley. I need to talk to you."

Dunham barely looked up from his plans. "Harvey. What's wrong?"

"We're missing two reels of transmission cable. Ten thousand feet."

"They'll turn up," Dunham said, finally abandoning his plans and pushing back his chair. "The boys in Power probably decided to move them to another location and couldn't be bothered to tell us." He shook his head. "Typical."

"Can I have the keys to the storage bay?" Van Norman asked.

"Sure." Dunham stood and fished a key ring out of his pocket. His eyes shifted to the crowd outside his office. "Who are all these people?"

"A group of engineers from Providence. They wanted to see the facility."

As Van Norman took the keys, Dunham shook his head, and I

overheard his parting remark:

"Hell of a day for a group of damn tourists."

Van Norman led us to a door at the end of the corridor with a sign that read "Main Generator Room." When he opened it, the thrum was loud. Peterson and the other man in overalls were waiting for us. Both held a coffee in either hand.

"Coffee, Mr. Van Norman, sir?" Peterson said above the din. "For you and your guests?"

Van Norman looked back at us, but we were taking our cue from him. "No, thank you," he said. "Not right now. Just leave it in the reception area." We brushed past them.

The thrum in the room came from three enormous generators. Each was a concrete drum thirty feet in diameter and twenty feet high, set into the rear of the building. Inside that drum, I knew, was a spinning turbine turned by fast flowing water. Steel stairs provided access to the top of each drum, and a concrete parapet along the back wall enabled access to all three drums from the top. Above each drum protruded the generator itself and a shorter, steeper stair of perhaps fifteen feet to the top, where a light showed that the generator was active.

Van Norman gestured for us to follow, as conversation was impossible in the generator room. He led us to an illuminated storage bay at one end of the building, closing the doors after we entered to reduce the noise. I saw tools, crates, metal rods, paint, and innumerable sacks of concrete—but no cable reels. There was an empty area that might have accommodated them. We examined the floor. There were a few flakes of wood—the kind that could come from a large wooden reel. At the far end of the bay were large doors for truck access.

To his credit, Van Norman attempted to explain to us the construction and operation of the dam and powerhouse, despite his concern for the missing cable. We feigned interest, of course, but eventually I managed to convince him that we were more interested in helping him solve the mystery of the missing cable. He seemed to appreciate that.

"The Chief Electrical Engineer and the Lead Mechanic both work for the Bureau of Power, not the Water Department. Apart from Dunham, they are the only ones with keys to this storage bay, and they haven't been here in days, according to those two." He pointed out Peterson and the other man in overalls.

As we walked back through the building, we came to an area where there was a dip in the sound level. I looked up and immediately understood why. The light above Generator 2 was off.

I pointed it out to Van Norman. He moved over to the generator, and we followed. At the bottom of the stairs to the concrete parapet, he paused.

"I'm going to check it," he told me. "Wait here." He turned to remove the chain from across the steps.

I put a hand on his shoulder. "I'm an engineer. Let me help you," I said.

I motioned for Susan and Helen to wait, then followed Van Norman up the access stairs.

At the top, we gained the parapet and moved onto the flat top of the concrete drum. A safety rail was in place around the edge. The generator protruded from the middle of the drum: eight massive steel arms reaching out from the center of the concrete cylinder, crowned by a conical steel section that held the generator winding, producing electricity. A steep access ladder led to the top, where the light was. Van Norman climbed the access ladder, examining the generator as he did so. I walked around the steel flanges, along the railing—and nearly fell to my death over the railing. I had tripped over something. A power cable about four inches in diameter.

I called to Van Norman, who was on the other side of the generator but couldn't hear me above the thrum. I walked round and waved my arms at him, motioning for him to come down. He did, and I led him to the cable, which began at the generator and disappeared over the side.

"Is that supposed to be there?" I asked.

"A high voltage cable lying where people can trip over it? No, it's not," he said. "The generators are wired to a transformer on the roof. From there, high tension cables are connected to a transmission tower. This cable doesn't belong here."

I leaned over the railing and waved at Helen and Susan below, pointing to where the cable ran down the side of the drum. They moved to trace it. Soon we were standing together at the base. The cable ran to the floor, and through a manhole plate with a notch in it.

Van Norman swore under his breath, looked up, and saw Peterson and the other man chatting idly nearby. He summoned them, waving his arms violently. They hastened to us.

"Who installed a power cable on this generator?" he demanded.

"I don't know, Mr. Van Norman, sir. You'll have to ask the Chief Electrical Engineer. That's Mr. Colson, sir."

"I know who it is, dammit," said Van Norman. "Go get a crowbar and remove this plate. Now."

The pair hurried off and returned with two crowbars. Peterson was about to lift the cover when he hesitated.

"Is it safe to lift this plate with a power cable running through it?" he asked Van Norman. The latter snatched the crowbar from Peterson's hands, stuck it in the notch, and with great difficulty lifted the notch side of the plate just above the floor. The other man used his crowbar to pry it off, then together they slid it to the side, revealing a hole with an access ladder. It was dimly lit and went down perhaps twenty feet.

Van Norman handed me the crowbar and started down the ladder. I handed the crowbar to Helen.

"You two wait here," I said.

Helen frowned. "Like hell, Professor."

Susan agreed. "Yes, like hell."

Cut from the same cloth, both of them. No point in arguing. I started down after Van Norman. Helen was right behind me, crowbar in hand.

CHAPTER
27

SOURCE OF POWER

Shila Ghiss

Climbing down the ladder reveals to me humanity's ape heritage. The drop is unnerving, but the climb down is strangely satisfying, as if I am somehow achieving my full potential as a human.

When I reached the bottom, I stand next to them in near darkness. I look into a sprawling, regular chamber between two cylinders of artificial stone—concrete—that stretch from floor to ceiling. The sound of roaring water fills my ears, and I realize that we are standing below the three generators, where, as Mr. Van Norman had explained, the water running down the canyon walls is piped into the turbines. Someone has hung a string of weak electric lights from the ceiling in the chamber's center, reminiscent of those in the King's Hall. Below them is a large box and a pile of rubble. The power cable runs along the floor towards it.

Horace yells above the roaring water to Helen Parker.

"I don't suppose you brought one of those electric—"

She produces an electric torch from her bag and hands it to him.

"—torches. Thank you."

She smiles, then produces a second torch and turns it on.

"You people do seem to come prepared," says Mr. Van Norman, pleased. "Like Boy Scouts."

"Engineers," says Horace.

"I'm a geologist," says Helen.

I do not say what I am.

Helen scrapes at the wall with the crowbar and examines its tip. It is covered in whitish dust and a few flakes of shiny silver and gray.

"See? I was right. Talc and mica schist. Mr. Van Norman, I hope your dam isn't founded on this material. It's subject to—"

"Delamination and slippage. Yes, we're aware of it. I can assure you, young lady, Mr. Mulholland considered the geology when he selected this site. And Mr. Dunham took borings prior to construction. The dam is safe. Which is more than we can say for Powerhouse No. 2. Let's see if we can find the rest of that cable."

We follow the cable to the pile of rubble. As we approach with our lights, the shapes resolve themselves into smashed wooden crates. Two of them have curves and spindles—the missing cable reels. Both are empty. We shine our lights onto the large box. It is made of metal. The power cable leads directly to it.

We are close, I realize. This is the strand that will lead me to the center of Sesh's web.

"It's a transformer..." Van Norman says. "Why would that be down here? Unless...here, help me move some this debris." We do so, turning them over. Tools and old, broken, bladed equipment. "Cable splicers," he says. "Jennings, lend me your torch. I want to check the other end of the transformer. I'll bet there's a cable leading away from it. Someone's built themselves their own private power supply." He walks around the transformer, stumbling a bit on the debris. "Aha!"

Then he screams.

His torchlight plays wildly on the ceiling from the far side of the transformer. Then he stumbles backward, into view. One of my people appears with him, jaws fastened to his shoulder, body wrapped about him. I recognize the size and pattern of the large scales on its head. It is one of the two guards who accompanied me to the surface, who snickered as I struggled to dress and speak. At the time, I found the guard annoying; but I had never seen it in combat: formidable and deadly.

Horace seizes the crowbar from Helen and charges forward. He swings it down on the guard's head. The guard shudders but remains fastened. Horace swings it again, grunting with effort. It releases Van

Norman, who topples backward towards Horace.

Now the guard turns to face Horace. It raises its head high above him, mouth open, fangs dripping. Its tail wraps around Horace's legs. I bound forward to stand beside him.

"Guard!" I hiss in our language. "Stand down! Do not harm him!"

It sees me, recognizes me. Its body freezes, but its head bobs slightly. "Shila Ghiss! You should not be here! You must—"

The crowbar rings as it meets the guard's skull. To my horror, Horace swings it again, and the guard releases him.

"Stop!" I cry, but it is no use. A third time he strikes, and the guard falls backward.

"Horace, stop!" I push him aside, grab Van Norman, and drag him back through the rubble.

From behind us, Helen screams, and I turn to find her face to face with the other guard. She holds an electric torch in one hand and a long, straight blade in the other—the blade with which Horace mistakenly stabbed me. It drips blood.

I run between them. "Back!" I say in English, waving my hands. And then, in our language: "I forbid you to harm these humans!"

But this one is different. "I'll take no orders from an ape-loving traitor!" it cries, bleeding from its neck. It lunges at me and knocks me down. There is a crack and ringing metal as Horace brings the crowbar down on its head. Helen stabs it with the blade. It falls and lies motionless.

"We must get back to the ladder," I tell them. "Van Norman is hurt, and there may be more of them."

We run back to the ladder. Horace climbs up while Helen examines Van Norman's wounds: two deep punctures, bleeding profusely.

"What...what was that thing? A snake...with arms and legs? A giant Gila monster?"

"No," she tells him. "Something worse. We're going to get help for you. Then we'll explain."

Horace calls down from the top of the ladder, barely audible above the noise of the water. "They've covered the hole! Peterson and his pal! They've put the plate back! I can't move it!"

Helen does not hear him. I must act quickly if I am to learn what Sesh plans. "Stay here," I tell her. "Take care of Mr. Van Norman. I will return in a few minutes."

"Where are you going?" she says, alarmed.

"Horace says the hole above is covered. I think I saw another way out."

I walk toward the rubble where the first guard attacked Van Norman, ignoring Helen's pleas to return.

"Where are you?" I hiss in our language. "Let me help you."

"Here," he says in English.

I find him sitting with his back against the metal box—the transformer. He has transformed back to his human skin. His legs are sprawled out before him. His head is broken and bleeding. He wears a technician's coat, filthy and stained with blood, the name "Colson" stitched across its pocket.

"Let me help you," I say again.

"I am beyond help, Royal One. Even you cannot help me now."

I examine him. His wounds are grave. The healing ointment in the briefcase may be powerful enough to help him—but the briefcase is in the car, out of reach.

"Is there another way out of this chamber?"

He points to the far end, opposite the ladder. He is very pale and breathing hard.

"The Inquisitor has lost his way," he says. "I should have seen it sooner."

"Why the power? What is he planning?" I ask.

"A machine…the entry cavern…the worms…" He begins to sleep.

I shake him gently. "What about the worms? Please, you must tell me."

But he will not tell me, or anyone, ever again.

Horace Jennings

We left the inflow chamber via a large hoist that surfaced to an outbuilding at the end of the parking lot. No doubt that was how they'd moved the transformer down there. The power cable led only to a hole in the floor, perhaps a foot in diameter. And with Van Norman unconscious and bleeding to death, we weren't about to start digging.

We didn't go back into the powerhouse; instead, we drove east, out of the mountains and down into Lancaster, to the first hospital we could find. By then, Susan had dressed his wounds and applied some ointments from the briefcase, which she said would help.

She had a theory about the serpent creatures. She believed they had developed a drug to make humans subservient to their will, and that they were adding this drug to liquor, coffee, and just about everything else we imbibed, making us compliant.

Helen and I were skeptical at first, but it explained the behavior of Mateo, McAfee, and Parish, as well as Peterson and his accomplice, who'd been pushing coffee on us at the powerhouse, and Dunham, the dam's Chief Construction Engineer, who seemed indifferent to what was going on right beneath his nose. Could it explain Sam Smith as well? I didn't know, but I preferred it to believing that the serpents were devouring and impersonating them all. It was a convincing theory.

Scholarly, observant, and intuitive, Susan River was a fine anthropologist and an excellent scientist. She'd also proven courageous and quick-thinking, taking on Parish yesterday and the serpent creatures today. I recalled how she'd stepped forward, hissing and waving at them. I also recalled Harry's warning to stay away from her.

Too late.

In Lancaster, a doctor no older than Helen ran a ten-bed hospital out of his mother's house. Seth Savage had a lot of medical equipment still in boxes and a stiff, white lab coat that smelled of starch. He examined Van Norman and admitted him promptly.

We told him Van Norman was attacked by a large snake, but he assured us that no snake was large enough to leave such marks. Then we told him that it may have been a Gila monster; he didn't believe that, either. When he was done closing Van Norman's wounds, I asked him to examine Susan's wound from the Del Monte.

"It is not necessary," she told him. "The wound is healing."

"If so, then you may need me to remove the sutures," he countered. "Let me examine it." She reluctantly agreed.

When he was done, I met privately with Savage in his small office to pay the bill. The walls were adorned with photos of horses and a framed medical degree from UCLA. I hoped his degree wasn't in veterinary medicine.

Savage put my check in a drawer, then folded his hands atop the desk. "Mr. Jennings, I'd like to talk to you about these two cases—their wounds. Mr. Van Norman's wound was caused by an animal bite. A large animal, likely not a snake. I've closed his wound and given him some plasma, but he'll need to stay here for a few days. I'd like to monitor him for rabies or venom, if you really suspect it was a snake. As for Miss River, her wound wasn't caused by an animal. It's a knife wound."

"It can't be," I said. "She told me she was bitten by the same type of animal that bit Van Norman."

"Impossible," he said. "The wounds are completely different. Hers is a laceration, not a puncture. Either she's delusional or she's lying."

I felt a flash of anger at this would-be doctor playing the detective; he was too young to be so cocksure of everything. But there was no denying his skill.

Dr. Savage seemed used to being doubted. He shrugged. "I thought you should know."

A short distance up the road from the hospital was a diner. While

Helen and Susan had a late lunch, I made a few phone calls. The first was to Harry's office.

"Electric Torch Investigations," a woman's voice answered.

I gave her my name. "I need to speak to Harry," I said. "It's urgent."

"I'm sorry, Mr. Jennings, but Mr. Raymond is out of town. But if you leave a number, I can have him call you as soon as he checks in."

I left her the number of Savage's hospital and thanked her. And then, purely out of curiosity, I asked, "Is this Mrs. Raymond?"

There was a pause, then tinkling laughter from the other end. "I'm sorry, honey, but I can't divulge that information. You'll have to ask him."

The next call was to Sam Smith. He answered the phone himself.

"Mr. Smith, this is Horace Jennings."

"Mr. Jennings! How are you, sir?"

"Well," I said. *Considering your henchman tried to run me down.* "I'm sorry Detective Raymond wasn't able to help your man Parish recover your missing materials. Apparently, he has another assignment out of town. It seems our business with him is finished."

"Ah," Smith said. "Well, how can I help you? Would you like to speak to young Mateo?"

"Yes," I said, surprised. "If you don't mind."

"Of course. Let me fetch him for you."

A few minutes later, I was talking to Mateo, who seemed as cheerful and excited as he'd been when I'd gotten him assigned to the Golden Gate Bridge project. He enjoyed working with Smith, he said. The project was nearly complete, and he expected to be heading back to San Francisco to see his family in a few days. If Helen and I were still in Los Angeles, we could travel there together. He couldn't have sounded more rational or reassuring.

I asked him if he was eating and drinking enough, and specifically, what he was drinking. Water, tea, lemonade, and the occasional soft drink, he said. He laughed at the question and told me I sounded like his mother.

He put Smith back on.

"You're a good man to worry so about him," Smith said.

Could I possibly be wrong about this man? Susan said he was dangerous; but Harry said *she* was dangerous; and Savage practically called her a liar.

As long as Smith was being so forthcoming, I decided on a more direct approach. I asked him if he knew Susan River.

"Yes, of course. She's a docent at the Southwest Museum. Introduced me to the work of Guillermo Meza. Why do you ask?"

"Well, sir, it's just that…she had some unkind things to say about you. Things I find difficult to believe." I felt like an idiot.

"I see," he said. I could hear the hurt in his voice. "I'm sorry to hear that. But it's my fault, really. She's a remarkable woman, and I—well, I misjudged our relationship. I'm sure you can understand how that could happen."

Most certainly, I could.

I apologized to him, and he assured me he took no offense. Mateo would likely head home in three days, he said, so there was no reason to worry about him. Smith had gotten the Martinez's bank account information from Mateo and had already wired them $5,000.

I returned to the table where Helen and Susan sat, wondering what I would say to each of them, privately, about my conversation with Smith.

I decided to say nothing.

CHAPTER
28

VALLEY OF THE DAMNED

Horace Jennings

The next day, we checked on Van Norman. Savage warned me that he, too, was delusional. It turned out that Van Norman had just recounted what he'd seen—what we'd all seen—beneath Powerhouse No. 2.

When Savage left the room, Van Norman donned his eyeglasses, his eyes growing larger in the black rectangular frames. He looked at each of us, imploring. "You saw it, didn't you? You all saw it."

I nodded. "But it won't do any good to tell people about it. No one will believe you."

"What…what was it? Some kind of snake? An alligator? A giant salamander?"

"We don't know," I told him, "but we're trying to find out. Don't go back to the dam, and don't call the police. We have reason to believe some of them are complicit in a conspiracy."

"A conspiracy?" Van Norman sounded at his wit's end. "To do what, for Christ's sake? Sell them to the zoo?"

I looked at Susan, but she had nothing to say.

"We're trying to find out that, too."

Before we left, Savage told me he'd received a call from Harry Raymond, who'd left a number where he could be reached. I called him from Savage's office and got a hotel called the Dow. They put me through to his room.

"I'm in Lone Pine," he said, "trying to track down the bastard who stole the museum rocks and took your boy's car. I told the PD it's a waste of time, but it's the only lead they have on the museum theft, and they won't let it go."

I briefly recounted the City councilman's return from the dead, Parish's attempt on my life, and the ambush at Powerhouse No. 2. I told him Susan's theory of the drug. It sounded like the ravings of a madman, even to me.

But Harry didn't scoff or chastise me, and that gave me pause. His only comment regarded Parish. "Drugged or not, he's always been an asshole. A dangerous one."

Then, to my surprise, he suggested the three of us come up to Lone Pine. "It doesn't sound like your boy's in any danger. And if your friends know anything about these rocks or why someone might steal them, maybe they can help. Dow Hotel, Room 215."

The road north wound through hills and peaks. At some points, red, rocky hills squeezed us into a narrow corridor; at others, they fell away revealing a vast brown landscape dotted with green sagebrush. With every mile, the mountains on our left grew taller, the land on our right, drier. To me, it was alien—the very antithesis of Providence, which was wet and green, urban and bustling. But a glance at Susan—eyes closed, window rolled down, hair tossed by the wind—told me it felt like home to her.

We soon entered a vast, flat valley that stretched endlessly before us, distant mountains on either side, sagebrush the only thing growing as far as the eye could see: Owens Valley.

"I have been told about this valley," Susan said. "I have been told that it was once green."

"Is that true?" Helen asked me.

"Yes."

It seemed impossible that an aqueduct—a concrete trough—had turned a lush, green valley, mile after mile of productive farms, into a desiccated wasteland. How could we have done such a thing? By what right? Had we considered the price before leaving others to pay it? I thought of all the marvels I had seen in Los Angeles, in Providence, in cities across the country. I wondered how many places like this we had created. I tried, as only a fool engineer would, to estimate the lives changed for the better versus those changed for the worse.

We passed by an animal carcass so quickly that I couldn't begin to identify what it had once been. I realized then the great, silent constituency of nature that was missing from my calculus, as things taken for granted so often are missed. One day, perhaps, the bill for our advances and hubris would come due.

Eventually we came upon a road that forked off to the right. Helen's map showed it forked around Owens Dry Lake, a place where the water had receded considerably during a drought ten years ago and had never recovered. Lone Pine was just to the north of it.

Soon after we passed the lake, we found ourselves in a place of spectacular natural beauty. To our left in the distance rose a long wall of white rock, ten thousand feet high, culminating in four craggy, majestic peaks. To our right were mountains in shades of tan, brown, red, and peach, illuminated brilliantly by the afternoon sun. Twin streams flowed along the valley; and in between them stood a small but vibrant town: Lone Pine.

CHAPTER
29

LONE PINE

Horace Jennings

The Dow Hotel reminded me of the Southwest Museum: white adobe walls, terracotta roof, and a long arcade running across the entire front. But this was merely a facade; inside was a swank lobby brimming with black-and-white floor tiles and art deco furnishings more fit for a theater than a Spanish mission.

Susan and Helen retired to our rooms, leaving Harry and me sitting at the bar, sipping ginger ale and listening to "Rhapsody in Blue" on the radio.

Harry eyed Susan as she left. "You gonna tell me what's going on between you and Miss River?"

"Depends," I said. "Are you going to tell me who answers your phone?"

"No."

"Well, there's your answer."

He held up his hands. I'd made my point.

Lone Pine wasn't very big. We set off to sweep it on foot. If Mateo's car was here, we'd find it.

Shila Ghiss

Someone is knocking at the door to my room—the room I share with Horace Jennings. I cannot answer or open it. With great effort, I have transformed back into a reptile, just to be sure I could do so.

The window is open and a cool breeze wafts in. It is blissful being able to taste the sweet, fresh air with my tongue again, to smell lilacs and robins and mice and know the direction of each without seeing them. Soft blankets and softer sheets pamper me as I slide through them, offering refuge from the bright daylight and the colors that my eyes can no longer see.

Again, the knocking. "Susan? It's Helen. I'd like to speak to you."

I cannot change back. Not now. The effort to become Shila Ghiss again has exhausted me. But I now know why: the blood transfusion.

After Horace stabbed me, I lost a great deal of blood—Shila's blood, the only blood capable of transformation. And my body can produce more of her blood only when it is in her form. If I do not spend more time as a reptile, I will be a mammal forever—a mammal called Susan River.

Would that be so bad?

I do not know. But Helen Parker will have to wait.

The knocking stops. Soon after, I fall asleep.

When I wake, it is late afternoon, and my room is quiet and undisturbed. I feel much better, apart from being hungry. I remember the knocking and realize I should talk to Helen Parker before I arouse suspicion. I transform back to Susan River, and I am rewarded by a view of white mountains bathed in orange light. After checking my appearance and brushing my hair, I knock on Helen's door.

She admits me to her room. There are maps spread across the bed—maps with innumerable fine lines running this way and that, illuminated in the afternoon sunlight that falls on the bed.

"Pardon the mess," she says. "Before our tour of the dam, I'd picked up some US Geological Survey maps of the San Francisquito Canyon. I'm only now having time to look at them."

She offers me a seat in her desk chair, rolls back a map sheet, and seats herself on the bed.

"I knocked on your door earlier, but I guess you were asleep. I wanted to thank you for coming to my aid back at the powerhouse."

"There is no need to thank me," I say. "And as I recall, you needed little help. You had a weapon."

"But you didn't," she says. "You stepped in front of me, waved your arms, and hissed at it. But it wasn't just hissing; there were other sounds. You can read their language; can you speak it, as well?"

Sunlight turns her face ruddy as she leans toward me. Her eyes are gray, piercing, with flecks of blue. No lie of mine will evade them.

"Yes," I say.

"How? If these creatures are as old as you say, if humans have never heard their speech, how can you speak it?"

I do not answer. I cannot.

"You know a great deal about these creatures. You have many theories about them. Back in the powerhouse, when I stabbed that creature, I was reminded of when Professor Jennings stabbed the serpent in the speakeasy basement. I began to form a theory of my own. Would you like to hear it?"

Again, I am silent. But I watch her carefully.

"I think you are one of these serpents. I think it was you the professor stabbed at the speakeasy. But I think you are helping us for some reason. I want to know why."

What can I do? Deny it? Admit it? Kill her? Run? *I am trapped. Ruined. Someone, please tell me what I should do!*

Before I can do anything, she has taken my hand in hers, gently. Her gray eyes are hard, but her hands are soft, warm.

"Friends help each other," she says. "Friends trust each other. Friends know each other's names."

I have had no one to trust. But I must trust Helen Parker now.

"My name is Shila Ghiss."

Horace Jennings

The streets were paved, and clean enough. We passed several men in overalls loading feed onto farm trucks, a grocery with an abundance of produce, and a barber shop.

"There must be some productive farms nearby," I remarked. "Probably fed by those streams. Looks like the valley isn't completely dry after all."

We walked on and came across a gun shop. Harry stopped.

"I'm going to have my gun cleaned. Jennings, do yourself a favor and invest in a pistol and shoulder holster."

"Absolutely not," I said. "I have no intention of becoming a pistol-toting…"

He cocked an eyebrow. "Thug? Goon? Assassin? Or just plain detective?"

I felt myself flushing. "You know what I mean."

"Sure, I know. You don't like guns. Keep that in mind the next time you run into one of those lizards."

"Reptiles."

"Whatever."

After the gun shop, we continued down the street. There were a lot of cars, none of them the Martinez's Model T. We came upon a candy store, outside of which a group of boys were comparing baseball cards. Harry bought some caramels. They were sweet and creamy, and they came with some baseball cards. When we were back outside, I held them up to the boys.

"What can I get for these?"

A near riot ensued, as they began shouting offers for the different cards I held, none of which I recognized. A boy offered me the Bambino, who, of course, I did recognize, and I traded him a card for it.

"Sucker move, Jennings," said Harry.

"Really? The Sultan of Swat? He's got to be worth more than all of those other cards put together."

He laughed. "No, you don't get it. Do you know how many Babe Ruth baseball cards there are? He's about as rare as that sagebrush out there."

I'd assumed the boys were creating teams, or collecting teams. It never occurred to me it might be about profit. Of course, Harry understood that.

"Well, it doesn't matter." I handed out my remaining cards to the boys, and the riot resumed as we walked away. "I don't follow baseball."

A truck with a canvas cover rumbled by, and I glimpsed some equipment—tripods, perhaps—as it drove away.

"Something's odd about this town," Harry said.

"Yes, I agree. A thriving community amid a dead valley. They have water, of course, and that may explain some of it. But there's still something strange about it."

Around a corner, and we came upon the Lone Pine Saloon. It was an impressively large wooden structure, and vintage, too, right out of the Old West, except its entrance had modern double doors instead of batwing swinging doors. Its large windows were blocked by what appeared to be room dividers. I could see bright light beyond them, though.

We were both thirsty, and the candy didn't help. I tried to open one of the saloon doors, but it was locked. "That's strange. Middle of the day, and I can see there are lights on."

A shout came from inside, and we heard breaking glass.

"C'mon!" Harry yelled. "Back door."

We raced through an alley, past downspouts and old wooden crates, knocking over trash cans, until we reached another alley behind the building. Sure enough, there was a rear door. Harry opened it quietly. He stepped inside and gestured for me to follow.

Inside was a dimly lit storage room, filled with so many crates and kegs, there was barely a footpath through it. Beer-soaked floorboards creaked as we inched our way forward toward a curtain at the other end. Light shone beneath the curtain from the other side. Two misshapen figures crouched beside it, their backs to us, peering through the curtain. Reptiles.

We stopped about ten feet from them. Harry reached into his jacket for his gun—then began patting his chest and side frantically. He opened his jacket to reveal, in the dim light, an empty shoulder holster. He'd left it at the gun shop.

He held up a hand for a moment, thinking. On the far side of the curtain, the sounds of breaking glass, grunting, and cracking wood told us that a fight was raging. Harry pointed to me, balled his fist, and pointed to the creature on the left. He pointed to himself, then the one on the right. I swallowed hard and nodded.

He held up three fingers, then put them down.

One. We stood slowly.

Two. We prepared to spring.

But before he could put out a third finger, the serpents sprang through the curtain and into the room beyond.

"Go!" Harry yelled, and we raced forward, through the curtain, and into whatever horror awaited us on the other side.

CHAPTER
30

THE HORROR BENEATH THE EARTH

Horace Jennings

I tackled my serpent, who was far lighter than I expected. Harry did likewise. I smashed my fist against my serpent's face. It was not hard and scaly, as I expected, but crunchy and fragile. In fact, I knocked his head clean off. In the bright light of the saloon, I was amazed to find a human head glaring back at me.

"What the fuck is wrong with you?" it said.

"Cut!" yelled an older man with a megaphone. "Who let these morons on the set?"

"Sir, do you mind?" said the serpent beneath Harry. He looked more like a shabby lizard man. "We're trying to make a movie here."

Actors and film crew alike cackled and guffawed: a big man with a handlebar mustache; the lizard man he was fighting, who was laughing so hard, he had to remove his headpiece to breathe; the man operating the camera, who had to keep from tripping as he staggered over innumerable electrical cords; a man operating a boom microphone, who let it swing down into the midst of the set; and others, including a familiar man behind the bar with a movie-star face. Everyone was laughing—except for the man with the megaphone.

"How did you get in here?" he demanded.

"I—we—" I pointed helplessly toward the curtain.

"Oh, I get it," he said. He walked across the set, which was littered with broken furniture and glass—all fake, no doubt—and over to Harry, who himself was laughing. "You having a good laugh, sonny boy? I hope it's worth it. Because I'm charging you fifty dollars for wasted props, wasted film, and wasted time." He turned to a young man with a pencil behind his ear. "Jimmy! Call the cops and have these two arrested!"

That sobered up Harry, more or less. "Now wait a minute. This was an honest mistake. Don't get your panties in a bunch. Here." He pulled out a wad of cash and peeled off six bills. "There's fifty plus an extra ten for the trouble." He held it out to the director, who snatched it out of Harry's hand.

"Fine. Now get the hell off my set."

"Come now, Joseph, I think we've done enough for today," said the man behind the bar in a British accent. It sounded real enough, but at this point I wouldn't bet on it. "You can probably use some of that footage." He laughed. "It's awfully genuine."

The director seemed to consider it. He looked at the cameraman. "What about it?"

"I got it all," he said. "We'll have to edit out the end, of course. And you'll need the clothes from these two for continuity. We can find two people their size."

"No," Harry said. "We're on a tight schedule. We've no time for this nonsense."

The man behind the bar walked over to us. "There's a haberdashery just down the street. Perhaps you could purchase something else to wear and leave your clothes here. I'm sure we can reimburse you. Allow me to introduce myself. I'm—"

"Colin Birch," I said, amazed. "I think I've seen all of your movies—*The Magician*, *The Sultan*, and of course, *The Cat and the Canary*—I've seen that one twice. You played alongside Clara Bow."

"She is a fine, lovely lady," he said genteelly.

"You gonna swoon, Jennings?" Harry asked.

I introduced us both, then asked Birch what we were both wondering. "What on earth are you doing here in Lone Pine?"

He smiled and swept the room with his hands. "Isn't it obvious? *The Horror Beneath the Earth*. My first science-fiction feature. And hopefully my last."

"I want this set cleaned up! I want you hooligans out of here!" When no one moved, the director's voice grew louder and higher-pitched. "Now!" He clapped his hands. "Or you'll find yourselves fired! Or in the hoosegow! Or both!"

"Come," Birch said. "I know a real saloon that's really open. Far from the madding crowd."

No one had told us that Lone Pine was a popular location for filming movies. We'd just assumed that Hollywood movies were filmed in, well, Hollywood. But the town, originally a supply point for mining operations, offered spectacular mountain scenery, clean, reliable streams, and a convenient supply point for filmmaking as well.

Someone had discovered this and shot a western there in 1920. After that came a slew of notable films, including *Riders of the Purple Sage* in 1925 with Tom Mix, *The Enchanted Hill* in 1926 with Jack Holt, and *Somewhere in Sonora* in 1927 with Ken Maynard. And now, *The Horror Beneath the Earth* in 1928 with Colin Birch.

We sat at a table in a little speakeasy Birch had found during his first day of shooting. It wasn't nearly as well hidden as the Del Monte, but Lone Pine was in the middle of nowhere, so it didn't need to be. The place had eight booths with padded benches and clean, shellacked wood tables, spacious and private. It also had excellent root beer, ice cold.

"Of all the strange coincidences," I mused aloud. "After everything we've seen."

An instant later, I realized I'd said too much.

Birch's blue eyes flicked to me, then to Harry. He stared down at his empty glass for a moment. Then he held up his hand. A waiter was on him before his palm left the table.

"Yes, Mr. Birch?"

"Another round, Francis."

"Yes, sir. Gin and tonic, three olives; bourbon, rocks; and a root beer." He hurried away.

"Hmm…now I wonder…what could you have seen?" Birch said, hand on his chin. "What would make you believe that two people in zip up costumes and paper mache masks could actually be lizard men from the bowels of the earth?"

His tone made clear he knew perfectly well what we had seen. He looked for confirmation, his gaze lingering this time, piercing. But we averted our eyes and remained silent.

"Of course, you're not the only ones who've been fooled by these costumes. A man was in here just a day or two ago, saying his sister-in-law saw one of our lizard men on a farm by Owens Dry Lake. We're trying to keep the film secret, but you know how rumors spread. We've had to lock up the costumes to prevent them from being stolen."

He let it go. We enjoyed the quiet of the speakeasy for a few minutes, punctuated by laughter from nearby tables.

"Now, you're probably wondering how the star of *The Cat and the Canary*—and an Englishman, to boot—could find himself making a monster movie in the middle of nowhere."

"Oh no," I said. "I wasn't wondering that at all. This film is going to be a talkie, isn't it? I saw the microphone. I'm sure it will be a hit, just like *The Jazz Singer* last fall. And your work in it will be acclaimed. But to be honest, I was wondering why the studio would cast a man with a British accent in a talkie that takes place in the Old West."

"Ah, but you didn't hear me deliver my lines." And then, in a voice that sounded disturbingly close to Harry's: "'Tell them to keep their doors locked and their guns handy. Those things are looking to eat soon, and they ain't hungry for cattle.'" I applauded this remarkable transformation, and Birch replied with a royal hand wave, capping it perfectly.

"Mr. Birch," I began.

"Colin, please," Birch said.

"Colin. If I may ask…*The Cat and the Canary* premiered in 1923.

Why haven't you made any films since then? Your public misses you."

"You are too kind," he said, his accent fully reasserted. The waiter returned with our drinks. "Thank you, Francis, you've saved us all."

He sipped his gin. "Do you know, I moved to New York City after that film. It's where I learned how to do an American accent. I had a wealthy friend there who had a lovely penthouse apartment. One day I read in the newspaper that something had crashed into it. A large bird, I presumed. I called my friend to ask him about it, and he assured me it was nothing. But he later told me that it wasn't a bird. It was a creature, to be sure; but it was a thing that could not be. It destroyed his apartment, and it nearly killed him. He and some friends had stumbled onto something. A plot of some kind. Something dire, terrible. And this creature, he said, was sent to kill him.

"Well, I didn't believe it, of course. Didn't talk about it or discuss it with anyone. And my friend…well, he was never the same. On the inside, I mean. So you see, I do understand."

He was quiet for a moment, and we heard again the laughter from the nearby tables. Harry and I both knew what Birch was saying. There was no friend. Birch had lived through a tale like ours. From his demeanor, I gathered it was not without tragedy.

"And now…well, I'm retired, really. But I thought it would be nice to make one of these talkies. Just for posterity, you understand. So that long after I'm gone, my voice will be remembered."

He raised his glass. "To *The Horror Beneath the Earth*," he said. "May it find my agent before I do."

Shila Ghiss

When we leave the town, Helen rides with Harry Raymond in his car, and I ride with Horace. He seems preoccupied, but he holds my hand, and I see no sign that she has told him the truth about me. I wonder if she rides with the detective to afford me the opportunity to tell him.

"His feelings for you have blinded him," she told me. "But eventually, he'll put it together. Tell him before it's too late."

We are heading back south, away from the four mountain peaks that bring to mind the stories Susan River's mother told her as a child—sacred mountains. I do not know if they are sacred; but they are beautiful in the morning sunlight—the light of the Father, itself sacred, or so I was taught. Brown and tan and red and pink, crowned with white against a blue sky.

I hear Sesh's words again. *"That is why we must reclaim it."*

And my father's words: *"The place where the Father and the Mother meet is beautiful,"* he told me once, when I was very young. *"Someday you will see it, if you are true, if you carry on with your duties."*

I have forsaken my duties, my ancestors, my people's future. Betrayed them. They will live out their lives underground without ever seeing this beauty. Because of me.

Less than half an hour after leaving Lone Pine, we pass the lake on our left, its muddy shores receded. Ahead of us, the detective's car stops suddenly. A car is stuck in the mud not far from the lake. There is a farm truck nearby, and men standing around it.

Harry Raymond swings his car to the left, off the road, and Horace follows.

Harry Raymond comes to Horace's window. "That's a Model T. Could be the Martinez car. Let's have a look."

CHAPTER
31

THE SAGEBRUSH LODGE

Horace Jennings

We walked a short distance to where five men were laboring to get the car out of the mud. They were getting nowhere fast. Harry checked the plate. It was Mateo's car.

Harry and I offered to pull it out with the Studebaker, provided they had an adequate tow rope. They had something better, they told us.

That's when they pulled out the shotguns.

A man with a broad-brimmed hat, grizzled beard, and long boots stepped forward. Harry reached for his shoulder holster, and the gun barrels swiveled toward him.

"Now, don't you folks do anything stupid," said Longboots. "We ain't here to steal your cars. We're just looking for someone, is all."

"Yeah?" said Harry. "Who you looking for, Farmer Brown?"

Longboots flipped his shotgun like a quarterstaff. The butt caught Harry on the side of the head. He went down like a dropped egg.

"You best mind your manners, City Boy."

Harry rolled on the ground, holding his head, while another man snatched Harry's pistol from his shoulder holster.

"You didn't have to do that," I said angrily. "You're the one short on manners."

He looked me over, and I did the same with him. He was younger, and I gathered he had no interest in beating me. "I'm in a hurry," he said.

"So are we," I replied. "We're looking for the man who was driving this car. Who are you looking for?"

"His friends," Longboots said. "And seems to me that might be you."

They loaded us into the back of the farm truck at gunpoint. For some foolish reason, they decided to blindfold all of us. I suppose I should have been frightened; but after everything I'd seen, I was more aggravated than scared. We were in the truck only ten minutes, and when they removed the blindfolds, we had a view of the lake, leading me to wonder why they'd bothered.

Before us was a rustic cabin on what had once been the shore of Owens Lake and was now solid, dry ground, the lake at least a quarter mile distant. A small sign before it read "Sagebrush Lodge." It had a porch, complete with rocking chairs, and a great room with tables, padded chairs, a fireplace, and doors to what I assumed were bedrooms. The smell of bacon told me the passage opposite the entry led to a kitchen. Were it not for the circumstances, it seemed like the kind of place I'd enjoy for a week or two in Maine.

They seated us and, curiously, offered us water, which we all declined. We heard footfalls on the porch, and through the windows we could see another four men seating themselves in the rocking chairs. We wouldn't be leaving here without permission, and nothing short of an apocalypse would change that. I didn't know then that one was close at hand.

Longboots introduced himself as Lucas Conway. "Why are you looking for the driver of that car?"

"Because it was involved in a robbery." Harry pulled out a badge, prompting more movement of shotguns. "Because it's my job. LAPD. So far, you're up to kidnapping and assaulting an officer. Anything else you want to add?"

"'That badge says 'auxiliary', and you're a long way from LA, City Boy. It don't mean shit in Owens Valley. How 'bout your friends here? How 'bout these ladies? They LAPD, too?"

I thought it time to jump in before Harry had us tied up and gagged. "Mr. Conway, the man who drove that car—he's a criminal. We're looking for his friends, as well. And they don't look like us, I assure you. They're...well, they're different. Have you seen anything strange around here, sir?"

He hesitated. I was onto something.

"I don't know for sure," he said. "But folks up here keep seeing—creatures, they say—and sometimes those folks are gone the next day. Whether something happened to them or they just up and left, I don't know."

"What do these creatures look like?" Helen asked, hunching forward in her chair. "Can you describe them?"

Conway looked wary, as if he were about to be made the butt of a joke.

I held up my hand. "We may have seen them, too."

"I ain't never seen them. But looks like we caught one. My man Fergus caught it snooping outside his house. Said he saw it coming out of that car. Had some of kind of rocks with it."

Helen gasped, and I was standing before I realized it.

"Rocks? When did he see it? Do you know where it is?"

Now Conway looked smug. "Sure do. Fergus is downstairs watching it right now. We're going to go take a look at it. So if you know anything about this thing, now would be a good time to tell us."

"Mr. Conway, these things are dangerous—very dangerous. They've killed several people already. If you've really captured it—well, it had better be chained up tightly."

"What is it?" Conway asked. "What're we dealing with here?"

I looked back at Susan, tried to gauge how much I could safely say. Her expression offered neither rebuke nor approval. "They're a kind of...reptile. Large. Intelligent. They may be able to alter their form."

Conway paused. The muttered curses and I-told-you-so's around the table told me they had no problem believing it. Or at least, less than we'd had.

"Well, let's go have a look," Conway said. They rose from the table.

"Hold on a minute!" Harry yelled over the scooting chairs and calls for action. "I'd like my gun back, please. That is, if you're not planning on murdering us."

Conway looked like he'd just eaten something that disagreed with him, but he handed the revolver back to Harry. "Here. But you can't take it into the basement."

Harry checked the chambers to make sure they were loaded. I could smell the oil, and the barrel gleamed in the sunlight. "Oh? And why is that?"

"Because the basement is stacked floor to ceiling with dynamite, City Boy. And I'm not planning on having this lodge blown halfway to San Francisco. So you can take your gun and stay here, or shut your mouth and follow us downstairs. Your choice."

Helen wanted to join us, but after hearing that the basement was loaded with dynamite, Harry and I wouldn't hear of it. Harry handed his gun and shoulder holster to Helen. "Here you go, doll face. Hang on to this for me. You ever use one of these before?"

"No," she said dryly. She opened it with a flick of her wrist, spun the revolver, then flicked it closed. "I prefer a rifle." She stepped out onto the porch and sat in a rocker. Probably not far enough for safety if the basement really was full of dynamite.

Susan seemed intent on joining us, and I didn't dissuade her. After the powerhouse, I wondered if she could somehow communicate with these things.

Two ancient oars hung over the mantle, probably dating from the days when the lake shore was a lot closer. Conway grabbed one and tossed the other to Harry. The other four men grabbed an assortment of random implements: a fireplace poker, a tire iron, a kitchen knife. Remembering the encounter beneath the powerhouse, I wasn't filled with confidence.

Conway must have noted my expression. "Don't worry, Fergus has the thing tied up. And if it gets free somehow, we'll handle it. No one expects you to fight it."

"I've already fought them," I said. "I just prefer a crowbar."

Conway led us through a door to a bedroom with a four-post bed and an enormous oak wardrobe. He kicked away a throw rug between them to reveal a large trap door. One of his compatriots heaved it open and began descending wooden stairs into the space below.

"Odd place for a basement," I remarked to Harry as we waited our turn to climb down.

"It's supposed to be a secret," he said. "That's the reason for all the nonsense with the blindfolds. The Owens Valley Saboteurs probably operated out of this lodge last year when they were blowing up the aqueduct." He shook his head and said quietly, "What a bunch of clowns."

He descended next. Then Susan. Then it was my turn.

Conway yelled up from below. "Last man down, close the trap door!"

At first I assumed he was joking. But as I descended below the floor, I looked down to see him staring up at me, hands on his hips. I grasped the leather strap on the underside of the trap door, and heaved it vertical; then, bracing its weight with my forearm, stepped back down and let it close.

The basement was about twelve feet down, deeper than I'd expected. Cool, damp air greeted me with a smell of sawn wood and...bananas? Or something that smelled like bananas. I descended the stairs carefully.

At the bottom, I stood next to Harry and Susan. We were in a long room with a wood floor, dimly lit by a single lightbulb hanging at its center. The room was filled with wood crates, stacked almost to the ceiling, except for a large space in the center that had been left empty, along with a path to reach it from the ladder, and a gap near the walls, where I could see tool racks. A few paces from us, Conway and his four men were conversing with an old man sitting in a chair, his back to us.

"Fergus, I need to know if—"

"Goddammit, Lucas, I been sittin' here since before sunrise. I need to get some sleep." He rose, wiped his hands on stained blue overalls, and handed something to Conway—a club. "Here. You watch the damn thing. It ain't going nowhere." He stalked toward us. We stepped aside to let him reach the stairs, but not quickly enough for his liking. "Come to enjoy the show? Outta the way, goddammit!" He climbed the stairs, shoved the door open, and disappeared, his foul mood punctuated by the slam of the trap door a moment later.

We approached the knot of men to see what Fergus had been guarding. In the open space beneath the lightbulb, a figure tied in heavy rope struggled slowly against its bonds. A reptilian figure. Next to it was a potato sack. Ornery as he was, Fergus had evidently decided to keep the thing fed. I did not want to know what was in the sack.

Conway stepped toward it and gestured for us to follow. We did, reluctantly.

"Do those things eat bananas?" Harry asked Susan.

"No more than apes eat mice," she said. When she saw that her point was lost on him, she added, "No."

"That's the dynamite you're smellin', City Boy." He stopped ten feet from the thing. "Well? Is that one of them or not?"

It was inhuman, but it looked wrong somehow. My heart pounding, I approached it, Susan and Harry with me.

A moan escaped the thing, and its struggles were feeble.

"Shit!" That was Harry.

My realization came in the same instant: another movie costume. I tore off the headpiece to reveal a woman's face, gagged, bruised, and bloody. She stared at me with wild eyes.

"What the fuck?" Conway said. "That's Gertie McCaffrey—Fergus's wife!" It was only then that I noticed what Conway was holding—what Fergus had handed to him. Not a club; a baseball bat. A Louisville Slugger.

"Oh, no..." Susan had opened the sack. Three stunning mineral specimens: cobalt blue.

Above us we heard thudding, scraping. Something heavy was being pushed across the floor.

"We've got to get out of here!" Susan cried. Her panic unnerved me.

We freed Gertie McCaffrey from the costume. She had been beaten badly with a blunt object—likely the bat. Harry tried talking to her calmly, asking her questions. She let out a piercing scream. Then, for a moment, she looked into Harry's eyes.

"That thing…that horrid, awful thing! My poor Fergus! It—it ate him! Bit by bit, it ate him! Until there was nothing left! And then—and then…it—it…" She screamed again and again, louder, an insane, tortured scream. My blood froze as I relived the feast in the basement of the Del Monte.

Conway's men were shouting. Two of them clung to the top of the stairs, shoulders against the trapdoor. "He's pushed something on top of it!" one of them cried. "It won't budge!"

We were trapped. But the horror had not yet begun.

Susan grabbed at her temples, her eyes wide, unfocused. "It's coming. I can feel it." She snapped her head around to look me in the eye. "It's coming! Do you hear me? It's coming! We've got to get out!"

The floor trembled. Dust and dirt floated down from the ceiling. We all froze. Amid the silence, I heard shouting from upstairs, then heavy footfalls, running.

"It's an earthquake," said Conway. "Don't panic. Stand here, in the center, away from those stacks of crates."

"No! No!" Susan cried. "We've got to get out! Run! Hide!" She grabbed Harry and me by the back of our shirts and began dragging us away from the center of the room. We fell back between the stacks of crates, toward the wall.

"No, you idiots!" Conway yelled. "Here, in the center, before those crates come down on your heads!"

I regained my footing, grabbed Susan's arm, began pulling at her. From upstairs came pistol fire, then a shotgun blast.

Then I felt it, in my head. Something enormous. Looking…

for me? Searching, as one might search for a bacterium through a microscope. Coming closer.

The floor shuddered again. Tools on the wall behind us fell, and the stacks of crates beside us rocked. The lightbulb swayed, and the circle of light swept back and forth over Gertie, Conway, and two of his men. The blue rocks slid across the floor, behind us.

The creeping feeling grew within me.

"Jennings!" Harry said. "The mineral specimens!" He picked one up, then grabbed the empty sack and stuck it through his belt. "We need these for evidence!"

"For God's sake! Is that what you're worried about? Something's coming! Hide!"

The floor shook violently. Crates tumbled, crashed to the floor, sticks of dynamite spilling, the sharp banana smell filling the air. The stacks above us fell together, forming an unstable tunnel of boxes. We huddled within and listened. From above came the sound of crashing plates and windows breaking. A final, violent, upward jolt threw us flat. The tunnel collapsed; dynamite and wood rained down on us.

A crack of stone thundered through the basement. Wood splintered and flew from the floor. The awful, creeping feeling filled my reality. I looked up toward the circle of light; where Gertie had been, there was now only a ragged hole in the floor, heat blasting out of it.

Things emerged from the hole. I beheld a group of tentacles, each thicker than a man's thigh, groping upward, outward. Where the tentacles met, a mouth rose; and behind the mouth rose a titanic, muscular, slime-covered worm. Conway stood dumbfounded before it, the bat still in his hand. He came to his senses and wound up to strike.

The tentacles struck first. One wrapped about his neck, two about his waist. They flexed, and in an instant, they pulled off his head and ripped his body in half. The two men standing with him attacked. One swung a fireplace poker at the thing's body, the other jabbed with a long kitchen knife. The poker bounced as if it had struck iron; the knife simply broke. The men turned to run, but a new tentacle caught each. One wrapped around the poker-wielder's chest and squeezed until an audible crackle sounded, blood spewing from the man's mouth and nose; the other lifted the knife-wielder from the floor and swept him into its mouth, his scream silenced immediately.

The thing rose higher from the hole in the floor. It reached the ceiling, then slid along it, mouth drooping, tentacles slithering through the air, groping, searching. It found the stairs, ripped them out in one piece, and shook them, the two men clinging and climbing away from it. One man managed to drop to the floor and run; the other was less fortunate. A tentacle wrapped around each leg. I turned away, closed my eyes; his screams ended with the sound of tearing flesh and bone.

In that instant, the thing's thoughts struck my mind like a lightning bolt forking and branching. I saw terrifying images of a molten red hell deep beneath the earth. A cold purpose lay in those images. I could almost understand it; but to do so, I felt, would unravel my mind. The images remained seared on me like a brand. It was searching for something—something it was due. And I knew what it was.

But I had to focus on what was before me: another tentacle, sliding along the floor toward us. I regained my feet and ran from it. It slid past me and wrapped around Harry's leg, lifting him until he was upside down.

"Jesus! Help me!" He dropped the blue rock he was holding, and before I could react, Susan ran forward with the two others that had slid past us. She cast them beneath Harry, near the one he had dropped. Instantly, the tentacle released him and he fell. He broke his fall with his hands, rolled on his shoulder, and ran away.

The worm pressed two tentacles together and picked up the three rocks. Then it rose high, pressing against the ceiling in the center until the wood gave way. Chairs, tables, and bodies fell through the opening onto the piles of broken crates and dynamite. I couldn't tell if the bodies were alive or dead; I only hoped none of them was Helen.

A moment later, the creature was gone, and the rocks with it, disappearing through the hole like a noodle through the lips of a starving man. Searing heat continued to emanate from that hole, and a red glow.

"The stairs!" I yelled to Harry, who stood atop a pile of debris, shaking. "Quickly! If that heat reaches the dynamite, this place will go up like the Maine!"

The stairs were battered but intact. With great effort, we heaved them upright on the debris pile, and we climbed up: Susan, Harry, then me. Somehow, all three of us were alive. For now.

CHAPTER
32

FORKED TONGUES

Horace Jennings

When we reached the top, I found the lodge ruined and empty. We moved everyone fifty yards away, though I doubted that would be enough if all that dynamite went up. Helen was alive, but two of the other four men were dead. Fergus—or the thing imitating him—had begun shooting them as they came through the front door. He killed two of them before Helen shot him through the window with Harry's revolver.

"I'm sorry about your friend Conway and the others," I said to one of the dazed farmers.

"Just promise you'll leave him to us when you're done with him, is all," the man said.

"Leave whom?"

Helen saw my confusion. "The man who attacked us—Fergus. He's still alive. They dragged him out of the lodge just before the floor collapsed. So we can question him. Or it." She pointed.

"It" still looked like Fergus—an angry old man in stained blue overalls—with bullet wounds to the belly. One survivor tied him to a tree. Beneath an old maple he sat, rope across his chest, hands bound behind the trunk. By the looks of it, that was hardly necessary; he wouldn't be alive for long. His eyes rolled slowly up to see me when I entered the shade beneath the tree and stood over him.

"My friend loaned you his car," I said. "He tells me you're a baseball coach. How'd your team do today?"

"Well enough," he said in a raspy voice. "Enjoy the show, sonny boy?"

"The car was a trap—you left it there knowing we'd come looking for it. Hoping to let the worms do your dirty work for you," I said.

He laughed, then grimaced, as laughing must have been unbearably painful with holes in his belly.

"You stole the cobalt specimens from the museum," I said. "Why?"

He smiled up at me. "For the investiture. But you ain't answered my question. Did you enjoy it?"

There was a big rock at the base of a nearby tree, almost the size of a bowling ball. I had an overwhelming impulse to smash his face with it. But that wouldn't help.

"Investiture. So you bestowed an honor on the worms. Gave them the cobalt as a gift. That's nice. When's the convocation? I'd like to attend."

That got his attention. "Invitation only," he rasped.

"It's not important, Professor," Helen said. She stepped into the sole patch of sunlight beneath the tree and addressed Fergus. "We already know a great deal about your civilization."

Fergus snorted, squinting at her. "You're just a lyin' little girl."

"Not at all. The Spanish flu, the earthquakes, the plans to enslave us. None of it's much of a secret," she said nonchalantly.

As always, Helen was an excellent bridge partner. But perhaps I wasn't—I didn't understand the tale she was spinning or where it was headed.

"But using the worms to disrupt our civilization—that's just stupidity. You know we rebuild and recover quickly. Just look at we what we've done with San Francisco. It's like the 1906 quake never happened."

His confidence seemed to waver for a moment. Helen seized the opportunity. "Yes, a complete waste of time. Though I will say, I'm impressed with your biology. How much of your victim's knowledge and traits do you retain?"

"You'll soon see, Missy," he hissed.

Susan had been standing a short distance behind us, listening. Now she edged closer, and Fergus saw her for the first time. He hissed, gurgled, and spat blood, a momentary loss of composure during which I could swear his pupils changed to slits.

"Shila Ghiss! You treacherous ape-lover! Been talkin' to Little Miss Smartypants here, have you? The Inquisitor'll flay you alive, I promise you."

She paled. And not from the threat, I realized. She was looking at me.

Fergus's head lolled back toward me as well, and a smile came to him. "You didn't know, did you, you stupid ape? You didn't know she's one of us."

Susan tried to get to him, but I held her back.

"She's good with the male folk, I'll give her that. I don't know if'n it's her scent or them chemicals she mixes up in the lab." He spat some more blood. His eyes found Susan's, and his smile broadened. "Why don't you tell 'im? Tell the ape how your daddy made that there virus that killed 50 million of 'em back in 1918."

Mary.

"Tell 'im how you swore to finish his work." His eyes, now slits, shifted to me: "Tell 'im how you devoured that poor woman as she begged for her life. Ate 'er all up 'til there was nothin' left. Tell him. He's taken a shine to you; the ape deserves to know what you are."

"I only want peace," she said, all but whispering. "Can you not share the surface with them in peace?"

"Peace?" He coughed and gurgled, his lips drooped, and he slurred his words. As his anger rose, his folksy vernacular fell away, leaving something cold and hard in its place. "You stupid, spoiled little princess! Peace with a faithless, vile race of greedy apes? They slaughter each other with their weapons and machines, they destroy the very earth that feeds us, and you want peace? You expect trust? We have no need of such partners."

"But you do," she said. "Instead, you partner with creatures you don't understand and can't control. I felt their thoughts. We are insignificant to them, except to collect baubles from the surface. You think they will answer your summons, oblige your requests? They won't. They will destroy us all."

He laughed and choked, a death rattle. "We will control them as easily as we control the apes. And you, Royal One—you'll die right alongside them. And good riddance to you." A hiss escaped him, and his innards seemed to leak out all at once. He slumped against the cord beneath his arms.

"And to you as well, you evil bastard," said Helen.

I took the rock and gave in to my base impulse, leaving his blood and brains beneath the tree. Then I pushed past Susan and left.

Shila Ghiss

Horace forces his way past me like a cold wind; I have lost him, I am sure. I turn to follow him, but Helen puts a hand on my shoulder.

"Don't. He's angrier than I've ever seen him. And he's wounded. Give him time."

Harry Raymond overhears this. He limps over to us, pale and shaken. "I don't know what the hell happened, in that basement or under this tree. But I'd say we're out of time. Let's go." He limps away after Horace.

When we reach the cars, Horace has already started the one he has rented and has turned it to face south. I accompany Helen in the old car belonging to her friend, and Harry Raymond starts his car. The three machines have only gone a short distance when the ground shakes with an enormous explosion. A cloud of dust rises behind the trees toward the lake. The Sagebrush Lodge is no more.

Sesh

"Sam Smith has done very well for himself," said the Commander, wandering around Smith's office and inspecting the photographs of the ships. "Does he still possess these vessels? They may be useful."

Sesh pulled the stopper from a bottle of brandy and poured himself a drink. What an imbecile, this one. Thank the gods that the war he'd been planning would never come to pass.

"Only a few," he said. "I—he—sold most of his ships. The remaining vessels are useful for discreet cargo transport, nothing more."

"Commander," said the Science Master, straightening her blouse and fingering her string of pearls, "I must stress what the Inquisitor said earlier. We must continue to act covertly until our science and infiltration have caught up. We must scale up production of the serum and introduce it to the public water supply, beginning with places where the manufacturing facilities for its production exist. This will enable us to produce even more. The effort will take several years, but once production has spread sufficiently, once we control the water supplies and occupy the key leadership positions, open conflict will be unnecessary, except for the final holdouts. By then, with the support of those we have subjugated, we will be unstoppable."

She is a wiser and far more capable ally, Sesh thought. How ironic that she is merely the wife of the Councilman. When the convocation was over, he would dispose of the Commander and find someone more appropriate for the Science Master to consume—perhaps Kent Kane, with his connection to the mayor. With the other councilmen under his sway, that would give Sesh effective control of the city government in what would soon be a time of great crisis.

"Well said, my dear," he said, smiling sweetly. "And may I say, you do the Councilman proud. If only I had such a mate."

She looked as if she'd eaten a rotten rodent. "Inquisitor, please! I remind you I am not the Commander's mate, merely his partner in a charade."

"Of course, I—"

"I will need a more suitable human skin at the earliest opportunity. Preferably a scientist. Perhaps this astronomer you mentioned—what's his name?"

"Edwin Hubble?" The woman must be mad.

"Yes. Hubble. He would do nicely." She reached into her purse, pulled out a compact, and checked her makeup. "Definitely a male, at any rate. I'd no idea how much effort human females go through to command attention."

"Speaking of human females, Inquisitor," said the Commander, taking his seat again, "have you any word on the whereabouts of Shila Ghiss? She knows of my involvement. If word gets back to the king…"

"The king?" Was this pantywaist actually afraid of a doddering old snake whose time was up? How could he possibly be our commander? "I assure you, Commander, the king is of no concern. And Shila Ghiss has been found. I will receive a report on her activities immediately after this meeting."

The Commander was not satisfied. "And what of her professor friend, who ran from my meeting with Kane? He nearly killed both of us at the Del Monte. Has he been found? I would prefer to deal with him myself," he said, scratching the wound on his neck.

"Commander, please, let my aides handle these trifling humans. The three of us have far more important work to do. Now, if I may?"

Sesh reached into a desk drawer and drew out two small jewelry boxes. "Here are your pendants for the convocation. Be sure to wear them prominently. We don't want any accidents when the worms arrive tomorrow."

"You are sure about this, Inquisitor?" The Science Master wrung her hands. "You can summon the worms, and control them safely? And your human protégé will be able to direct them to the correct locations?"

Sesh took her hands into his own and drew her close. She was not unattractive, the councilman's wife. Her features were soft, delicate, her perfume alluring, and her dress and bearing very feminine.

"The boy is very capable. I trust him."

The Commander snorted. "Too much, I think."

Sesh barely heard him. "I assure you, my dear," he said to her. "All will go well. There is no cause for concern."

"Come," the Commander said gruffly. He stood, snatched her hand from Sesh, and yanked her out of the chair. "The Inquisitor has work to do." He scowled at Sesh for a moment; then they both left.

Ten minutes later, Parish entered his office. His first time in this room, Sesh realized. Parish swiveled his head, taking in the paneling, artwork, oriental carpet, and every object of value as if he were planning a robbery. His broken nose and black eyes made him seem even less civilized and far more sinister. And the news he brought of what had transpired beneath Powerhouse No. 2 was alarming indeed.

"Take McAfee and anyone else you need," Sesh told him. "Take personnel from the Del Monte—from this house, if necessary. Secure the convocation site. And have someone get up to Owens Lake and confirm that the investiture was successful. There's been no report." When Parish was slow to move, he added, "That was not a suggestion, Detective."

Parish turned and left without a word.

Sesh called the Del Monte and reached McAfee. "Did you buy yourself a new stiletto?"

"Yes, Mr. Smith. Thank you for that, sir."

"You're welcome. Mr. Parish is going to ask you to join him on a trip to the San Francisquito Canyon to secure an important site. Please give him your complete cooperation. And once you've made certain that the site is secure, I want you to put your knife in the back of his neck. Do I make myself clear?"

"Yes, Mr. Smith. Crystal."

CHAPTER
33

RECOVERY

Shila Ghiss

The four of us stand in a dilapidated, derelict old barn by the side of the road. Horace has pushed the door open, throwing light into the space. There is nothing in it but dirty hay and ruined farm equipment.

He paces back and forth like a caged animal, seething. "You lied to me—to all of us—from the beginning. We're trying to save a boy's life, and you fed us half truths and lies. You played me for a fool. But now it's over."

"Professor—" Helen says.

"Enough! You're part of it, aren't you? Sharing her little confidences. Angry at me for thinking about taking a job as a City Engineer, making something of myself. You'd prefer it if I were a widower for the rest of my life, wouldn't you? A washed up, broken down old professor, good enough to help you find work but long past being able to accomplish anything on my own. That's what you'd prefer, isn't it?"

"You know that's not true," Helen says. Her face is hard, but her eyes are wet.

Harry Raymond leans against something that might once have been a tractor. "You're being an ass, Jennings. It's not the girl's fault. People lie. You don't need to be a snake to do that."

"Reptile," Helen corrects him, wiping back tears.

"Whatever. Everybody lies. Hasn't a broad ever lied to you before?"

Horace glares at him. "I've always assumed the people I care about are honest. Clearly, I've been mistaken. Look who I'm talking to: a married man with two kids and a floozy answering his phone."

Harry's face darkens. "That's my wife, you asshole."

Horace waves his arms violently and kicks at the hay. "But that's all nothing. That's all meaningless. Because the best liar, the queen of false faces, is standing here before us. Have you enjoyed yourself, your highness? Have you enjoyed watching us try to unravel your mysteries while we bleed for you and search for Mateo, only to find him licking Smith's boots?"

"No," I tell him. "You are wrong. I love you." The words are like sand sliding across stone. I can barely get them out. "I would never—"

He silences me with an outstretched hand. "Shut up! You're not even human. I won't listen to any more of your lies. Not a single one. Never speak to me again, unless it's with a fact you can back up with evidence."

The barn is silent. The wind blows the door open further, rustling the hay, letting in more light.

I know what I have to do.

"Horace, that night in the speakeasy's basement. You and Helen were trying to walk past a serpent that blocked your way. That serpent was Sesh, the Inquisitor. You know him as Sam Smith. He is the one planning humanity's destruction. You thought he was letting you pass, but he was planning to attack you. I was there, I heard him. That is why I restrained him."

"You're saying that you were the other serpent? The one I stabbed? *You* saved us? What nonsense! I'm not fool enough to believe any more of your lies."

"I understand," I tell him. "You need proof. Let me show you where the blade struck. If you still believe I am lying, take my life. I won't resist."

I remove my clothing, one piece at a time, and they begin to avert their eyes. But when I am finally naked, I cry out to them: "Look!"

They watch, gasping, as my head flattens to a diamond shape, my arms and legs shrivel, my body lengthens and grows a tail. My skin hardens to scales, and I lie back in the dirty straw. I curl the tip of my tail up and over me, pointing to the place on my side where the scales are parted and missing.

I hear only one word in the barn's silence, uttered softly by Harry Raymond.

"Jesus."

I lie there, waiting, offering them a chance to put an end to me. I welcome it.

Horace walks slowly toward me. For a moment he stands before me, gazing down, his eyes wide. I recall my revulsion when I first saw Susan River; I imagine he feels that same disgust as he looks down at me. He pulls the long knife from its sheath.

He casts it aside. Then he falls to his knees, head in his hands. I hear him weeping, but I do not know if it is pain, regret, or remorse. Perhaps it is all three.

I transform back. When I am again Susan River, I touch his shoulder. He puts his jacket around me and embraces me.

"I'm sorry," he whispers finally, overcome. "I didn't know."

"Nor did I. But we need never be sorry again. There is no love without sacrifice."

Horace Jennings

When we showed up at Savage's hospital, there were no unopened boxes of equipment; all was neat and orderly. Everything was brighter and whiter (if that was possible), and I realized he'd installed more lights. One could probably eat off any surface in the building. Two men even younger than Savage followed him around in lab coats.

He regarded us disapprovingly and lined us up for a cursory inspection. He began with Harry.

"How'd you get this bump on your head?" He touched the spot where Conway had clocked him with the butt of a shotgun.

"A disagreement," Harry said, wincing.

"Mmm. And what's wrong with your leg?" Harry had been limping ever since the worm had grabbed him. "That a disagreement, too? Pull up your pants leg." Savage knelt beside Harry's leg.

Harry raised his cuff a few inches. When he received only a glare from Savage, he rolled his eyes and pulled the pants leg up above the knee. Helen gasped. A deep purple bruise with dark circles wound around his knee and thigh. Savaged gaped in disbelief and looked up at Harry, who shrugged.

"You should see the other guy."

He gave Harry a disgusted look and moved on to me. The smell of starch reminded me of my last visit to the tailor some time ago. I hadn't realized it, but I was sore as hell and riddled with abrasions and bruises.

"What's your line of work again, Mr. Jennings?" Savage asked, as he held my arm and studied the bruises.

"Professor of civil engineering," I replied. "Retired."

"Uh-huh." He moved on to Susan, who looked considerably worse than me. Shredded clothes, bloodied forearms, and the knife wound still healing on her side.

"I'm surprised at you, Miss River. You seemed like a woman of some refinement."

"Looks can be deceiving," she said.

Son, you've no idea.

Savage shook his head, then examined Helen, who was unharmed. "Well, I'm glad to see that at least one of you knows how to avoid harming herself or others."

Harry snickered at that. "Yeah, she's harmless, alright."

Savage was not amused. He stepped back and addressed all of us. "Now see here. I don't know what you hoodlums are up to, but I recommend you stop before you get yourselves killed, as your friend seems determined to do."

He noted our confused expressions and let out an exasperated sigh. "Van Dyckman, or Van Gogh, or whatever his name is. Mr. Snakebite."

"Van Norman?" I asked.

"Yes. Checked himself out this morning before I came down. He was still weak and delusional last night. I knew I should have restrained him."

It wasn't hard finding Van Norman. I guessed he'd try to take a bus back to LA. There was only one bus stop in Lancaster, and only one bus each day to LA, and Van Norman had missed it. I found him at the same diner we'd been to two days ago.

He wasn't happy to see me. Once I bought him a meal and offered him a ride back to LA, however, his outlook improved. Mollified, perhaps, but not satisfied. Engineers are like that when something doesn't fit, doesn't make sense: we can't let it go. In that way, I suppose, we're not unlike detectives.

Again he asked us about the thing that attacked him. I didn't tell him what I'd learned from Susan—or Shila: that the thing that attacked him was intelligent; that it was a youngster, a guard, doing its job; that she herself was one of them, and royalty, to boot; and that they were trying to take over the continent, if not the world. He'd been through enough already without me driving him over the edge.

Instead, I told him we were going to investigate a place near Santa Monica where we might get some answers, if he was interested. He was.

That afternoon, I found myself scrabbling through the brush up the hill toward Smith's house. We'd left Harry's and Mateo's cars in Santa Monica and driven the Studebaker halfway up the hill, then off the road. With Harry's bad leg, it fell to me to do some reconnaissance.

There were no cars in the front circle, and none in the back, either. No lights on, and no figures discernable through my field glasses. The house appeared empty. With its shades down and curtains drawn, it no longer squinted at me; it slept.

An open but screened window on the ocean side gave me access.

According to Harry, that reduced the potential charges against us from breaking and entering to trespassing. But I was beyond caring.

We crept into Smith's office, Harry with his gun drawn. It was empty. I searched his desk, which Harry unlocked without breaking it. Inside, I discovered a second journal similar to the one I'd found at the Del Monte. Only this one wasn't written by Sesh; it was written by Smith—or more accurately, by Sesh in Smith's form, partly in English and partly in, well, Serpentese. Susan sat down among the pottery, seascapes, and ship photos and began reading through it.

"We need to check Mateo's room," Helen whispered. "Upstairs."

I crept up the carpeted staircase, expecting shouting or gunfire at any moment. There was only the ticking of clocks and, from some open windows on the second floor, the sound of the ocean against shore far below.

Mateo's room was grander and better furnished than my bedroom back in Providence. Helen clung to his familiar clothing in the closet while Harry and I searched the wardrobe, bureau, and desk. Van Norman merely looked out the window at the sea.

On the desktop was a map of California, with many points marked with crosses. Some points were in municipalities, some were in valleys, and some were in the mountains. In the north there were a few points marked off shore.

"There's no pattern that I can see," I told Harry.

That drew Helen like a moth to a flame. She studied it for a moment. "It's not minerals or oil or water," she said.

"Could it be some kind of…battle map?" I asked. I felt stupid for even suggesting it.

Helen laughed. "From 'General Martinez?' I highly doubt it. Perhaps some infrastructure that we're not aware of. Mr. Van Norman, would you have a look, please?"

Van Norman stepped over and removed his eyeglasses, revealing dark circles and crow's feet. He ran a finger along the line of crosses. It took him only a few seconds.

"These locations are right on the San Andreas fault."

"Good Lord!" I said. "Are you sure?"

"Positive," Van Norman said. "We're not in the habit of building dams on fault lines. The Bureau of Water Supply has been working with Andrew Lawson for years, and I've practically got the fault map memorized. This part of the fault, for example," he said, sliding his finger along the map. "It runs in a straight line, from Palmdale to Mount Baldy."

"How could I have missed that?" said Helen.

"Do you think they are trying to activate the fault somehow?" I asked her. "If it's true that they caused the San Francisco earthquake in 1906, what's to stop them from doing it again?"

Van Norman looked at me as if I'd lost my mind. "The fault runs more than *ten miles deep*," he said, a teacher explaining geology to a slow student. "It's impossible to reach the bottom of it, by any means. And even if they could somehow reach it, there's not enough energy in the world to force it to slip. If you're thinking of the power line we found below Powerhouse No. 2, I'm here to tell you that 115 kilovolts won't make any difference. You might as well try to move Mount Everest by blowing on it."

"Mr. Van Norman," Helen said, "we have proof that these creatures—or at least Sam Smith—have been studying plate tectonics and the effect of convection currents in the earth's mantle on continent formation. That can't be a coincidence."

Harry shook his head. "You people amaze me. You're great at theorizing and explaining. But when it comes to listening, you're as deaf as my Uncle Howard. Didn't you hear what your part-time snake said? Don't you remember what we saw at the lodge this morning? They're summoning giant worms. That's what the stones are for. They've got some kind of device that draws power, and they're using it to direct the worms to the fault line. They're going to crack it open—not from ten miles above, but from right below."

Van Norman paled and took two steps backward. "You—you're all insane! First giant serpents, now giant worms! You can't possibly believe that."

"My words exactly, pal," said Harry. "But that was last week."

"If it's true," Helen said, "if they can do this—they're not just going to cause an earthquake; they're going to break Southern California."

From downstairs came the sound of breaking glass.

I ran to the top of the stairs. "Susan! Are you alright?"

"I'm fine," came her voice. "It wasn't me. There's someone else here."

CHAPTER
34

ARRANGEMENTS

Horace Jennings

I found a broken plate in the kitchen. A few minutes later, after searching the basement, we found the person who broke it: the servant in the black and gold livery. He emerged into the dim light from behind a stack of dusty wooden boxes, a middle-aged man incapable of looking anyone directly in the eye. Harry nearly shot him.

"Jesus, you moron! What are you doing down here? And what were you doing in the kitchen? Fetching tea?"

"N-no, sir, I don't care for tea, sir."

Harry swore and holstered his gun. "Don't care for tea, huh? Guy's okay in my book."

Once I convinced the man that we weren't robbing the house, that Harry was a police officer, and that the sunroom was a better place for questions and answers, I learned a great deal from him.

He'd once been the butler during Smith's wealthy heydays, the head of all household servants. He'd stayed with him during his sad decline and despondency after Albert's death. Some years ago, he said, Smith disappeared for several weeks. He feared the worst; but when Smith reappeared, he seemed happier, driven, though rather forgetful.

"But so many people coming and going at strange hours—it was hard for me to keep up with them all. I thought it might be some kind of illegal business Mr. Smith was getting involved in, but I don't know, and it's not my place to say.

"One day, he comes back from San Francisco with Mr. Martinez.

The best day in a decade! He's happy again. That boy's saved his life, if you ask me. I know he reminds Mr. Smith of young Albert, but it's more than that. He gives him strength. Purpose. He even helps me out around the house. He's a fine lad, that one."

Harry pressed the man about Smith's plans. All the servant knew was that there was some big event that the both of them were going to tomorrow afternoon, and that they might be away for a day or two. The servant was to see that the larder and all the house supplies were restocked by tomorrow evening. We all found that ominous.

"Tomorrow evening?" Harry pulled at his lip. "You don't have any idea where they went?"

The servant shook his head.

"Wherever we're going," I said, "we'd better get there tomorrow morning."

Shila Ghiss

Horace steps into Sesh's office, closes the door, and seats himself in one of the two chairs on the other side of the desk. We are alone. "Anything in Smith's journal?" he asks.

"Many things," I reply. "All of them troubling. But none of them detail his plans for this 'convocation.'"

"But you know where it will be."

"Perhaps," I say. Horace extends his hand to me, and I rise to take the chair beside him, so that the desk is no longer between us.

He takes my hand. "I'm sorry for what I said. Please believe me. I know I've been a fool, but I need you to trust me now. We can't have any more secrets between us."

I put my hand to his cheek. "I have trusted you and believed in you since the day we met. I still do." I slide my hands around his back, draw him to me, and kiss his cheeks, his lips. All the while, he trembles—whether he fears me, knowing what I am, or fears some dark fate, I don't know. He is determined but frail, this man. I have seen him break. Yet he persists. I wonder if he has the strength to face what is coming. I wonder if he has the courage to love me.

But I might ask these questions of myself as well.

I recount what I learned from Sesh's journal, recovered in the speakeasy: that he poisoned my father and may plan to poison our king as well.

"Sesh has always been self-serving. He desired me as a mate, but only because my uncle is the king. Now he uses his knowledge of the surface, of humans, to plan a world in which he reigns supreme. And yet…"

"And yet?"

"His writings in this journal—Smith's journal—are those of a conflicted mind. He loves me; he wants me dead. He admires you; he wants you dead. He detests human beings, but he becomes more human with every page I turn. Even the writing changes from our language to yours. The one constant is Mateo Martinez."

"Yes," he says. "He told us that Mateo reminds him of his son, who died in the Great War. His manservant told us the same thing."

He doesn't understand, because he does not know what it is to consume a human mind. And that is something I can't, won't, explain to him. "He cares for Mateo. He loves him as much as Smith loved his own son. Perhaps more. Horace, I don't believe Sesh would ever harm Mateo. But neither will he give him up, ever."

He is silent for a moment, his crow's feet deepening. "Neither will I. I gave up on him once before. Never again."

Horace Jennings

We agreed to spend our last evening at the Culver Hotel and drive together in the morning to the San Francisquito Canyon. Van Norman wouldn't be joining us; he was in no shape to do so, and if things went badly, we needed someone to tell our story, even if no one believed it. But I kept both journals, Sesh's and Smith's, and I continued writing in mine.

It was nearly sunset when we accompanied Harry to his home, the location of which we were sworn to forget. It was a modest but well-kept ranch in one of LA's many growing neighborhoods. Helen and I were intensely curious about his domestic life, and we watched him as he parked his car and made his way through the little gate, up the walk, past a bicycle, a tricycle, and two baseball gloves that had been left on the porch steps. Light shone from the screened windows, and we heard a woman's voice speaking softly and laughing—the same tinkling laughter that I'd heard on the phone. Harry stood at the front door between two large planters filled with marigolds. Then he brushed himself off, opened the door, and disappeared.

He emerged ten minutes later. I'd heard no arguments or protests, but I saw two round little faces peeping out the front windows from behind the curtains.

"Everything alright on the home front?" I asked when he'd closed the passenger door.

"Fine," he said, his voice breaking a little. "Drive."

I made one more stop at the Biltmore to collect our remaining clothes and pay the bill. I found the plaque Ellis had given me, still in the trash. I pulled it out, wiped it carefully, and put it in my suitcase. Then I called Kent Kane.

"I do apologize for running out at breakfast the other day," I told him. "Something came up. I suppose you've found someone else for the City Engineer position."

"Not at all," he said. "We'd still like you for it, if you're interested."

"Really?"

"Of course. What makes you think we'd change our minds?"

"'We?'"

"The mayor, me, and the Councilman."

"*The Councilman* wants me to be City Engineer?"

"Yes. What's going on with the two of you? I saw the way you looked at him when you ran out. You two have a history?"

"Not really." *Not unless you count me stabbing him in the throat while he was trying to digest someone.*

"Well, whatever happened between the two of you, it's history. He says it's going to be a new world here in Los Angeles."

"I'm sure it will, if he has his way."

I declined the job, told him the Councilman was a killer, and wished him well. I hung up while he was still asking questions.

CHAPTER

35

POINT OF ENTRY

Horace Jennings

I rose early, before Susan. It was Monday, March 12th. The forecast called for a warm, dry, beautiful day with azure skies spotted by a few puffy clouds. At dawn, however, it was dark and chilly. I couldn't be certain how much time we had—how much all of Los Angeles had—but I had to assume the worst.

I put my affairs in order, writing first to Charles Ellis, then to my department chair, then to Mrs. Martinez. I told her we'd found Mateo and were doing our best to bring him home. I said nothing about what we'd found. I wondered what Harry might have said to his wife and kids, and Helen to her parents.

After reconciling with Susan, I realized how much I needed her. I began to imagine a life with her, strange as that might seem. I wished I could spare her this last journey; but only she could find the convocation site. It was near their colony, she'd said. Somewhere near the point of entry.

We left the hotel sporting work pants and satchels: Susan, Harry, Helen, and me. Helen wore the same outfit she'd had in the photo with Mateo: rough spun jacket, pants, hiking boots, and a belt with a rope and hammer. At her side was a sheathed machete.

"What are you planning to do with that?" I asked.

"Whatever I have to," she said.

The streets were quiet. Soon, I knew, they would be alive with people, trolleys, cars, and the occasional horse-drawn carriage. On the sidewalks, white collars and blue collars, baby carriages and bicycles. We left town in the Studebaker, passing orchards, orange groves, and farms; service stations and grocery stores; and many a billboard promising quiet neighborhoods and a good life to come.

Behind the wheel, I wondered how much of what I had seen would still be here tomorrow.

And if we somehow stopped what was about to happen, what then? Would we lose all of it anyway through some foolish, man-made apocalypse, the way we'd lost a generation to the Great War, or Owens Valley to the aqueduct?

When we reached the dam, I took the road along the canyon rim, passing the turnoff that led down to Powerhouse No. 2. I stopped at an overlook with a commanding view of the canyon. From up here its floor was tan and brown directly below, black with shadow at the base of the east wall, and verdant where a river wound along the middle. Susan and I strained our eyes looking for the entrance while Harry and Helen scanned it with field glasses, hoping to spot any people, vehicles, or equipment that would indicate where it might be. There was nothing.

"If things are happening tonight, maybe we just got here before anyone else," I said to Harry. "That was the plan, wasn't it?"

"Jennings, your optimism is touching," he replied, peering through his field glasses.

"Susan, are there any landmarks that might tell us where we should be headed?" Helen asked. "An unusual tree or rock formation?"

She smiled wistfully. "This is my first time on the earth's surface. Every tree and rock is unusual to me."

That silenced all of us.

Eventually she said, "It took us more than an hour to walk from the entry cavern to the powerhouse, if that helps."

It did. I gauged it at perhaps three miles. That meant I had driven past it, which meant it was underground and not visible from up here. If we were to have any chance of finding it, we had to get down to the canyon floor and approach it from the powerhouse.

I backtracked to the turnoff and drove the switchbacks down to the powerhouse. There were cars in the parking lot and people heading into the building, but no one paid any attention to us as we drove past.

The road narrowed, and the pavement became spotty as the Studebaker bounced through the brush along the rushing river. After about two miles, I found an outcrop of rock and trees. I parked the car behind it, and Helen used her machete to cut some brush to camouflage it from above.

Once on foot, we left the road to walk among the trees, rocks, and shrubs closer to the canyon wall, out of view. Harry had a hard time of it with his injured leg, but not a word of complaint passed his lips.

Walking here, the four of us, towards who knows what. It was foolish. But there was no one to turn to for help, not the police or anyone else. I asked Harry about it one final time, even though it was too late now.

"There are guys I could have called," he said. "Guys I trust. But what's the point? Either we're crazy and we'll prove it to them, or we're not crazy and we'll get them killed along with us. Have you given any more thought to how we're going to stop this show?" he asked.

"I'm going to reason with Smith," I said.

Harry looked up at me, almost stumbling into a cactus. "Christ, Jennings. You know that won't work."

"So you've told me," I said. "But Smith admires me, at least according to his journal. Maybe he'll listen. Anyway, reason is my strong suit. We work with what we've got. You?"

"I've got something more violent in mind," he said. "Let's hope it doesn't come to that."

Susan signaled us to stop. "See the sand here?" she said quietly. "I recall the ground being sandy where we left the entry cavern. We are close."

She conferred with Helen, who raised her field glasses and began slowly sweeping the canyon wall. She stopped suddenly and gestured for us to get down.

We crouched in the brush. Helen handed me the glasses and

pointed. I looked.

A cave mouth. And a shadow moving within it. I made out a hat and a flash of metal. I pointed it out to Harry, who raised his own field glasses.

"Well," he said. "Shit."

Shila Ghiss

"That's a rifle he's carrying," Helen says. "I don't suppose either of you brought a rifle."

"I left mine in the car," Horace says, which is odd, because I haven't seen a rifle in the car or in our room. I realize that this is sarcasm, a facet of human language that eludes me.

"We're not going to shoot it out," Harry says. "This isn't the OK Corral. And if you think I'm going to sneak up on him, think again. I'm not a commando. We need a way to get behind him."

I think back to my time in the entry cavern. I spent most of my time blind. I remember the sound of the rolling stone door that led from our colony to the cavern. I remember the ramp that led up and out to the cave mouth. There was no other entry.

Wait.

The flat stone warmed by the light of the Father; and when I removed the blindfold, the fresh air, night sky, and stars through the hole in the cavern ceiling. The hole!

"There is an opening in the ceiling of the cavern," I tell them. "From below, I could see the sky."

"That might work. Maybe we can use it to get past the entrance," Horace says. "Do you remember where it was in relation to the cave mouth? Can you help us find it?"

I explain what I saw to Helen. She discusses the rock formations of the cavern and the reason for the opening until Horace grows impatient and asks her to just find the damn hole; then she becomes petulant. Such good friends, but so little patience with each other! She tells me what she knows about the rock formation as the two of us crawl through the brush, looking for the opening. I find her explanations fascinating.

We find the hole: a gap between large rocks. Helen waves me back and inspects the rocks without going near the hole; then she joins me and waves the others over.

"No talking," she whispers. "Our voices will carry down into the cavern. The hole is on the other side of that rock."

"Big enough to fit through?" Horace asks.

"Yes. I'll tie a rope around one of those boulders and lower myself down," she says.

Horace raises an eyebrow, and I recognize this expression.

"Why *not*?" Helen says in a hoarse whisper. "Have a little faith. I've done it plenty of times."

"Shhh!" Horace hisses. "Not with a bunch of armed men waiting for you."

"A), We don't know there's more than one man, and B), clearly you've never been to a gold mine in Montana."

Harry Raymond mutters to himself, while Horace and Helen continue arguing. "I only have to get far enough down to see." "They'll hear you before you can see them." While they argue, I walk back behind the rock, to the hole. I slip off my clothes and transform.

There is no pain, only a slight fatigue; then the wonderful, familiar feeling of my body. I coil and slide my head down silently into the cool darkness of the cavern. I feel Susan River in the back of my mind, and a memory comes: she dives from a rock into a deep, cool lake. She is an excellent swimmer.

I look all around. My tongue tastes the air. There is no one here. Tracks in the sandy floor lead down the ramp and away from the cave mouth, to the back of the cavern, past the round stone door, now closed, to a passage I have never seen. Light shines from that passage.

I bring my head back up into the sunlight. They are still arguing.

Horace: "How will we get out?"

Helen: "Let's worry about getting in first, shall we?"

Harry: "At this rate the worms will open a new hole for us."

I can easily span the distance from the surface to the flat rock below. I sweep my clothing into the hole and slide my tail down after it, resting my head and forearms on the surface. Then I wait. The sun feels wonderful on my head and back as I listen to my friends' whispers beyond the rocks.

Horace: "Wait! Where is Susan?"

Helen: "You don't suppose—"

Harry: "Nothing but trouble, that broad."

Horace Jennings

Helen slid down Shila's body first, quickly and easily, with a broad grin on her face, practically begging to do it again.

I was slow, plodding, and careful, whispering apologies the entire way down, torn between not wanting to hurt Susan and not wanting to break my fool neck.

Harry wanted no part of it. He considered becoming a commando after all. But in the end, he straddled her neck and wrapped his arms and legs around her. She lowered him to the floor of the cavern as if he were at the end of a see-saw.

Once we were down, Susan—Shila, I suppose—slid silently toward a passage with a dim light. I put her clothes in my satchel and followed her, Helen and Harry behind me.

The passage ran perhaps thirty feet, then opened into a round cavern perhaps sixty feet in diameter. Floodlights had been placed around the room, drawing power from a panel mounted just above the floor. They were aimed at the center of the cavern where on a wide plinth squatted a hulking shape of black metal: a machine.

It was bell-shaped, perhaps eight feet tall and wider at the base. I wasn't sure about the metal—cast iron, or perhaps steel. Atop it, three long, curved arms, each tapering to a rounded end, rotated slowly, silently.

Remembering the cavern beneath Powerhouse No. 2, I advanced carefully, craning my head all around, expecting an ambush. The machine's smooth, complex curves had not a single straight edge except at the bottom, where it met the plinth. We circled it. The far side held nothing different.

"What in God's name…" Harry whispered.

"No idea," I said. "I've never seen anything like it."

"Can we turn it off?"

I looked around it. There were no controls, gauges, or buttons of any kind; no holes or openings; no joints, seams, or even edges. There was no exposed cable, and no way to disconnect it.

"I don't see how. I'm sure this power is coming from the dam. But it's not part of the power grid. They didn't want it to be vulnerable to shutdown. So instead of using the transmission towers, they've somehow run it underground. Based on the position of that outlet panel, the transmission cable runs beneath this cavern."

"Alright then," Harry said. "What's our next move?"

As the three of stood there and considered what to do, Shila coiled next to me and put her head under my arm. Strange, and strangely comforting it was.

In the bright light of the cavern, I saw her clearly for the first time: a creature of green scales and black stripes, diamond head perfectly proportioned, golden eyes with slitted black pupils, short but powerful arms and legs with claws that were curved and appeared prehensile. She was a marvel of nature and beauty come from the depths of the earth: an emerald. I caressed her head with my fingers, and her tongue flicked in and out.

"I'll bet she could take out the guard at the entrance," Helen said.

"Considering what she did to Parish in Chinatown, I'm sure she could. But what then? When the others come, they'll know we're here." I thought for a moment. "I was counting on ruining their preparations to buy us a few days. But we can't take on an army, and we can't disable this thing. We need help."

"Ghiss," Shila hissed.

Helen glanced at her, then back at me. "What about the power station? Maybe a call to Van Norman?"

"Ghiss," Shila hissed again.

"Jennings, your snake is trying to tell you something."

Shila's head rose high above the three of us, higher than the machine, until she nearly touched the cavern ceiling. "Ghiss-ss-ss!" she hissed, loudly, clearly agitated.

"I'm sorry, dear, I don't understand you. You may need to transform back." I opened the satchel and held up her jacket. "I have your clothes here—"

"No, Professor, she's saying a name. 'Ghiss.' It's what Fergus called her back at the lodge: 'Shila Ghiss.'"

"Her name? Why—"

"Her family name. Her uncle is the king, remember?"

"Ghsah…Ghiss," Shila hissed, and finally I understood.

"Alright…so, King Ghsah Ghiss?"

She bobbed her head, just as I'd seen Sam Smith do, as a human and as a serpent. She led us back down the passage to the entry cavern. To our right, the cavern wall was a round inset of gray stone.

Helen examined it. "This isn't natural stone," she whispered. "It's manufactured." She ran her hands along it, then turned back to Shila. "I see some holes in the surface on either side. Any advice on how to open it?"

Shila did something strange. She coiled herself into loops, then rolled along the cavern floor. Helen surmised that the stone door rolled, and we eventually found beneath a stone the metal pipes to be inserted into the holes as handles. The three of us pushed and pulled, and with great difficulty, we rolled the door back. Shila slid into the opening, dimly lit from beyond with a faint green glow. She buried her head in my chest.

"We'll have to work on our communication, darling. Good luck, and hurry back. With help, I hope."

She disappeared through the opening, hissing as she went.

Harry whispered after her. "And next time, keep your clothes on!"

CHAPTER
36

OLD FRIENDS

Horace Jennings

We finished rolling the heavy stone back in place and hid the metal pipes, making sure all the while that the fellow with the rifle hadn't heard us. But he had.

In fact, he was standing in a deep shadow to the side of the ramp, his rifle pointed straight at us. All we could see was the barrel.

"Come up here where I can see you. No sudden moves."

Harry and I exchanged glances.

"I know this guy, I think," Harry whispered.

He and I began walking toward the ramp. "Stay here," I whispered to Helen.

The rifleman wouldn't have it. "Her, too. Hands up, all three of you."

When we got within ten feet of him, he stepped out of the shadow. Broad hat, thin nose. "That's far enough."

"Yarnell?" Harry said. "Shit, what are you doing here?"

"Raymond," he said, squinting at Harry. "I might ask you the same question."

"Same as you," Harry said. "Working for Smith. The money's good, the work's fine. But dealing with Parish…" He shook his head.

"I know," said Yarnell, the rifle drooping slightly. "What an asshole. And you know McAfee? He's along for the ride, too. They'll both be here soon."

"Yeah," Harry said. "I got it all from Parish. Now, will you stop pointing that rifle at us?"

Yarnell lowered the rifle, but his finger never left the trigger. "Tell me how you got in here."

"Oh, for heaven's sake," Helen said, huffing. "From down below. We're authorized."

Yarnell's eyes flicked from Helen to me, then back to Harry. "Who are these two?"

Harry laughed. "I can't tell you that. They're authorized for this shindig, and you're not. You know how it works."

I expected trouble from Yarnell after that, but I was mistaken. He laughed as well. "Alright, alright, no need to rub it in." He turned his back to us. "C'mon, I got some grub near the entrance." He began walking. "How are Blanche and the kids?"

Harry didn't follow; his expression had changed. He had the same dead eyes he'd had back in the warehouse when we were hiding from Parish and McAfee. He pulled his pistol, cocked it, and aimed it at Yarnell's back.

"Yarnell, stop. Don't move."

Yarnell turned, and his rifle swung around with him, leveled in our direction. Harry shot him twice in the chest. He fell backwards.

I knelt and felt his neck for a pulse. There was none.

"Jesus Christ, Harry! He was drugged by Smith! He was your friend! Did he have to die?"

He shoved his gun back into the shoulder holster and looked down at me with those dead eyes. "Get used to it, Jennings. A lot of people are going to die today. He won't be the last."

Shila Ghiss

From the stone door, I slide to the end of a corridor with no openings. There I find the long, sloping passage leading down to the cells. The lichen casts a pale, dim glow all the way to the bottom of this narrow passage, though I can barely see it. I seem to recall twists and turns when the tracked carrier brought me this way, bloated and groggy. Could this be right? It must be.

I begin the descent, muscles in my back and front flexing and extending alternately as I slide along. Again, I feel the thrill of my natural form. Humans are fast on their long legs and can cover long distances at speed. I am slower; but I will never fall.

I hear two pops from somewhere above, beyond the stone door. I hope my friends are alright.

Friends. I felt myself smile inside, though my mouth does not smile and my face has no such muscles. *I have friends.* When I left here, it was to help destroy humanity, or at least subjugate it; but that Shila is gone, never to return. This Shila has friends; has feelings for a human male; has mated with him. This Shila will ask the king to spare all humans, will ask him to aid them against his own kind.

Each thought is madder than the last.

Onward. Downward. I reach the end of the passage. But it is not the end; instead, it merely turns sharply and continues downward. And when I reach the bottom, it turns again. On and on, for what seems like hours, I crawl along.

Eventually, I reach a familiar flat, damp passage with a floor of sandy soil. Round stone doors run along its walls. Coiled at its end, where the passage leads to the lower levels, is the young guard who stood outside Susan River's cell. He is young—younger and smaller than the guards who brought me to the surface. I recall his skin was tight, overdue to be shed to allow his body to continue growing. Now it is shiny, radiant, and new. He coils around his spear, gripping it in his claws just as he did a lifetime ago, or so it seems.

"May the Father watch over you," I say from the shadow.

"May the Mother nourish you," comes his reply as his eyes seek me. "Who—"

I emerge from the shadow. "Your new skin becomes you, youngling," I tell him. "May it serve you long."

I half expect a human expression from him, but of course there is none. Instead, he coils more tightly around his spear, raises his head high, and his eyes narrow.

"Shila Ghiss! I was told you left the colony."

"Indeed, I did. And now I have returned. Why does that surprise you?"

"You cannot be here. You…you are a traitor."

I misheard him, or perhaps it was a jest. I do not believe him. For a moment, it seems he does not believe it, either. Then I see his eyes and head become still. I know then it is no jest.

"The treachery belongs to Sesh and others. The Commander. The Science Master. Sesh killed my father, and the others plot with him to kill the king. I must warn him."

I try to slide around him, but his head, body, and spear move to block me. "You shall not see Ghsah Ghiss," he hisses. "You shall stay here, in this cell. I will advise him of your return."

My blood burns as I listen to this foolishness. "You? You will delay my urgent business with the king? You will advise my uncle of his niece's return? I think not."

Now his mouth opens wider, and he displays his fangs. I do not bother; we are beyond displays and warnings. This is a fight to death. Among my kind, there is no other way.

His head stands tall and straight on his coil. He leans to the left, a stalk in a breeze, then to the right, as he looks for an opening. I keep my head low and slide along in a crooked path, left and right and left again, building the S-shaped spring that I will unleash upon him.

The guard is younger and faster, but I am larger and more powerful. His spear, a symbol meant to intimidate humans, puts him at a disadvantage. Against me, it is nothing but an impediment.

He soon realizes this. He releases the spear and slowly begins uncoiling from it—too late. I spring forward. My jaws close on his new skin, just below the head. I puncture his crisp scales with my fangs. My tongue takes in his blood and pheromones. Heady, delicious.

"No!" he hisses. "Stop!" But I cannot stop. I will not. My jaws clamp tighter, my fangs deeper, my body wraps around his and constricts ever tighter.

Minutes pass. I wait patiently for him to die. When he does, I slide past him, downward, to the familiar levels of the colony.

Horace Jennings

We took Yarnell's rifle and hid his body.

"The gunshots will attract the attention of anyone within a few miles. This will probably be your last chance to leave," I told Helen. "You should take it." I handed her the car key.

"Thanks," she said. "But not without Mateo." She flipped the key to Harry, who caught it neatly. "Here you go, Detective."

"Don't be a smart ass," he said. "Our odds of living through this are low, and dropping every minute. Do yourself a favor and get the hell out of here."

"Me? Why don't you get the hell out?" she shot back. "You're the one with the family. They need you. You've got no reason to be here, and no stake in this. Professor, tell him his contract is terminated."

Harry flipped me the key, swore, and stalked back down the ramp.

"Honestly," Helen said. "I don't understand that man. Stubborn as a mule."

I let out a sigh. "He knows the score, Helen. He just killed a friend. I'd say he's got stake enough." I gave her my binoculars. "Stay here and watch for Parish. He'll be here, eventually. Can you handle this?" I asked, offering the rifle.

"You really have to ask me that after the lodge?" She took it. "I'm no Annie Oakley, but I can shoot."

"Good. Anybody comes near, start shooting." I picked up her tool belt.

"What are you going to do with that?"

"I don't know. Practice my mechanical skills, maybe."

I found Harry back at the machine, staring at it with a hand on the back of his head.

"What do you suppose this metal is?" he asked. "Cast iron?"

I gave it a hard rap with Helen's hammer. It rewarded me with a sharp, ringing CLANG! Steel, judging by the ring. At least a half-inch thick. Maybe with a coating of some kind. I told Harry as much.

"Jesus. How much dynamite do you suppose it would take to crack it?"

"Dynamite? I don't know. Quite a bit, I'd imagine."

"More than two sticks?" He pretended to inspect the floor as he said this, and that told me all I needed to know.

"No! You didn't!"

But he did. He pulled two sticks of dynamite out of his satchel, and the smell of bananas filled the air. I wanted to throttle him for putting us all at risk countless times since leaving the Sagebrush Lodge. But the dynamite looked dry, and the pile in the basement hadn't gone up immediately despite the violent shaking. Perhaps it was relatively stable. Perhaps.

But it was not nearly enough to destroy the machine, and I told him so.

"Not enough for the machine, maybe," he said. "But plenty for the people operating it."

No. "Harry, Mateo might be one of those people."

"Yeah, I know," he said quietly. "Look, Jennings, if it comes to it, you can warn him. Or you can save the West Coast. You decide."

Sesh

Sesh's first clue that something was wrong at the convocation site came when a bullet punctured one of the Packard's tires. He backed the car up and ordered everyone out into the brush.

His first thought was Mateo.

"Are you injured, my boy?"

"No, sir," Mateo answered. "I'm fine."

"Good. Stay behind the car until I tell you otherwise. Councilman, if you and your wife would remain here as well, I will find out what's going on."

"We're coming with you," said the Commander. They stood and came out from behind the car.

"No. Stay here, please, sir. It's not safe."

"I'll decide what's safe and what isn't," he said. "Let's move."

The three of them scrambled toward a tree where a man with big ears was peering at the canyon wall with binoculars.

Sesh started to speak, but the Commander cut him off. "Who's in charge here?"

"Detective Parish, sir," said McAfee, pointing him out. Parish was leading a group of three men circling to the right, while another three men were circling left. Two men in the center were lying face down, motionless. "There are several people at the cave mouth. One of them has a rifle and is a pretty good shot. Another has a pistol. They've been shooting at anyone who gets close. They've killed two men already."

"Who's been—" Sesh began.

"Keep them busy for a few more minutes," said the Commander. "That ought to be enough time. Inquisitor, Science Master, with me. We'll enter through the oculus and take them from behind."

They shambled to the group of rocks that marked the oculus. Their human skins, chosen for knowledge and status, were not terribly strong. Once they transformed, however, Sesh felt his strength and confidence returning. It had been long since he'd assumed his true form.

The Commander was a windbag but admittedly impressive in the skin the Father and Mother intended: an enormous, muscular body of black and gold, second in size only to the king. He had a wide head and long fangs, and he was more than a match for any man. The Science Master, smaller, was solid black and extremely fast.

They slid silently and quickly into the dim, cool cavern; they were up the ramp before any of the humans knew they were there. All three struck simultaneously: Sesh's jaws snapped closed on the arm and shoulder of Professor Jennings; the Science Master darted past the two men and flung herself around Helen Parker's neck; and the Commander sank his fangs into the detective's torso, lifting him from the ground and shaking the man until his gun clattered to the ground.

The Science Master opened her mouth, revealing dripping, venomous fangs.

"Don't kill them!" Sesh cried. "I have questions for them. I need them alive."

When the three humans were still, the Commander released his grip on the detective. "They'll live, Inquisitor. For a short while, anyway."

CHAPTER
37

CONFINEMENT

Shila Ghiss

As I draw near to the main levels of the colony, I pass workers and caregivers, and many scientists. We are a race of scientists, you see, though our knowledge is limited beyond our primary fields: chemistry, biology, materials, and geology. Unlike humans, there are none among us who are ignorant or illiterate, nor are any too proud for menial labor. We do what we must to maintain the colony, to improve our race, and to prepare for the day when we will reclaim the surface world.

Our colony is modest, and most of us—more than six thousand—hibernate to prolong our resources and lives. For this reason, I know most of those who I now pass, and they certainly know me, niece of the king. But I see no heads bob as I pass, no tongues tasting the air, and no eyes meeting my own. It finally becomes clear to me: I am an outcast.

I turn the bend in the passage to the King's Hall and find a strange sight: five younglings a short distance ahead, blocking my path.

"Do not delay me," I warn them. "I must speak to the king."

They do not speak, nor do they move.

No matter. I will endure what I must, do what I must. And I must reach the King's Hall. I continue toward them.

Too late do I see the device. It activates, and I am bathed in a cold blue light. I feel my blood cooling and the strength leaving my extremities. I know this feeling: a stasis field. I use it to make subjects ready for hibernation; now I cannot overcome it.

Minutes later, they are all over me, wrapping and coiling and dragging me down the passage, past the King's Hall, down to a lower level where we place those who are troubled or defiant. There are none here but me.

They drag me into a cell and roll the door shut. The blue light is gone, but the process they have started cannot easily be stopped. My thoughts break down. They become confused, muddled.

My last thought is for Horace…

Sesh

"The convocation chamber is secure," Parish announced.

Undeniably true, Sesh thought. The three rebel humans were disarmed and dying in the entry chamber, Shila was nowhere in sight, and the machine was undamaged and powered. Apart from a dead bulb on one floodlight, a little masonry work to be completed, and the chairs and lectern to be brought in, the chamber was ready. But this did nothing to assuage Sesh's anger. The fight made him appear weak and unprepared before the Commander, who Sesh had to admit, had known exactly what to do.

"Of course it's secure, you stupid ape!" he said. "It's secure because *we* secured it: the Councilman, his wife, and me. Were you not told to have it secured prior to our arrival?"

Parish's face reddened. "What the fuck do you think I've been doing?" he bellowed, the veins in his neck and forehead straining. "I've had to be everywhere at once because that asswipe McAfee—"

Sesh slapped him hard across the face while the Commander and Science Master looked on in amusement. "Don't *ever* speak to me like that again, or I'll flay you from the toes up and give you to younglings to eat. Now go fetch McAfee and bring him back here so you can both apologize to the Councilman and his wife. Do you hear?"

Parish nodded slowly, muscles bulging, face twisted. He'd barely reached the passage to the entry chamber, dodging men carrying a lectern, when he screamed, "McAfee, you fucking asswipe, get in here!"

The Science Master quailed. "You must increase his dosage, Inquisitor. He's dangerous, out of control."

"I've already increased his dosage to five times the maximum. His disposition makes him extremely resistant to it. Most humans would be automatons at this dosage level."

"He needs to be put down," said the Commander. "See to it."

He sticks his stripes in my face, just when I was developing a little respect for him.

Parish returned a few minutes later with McAfee. Sesh had them line up facing the Commander and Science Master.

"Detective Parish, step forward. I want you to kneel before the Councilman and apologize for your earlier outburst."

"But he—"

"I will deal with Mr. McAfee. Apologize. Now."

Parish stepped forward and took a knee. As he stumbled through a less than heartfelt apology, Sesh said quietly, "Mr. McAfee, Detective Parish just told me that the convocation site is secure. Do you recall what to do next?"

"Yes, sir," McAfee said. A bright new blade flashed in the floodlights. McAfee brought it down into the back of Parish's neck, hard. The first strike spouted a spray of blood, but the second strike, as Parish rose, severed his spinal cord and nearly his head as well.

The Commander looked down in shock as Parish spasmed on the cavern floor.

"As you suggested," said Sesh. "The Science Master and I are going to bring in the boy now, and give him final instruction. Soon we will be ready to begin. May I ask that you remain here and keep the chamber secure?"

"Of course," said the Commander, recovering himself. He immediately began barking orders to McAfee. "Put the knife away. Remove the body. Clean that up. And fix that floodlight."

Sesh smiled to himself as he and the Science Master left the chamber. The Commander was not a strategic thinker. He was at his best when he had a limited task directly before him. Like changing a lightbulb.

"I think we need a new bulb, sir," he heard McAfee say.

"Probably just loose," said the Commander. "Here, let me—"

The explosion threw Sesh and the Science Master to the floor.

Horace Jennings

The ground shakes. The great white worms have come. Too many to count. Iron-hard tentacles entangle me, drag me down through the earth, toward hell. I'm burning…

I awoke to an explosion rocking the floor of the cavern. I heard sand and rock falling from the ceiling. My shoulder felt as if two hot pokers were being held against it, pain so bad I was nauseous. Reality was no better than my nightmare.

"Jennings…"

Harry's voice, a whisper, next to me.

"Jennings."

It was dark, but I heard running all around me. I rolled my head to look for Harry, not daring to move anything else for fear of losing more blood. A last bit of twilight leaked through the hole in the ceiling, falling on his face. He was pallid as the moon, but he smiled nonetheless. In the distance, people shouted.

"Good job," he whispered.

"Hush," Helen said to him, her own face streaked with tears.

The dynamite. My little wiring job must have worked. "Was that the—"

"You, too. Hush. They haven't killed us just yet. Don't give them a reason to." She pressed a damp, sticky cloth against me, and the fire in my shoulder leaped up. "I'm sorry." Her voice was just a squeak. "There's not much I can do. You're both losing too much blood…"

Tears fell from her face. She sniffed and wiped them away.

"Helen…the healing ointment…my pack…"

"They took it," she said, barely in control of herself.

"Find it. Leave the pack, if you have to. Just take the jar of ointment. I marked it with a cross. Go now, while they're still confused, disorganized. Hurry."

She looked left and right, a squirrel checking for dogs. Then she scampered off.

I drifted in and out of consciousness. Harry groaned beside me. The sounds of mayhem continued: shouting, cursing, people running, heavy things being pushed through rocks and sand.

Eventually I heard another voice. It was close, next to me—strong and confident.

"You're a clever man, Professor Jennings." Smith's voice. "I should be angry. In fact, I should pick up one of these rocks and crush your head with it, as I understand you did to my best servant. But I won't. And do you know why?"

I opened my eyes, but it was too dark to see. His faint cologne told me he was close. "You don't like getting your hands dirty?"

Smith laughed. "Because I like you. You're clever. Resourceful. People respect you. Even me. Even Shila, and she respects no one. Somehow you've convinced her that your race is worth saving, and our race—hers—is not. That's a rare gift."

"Sesh—that's your name, isn't it?"

"It is," he said.

"Sesh, your people are very much worth saving. You're far older than we, I know. You have knowledge of the earth, of history—my people's history—that's invaluable. And humans—well, we're flawed. Greedy. Frightened. We kill each other. But not all of us are like that. Many of us are good, like Mateo. He's worth saving, isn't he?"

He was silent, and for a moment, I allowed myself to hope I was getting through to him. The shouting died down, and lights were coming on in the convocation chamber. Some of it washed down the passage to this cavern, faintly illuminating him: a thoughtful-looking man in a business suit, kneeling beside me.

"I know you care for Mateo," I continued. "So do we. That's why I'm here. Let us take him home. Then you can decide what you want to do. Our race has achieved a great deal. You can learn from us. And perhaps we can learn from you. Your knowledge of our past may bring us together and keep us from killing each other. The world is big enough for us to share. Many of us would welcome you, just as my friends and I have welcomed Shila."

He paused a moment, his face kindly, but his eyes restless, first flicking up, then down, then finally focusing on me. "A rare gift, indeed," he said. "If more humans were like Mateo, certainly. If more were like you. But in my experience, most humans are like Parish—angry, brutish, violent. I expect once we have risen to dominance again, we'll dispose of them the way I disposed of Parish—using other humans to deal with them." He chuckled to himself. "I suppose you're right, Professor. I don't like getting my hands dirty."

Someone came by and dumped a pile of glowing moss on the ground. An alien green luminescence lit his face from below, carving it into a demonic, ghoulish mask.

"You've done me a service, Professor Jennings, even if it was unintentional. Your explosive device rid me of an annoying rival. So when we're done cleaning up the chamber, I'm going to invite you and your two friends to witness the convocation. Assuming you don't succumb to your wounds, of course. And if you're respectful and cause no further trouble…well, we'll see how you might fit into our plans." He stood. "I understand the position of City Engineer is still available."

Shila Ghiss

Someone speaks to me.
I am very tired. I must sleep.

The voice calls my name, but I am too tired to answer. Sleep.

Later, my dream fades, and I wake.

Someone speaks to me. I try to listen.

"Shila."

My name.

"Shila!"

I wake. I am in the cell. Someone is here with me.

The king. My eyes see only a blur, but I taste his scent, and I know his voice.

Mine is little more than a raspy breath. "Uncle…"

"Shila," he says sternly, "you killed a member of this colony. A guard."

"Yes…" I want to sleep.

"Is that all you have to say?"

Sleep.

"Shila!" he roars. "Attend me, I command you!"

His angry voice pierces the fog, and I wake. My eyes clear. His huge body hovers over me, his faded vestments flapping above me.

"Why have you done this?"

"I needed to see you, Uncle. The guard…he wanted to lock me in a cell. He called me a traitor."

"And are you?"

I try to move, to raise my head, but succeed only in rolling.

"Answer me!" he booms.

"I am loyal, Uncle. Always. Surely you know that. But Sesh has betrayed us all. He poisoned my father. He builds his own empire on the surface. His human form has distorted him. He conspires with the Commander and the Science Master. He plans to kill you and take your place as our leader on the surface."

"How do you know this?" he asks, and his head swings low to meet mine.

"His actions speak for themselves, and he makes his intentions clear in his journal. I have read it."

Now Ghsah Ghiss draws his head back above me. I surprise him with these words.

"Where is this journal?"

"I don't—the surface. It is on the surface. A human may have it."

"A human! Now I see," he says. "I am told that a human was found in the sleep chamber the day you left for the surface. That it escaped through the evacuation shaft before it could be caught. It has taken more than a week to seal the shaft; we can only pray that the humans do not investigate further. This is your doing, is it not?

"Uncle, please listen. Sesh is mad. He plans to rally the great worms to destroy the humans. He may destroy a good deal of the surface as well. He has become very dangerous. We need your help immediately, in the entry chamber."

"'We?'"

"The humans in the entry chamber. They sent me back to—"

"Now humans in the entry chamber! With knowledge of our colony! Sesh spoke the truth. You ARE a traitor! You would expose us to them." He calls for the guard.

"You don't understand."

"I will hear no more. Give your pleas to the Father and the Mother. Tomorrow, I will pass judgment."

My blood heats quickly, and I raise my head. My fear of the king is gone, replaced by anger at his refusal to hear me.

"You are a great king, but a foolish uncle, if you would condemn your only surviving kin on the word of Sesh—the very schemer who curried your favor as he slew your brother. Listen with your heart, Uncle. It knows better."

But the guard rolls back the door, and the king slides out. My life, I believe, is nearing its end.

CHAPTER
38

CONVOCATION

Horace Jennings

I woke to Harry's voice.

"I'm finished..." he said. "Just leave me."

Then Helen: "Blanche is expecting you back home. I'll let you know when you're finished."

The entry cavern was illuminated in green. Men were carrying bricks and buckets into the passage to the convocation site. A woman in a floral blouse and pearls directed them. I looked over to see Helen pouring something over Harry's wounds from a metal flask.

He winced. "Goddammit!"

"Don't be such a baby. It's just alcohol."

"My best bourbon. It's for emergencies. And me dying is top of the list."

She ignored him, unscrewing a ceramic jar with a red cross painted on it. She began fingerpainting him with a yellow cream.

"What's that?" he protested.

"Poison. Thought I'd give you an express ticket out of here." She produced a clean bandage and dressed his wound. "Ok, Professor. Your turn."

The bourbon stung like hell, but the cream was wonderful for the pain.

"I see you found the satchels," I said as she taped me up with a new bandage.

"Yes. I left them. If we get the chance to leave, I can—Mateo!"

I stood to see Mateo walking Sesh down the ramp: a Boy Scout helping an elderly man safely across a road, smiling and chatting as if the world weren't about to end.

Helen ran toward him. The woman in the floral blouse caught her by the arm and flung her to the ground.

"Down, you, and keep quiet. Not a word to him. Or I'll finish the job I started this afternoon."

Helen got up, put her hands to her hips, clearly about to do something foolish. I was almost relieved when three men dragged her, kicking and biting, to the other side of the cavern. Sesh and Mateo strolled by me as if enjoying a sunny afternoon.

An hour later, the three men returned, along with Helen, a bruise along the side of her face. They pushed her down to where Harry and I were sitting.

"Are you—"

"I'm fine," she said angrily. "Everyone here has a billy club. God, what I wouldn't give for that rifle. Or Harry's pistol."

"You and me both, sister," he said. "I can't believe we let them take us the same way we took Yarnell. We should've had someone watching that hole."

The activity in the entry cavern had stopped. Most of the remaining men began filing up the ramp and out into the night. A few headed down the passage to the convocation site. Then all was quiet. I got the feeling that whatever was going to happen, it would happen soon. And neither Shila's people nor the police nor anyone else would prevent it.

I don't believe in God. Or I didn't, after Mary died. To me, God was an empty promise parents made to children to get them to behave. But learning that Mary's death and all the others had been the work of an individual changed my thinking. I couldn't believe in some supernatural plan, for good or ill. But fear and greed, hubris and stupidity? They were everywhere—from the Argonne Forest and the Belgian Congo to Owens Valley and Chinatown.

So like many others before me, I made a deal with the God I didn't believe in, right there in the cavern, while Harry lamented his lack of cigarettes and bourbon, and Helen insisted we had to save Mateo so she could throttle him. I told him I didn't need a miracle or divine intervention; just a break. Just another foolish mistake by a human or a serpent: one that would allow us to escape and somehow save humanity, despite ourselves. Just one lousy break, and I'd believe in divine providence for the rest of my days.

Madam Pearls returned with her goon squad. She wore a pendant with a large blue stone that clashed with her pearls. "It is time," she said. "Stand."

We did, with effort.

She addressed Helen and Harry. "You are permitted to attend the convocation. Do not attempt to distract or communicate with your friend, or you will regret it, I promise you."

"Christ, lady," I hear Harry say. "Ever hear of breath mints?"

She turned to me. "In defiance of all reason, our Inquisitor has invited you to stand with him during the convocation." She handed me a small box—the kind that might contain a wristwatch. "Here."

I opened it; it held a pendant like hers, complete with a cobalt stone. "May I ask its purpose?"

"Protection," she said. "Put it on."

I did. She marched us into the connecting passage, brightly lit by floodlights.

"It belonged to our Commander. You knew him as the Councilman. He died as a result of your sabotage."

"I see," I said, examining the stone as I walked. "This wasn't particularly effective, then, was it? And may I ask who you are?"

Her lip curled in contempt. "His wife. Science Master."

The woman from the basement of the Del Monte. "Master of Science, eh? Good for you. I hold a doctorate."

—◊—

The convocation site looked different from when I'd left it. It was no longer round. The dynamite had blasted a ragged alcove where I'd planted it, and the ceiling had partially collapsed, leaving it open to the sky, admitting the cool night air. I imagined that the floodlights shining through the hole created a beam of light into the heavens. Perhaps someone might see it and investigate. A vain hope, I knew.

The machine was completely undamaged, as I'd expected, the strange three-armed carousel atop it spinning merrily. A dais had been erected on one side of the chamber, and on it, three chairs, with a lectern before them. Along the other walls were wooden chairs, and seated in them, men in work clothes who seemed my age, none of whom I recognized. Helen and Harry took seats among them.

In the center of the chamber lay a peculiar vanity: a small reflecting pool, its bottom some black stone or perhaps a stiff waxed fabric, its sides smooth brick, less than a foot high, and hastily constructed. Filled with water and perfectly still, it reflected the lights above like a mirror. I couldn't imagine the reason for such a pointless contrivance, but I dreaded finding out.

The Science Master led me to the dais, and we seated ourselves. A few minutes later, one of the men standing near the passage pulled something from his pocket and blew on it: three clear notes. Everyone rose.

Sesh and Mateo entered, walking solemnly to the dais. Mateo didn't notice me until he gained the dais. He stopped in his tracks, his eyes filling with tears.

"Professor! Oh, sir, I'm so glad you could be here! I was worried, but now I know everything will be alright. But you're injured! What on earth—"

"He'll be fine," said Sesh. "He's here to support you, and he's very welcome." Sesh guided him to the seat between the Science Master and me. Once he was seated, Mateo gripped my wrist and smiled broadly.

The whistle blew again, three short notes. Sesh took the lectern, welcoming his audience and asking them to be seated.

"Some of you have been with me for many years," he said, "and some of you are new. But veteran or newcomer, you know what this convocation means. Tonight, we bring about a new world, long awaited and filled with hope. I'm reminded of a much younger man who risked his family, fortune, and reputation to build a great enterprise. Those who sailed with him risked everything as well. We saw hardship and high seas and deadly weather, together, while our families awaited us…"

He went on babbling about sacrifice and suffering, a bizarre amalgam of the histories of Samuel Smith, shipping magnate, and Sesh the Inquisitor, champion of the dispossessed. He saw no difference between the two.

His audience nodded, cheered, and wept as if they'd lived these histories with him. *Perhaps they had. Perhaps he'd chosen them because they had.*

His speech came to a close, and the man who blew the whistle drew a different instrument: a recorder. This time he played not a note, but a melody—one I recognized from my young and brash days, an old sea shanty: "Leave Her Johnny".

No sooner had he finished playing through the melody once—beautifully and moving, I might add—then, to my utter shock, the audience stood and began singing:

> *I thought I heard the Old Man say,*
> *"Leave her, Johnny, leave her."*
> *Tomorrow ye will get your pay,*
> *And it's time for us to leave her.*
>
> *Leave her, Johnny, leave her!*
> *Oh, leave her, Johnny, leave her!*
> *For the voyage is long and the winds don't blow*
> *And it's time for us to leave her…*

Verse after verse they sang. Sad and sorrowful it was, and somehow, despite all I knew and all I'd seen, despite everything at stake, I felt sympathy for these men—them and everyone like them: the dispossessed, leaving behind all they knew, be it good or ill.

Perhaps that flash of compassion was as much human nature as the greed, fear, and violence I so reviled.

The shanty came to a close. Sesh led us down from the dais to the machine, where the four of us surrounded it. Mateo helped me down the steps, just as he'd helped Sesh down the ramp.

"Bring your pendant to the machine, Professor," Mateo said.

"Why?" I whispered.

"It will bring it to full power, so the worms will hear the summons."

"Mateo," I whispered. "Listen to me. I've seen one of these worms. They're destructive beyond imagination. Just one of them ripped people apart and destroyed a building. Do you really intend to bring twelve of them into this room? None of us will survive that."

Mateo laughed as if I were a child afraid of the bogeyman. "They're not coming into the chamber, Professor. They'll be miles below it. We just need them close enough to hear my message."

"And what message is that?"

The Science Master shoved me from behind, and my pendent stone swung against the machine and stuck there—magnetized. Then she pressed her own chunk of cobalt against it.

The lights dimmed, and an audible thrum came from the machine. It rose rapidly in frequency: a hum, then a whine, a whistle, a scream. The chain around my neck held me so close to the machine, I could hardly bear it. Then it was quiet, the sound rising beyond the range of our hearing. The lights came up, the cobalt stones released, and the four of us stepped back. The machine grew warm, then hot. The arms above were spinning like a propeller.

Sesh led us back to the dais, taking Mateo's seat between the Science Master and me.

"What do you think?" he asked me.

"I think I'm glad you're not planning to bring a dozen worms into this chamber."

He laughed, just as Mateo had. "We're not fools, Professor."

"May I ask why the sea shanty?"

He smiled. "A personal choice. It reminds us of our roots. Also comes in handy when there's work to be done. Did you enjoy it?"

"As a matter of fact… yes, I did. It was moving."

He clapped me on the shoulder, then turned his attention to the lectern. I checked my watch. It was almost midnight.

Mateo stepped up and spread a sheet of paper over the lectern. It seemed he was about to speak, but he said nothing, his head bent.

"Is he alright?" I asked.

"He's fine," said Sesh. "He's just collecting his thoughts. Once the worms reach the summoning point below, he'll have to tell them where to go. And as you can imagine, things look different ten miles down than they do on a map."

"Sesh, have you ever actually seen one of these worms? Communicated with one?"

He gestured for me to lower my voice. "No," he said conspiratorially. "But I've studied them carefully, through the records of my people and yours. I was apprehensive at first, as was Mateo. But he's been working very hard. And your presence here has boosted his confidence. Thank you for that."

My reply was not nearly as genial. "I'd say 'you're welcome', were it not for the fact that you're going to destroy Los Angeles and kill who knows how many people."

"Destroy the city? Poppycock. It's my home; why on earth would I want to destroy it?"

The Science Master rose from her seat and stepped forward. I'd assumed she was going to check on Mateo; instead, she moved to the edge of the dais and looked down at the reflecting pool.

"Isn't your home in the colony below us?" I asked.

"No more than yours is in the trees. We're going to live on the surface."

"Movement," reported the Science Master. "The water ripples."

"In our cities?" I asked.

"Why not?" Sesh replied. "San Francisco is beautiful. And Los Angeles, well, the buildings and infrastructure are superb. My own home is quite comfortable—"

"You keep talking as if you're human. But you're not human, are you? And our human buildings and conveyances won't serve you in your true form, will they? You'll have to destroy them, even if the worms don't."

The ground trembled as if a freight train was rolling by.

"They are approaching rapidly!" the Science Master shouted above the rumble. Her voice was shrill. She clutched at the cobalt pendant hanging from her neck.

"We'll adapt them," Sesh said, and again his eyes shifted up and down, restless, searching for something.

"No, you won't. You love them as they are. You love being human, don't you? Singing sea shanties and pretending Mateo is your son. But he's not your son. What will your people do when they find that their leader is a human? That he's no better than the apes who drove them underground in the first place?"

The ground shook harder.

The Science Master turned to face us, ashen-faced and wide-eyed. "They are here!" she cried. She looked around wildly as if she expected the worms to burst into the chamber.

Mateo thrust his arms in the air. "Hear me!" he yelled, trembling, his eyes closed.

Thoughts screamed in my head—thoughts that were not my own.

WE HEAR, they said, and with those thoughts I felt an awful foreboding, as if an ant had summoned a herd of elephants to help it build an anthill.

Sesh felt it, too. He paled, gaping at me with wide, wild eyes. "Oh, God!" he gasped. "It won't work, will it? A controlled slip of the fault?"

"No," I said quietly. "It won't."

He leaped from his seat in panic and locked eyes with the Science Master, who no doubt had come to the same conclusion.

Then, without warning, the machine hummed to a halt, and the lights went out, plunging us all into darkness.

CHAPTER
39

FIVE MINUTES

Sesh

The plan was falling apart. "What's happened?" Sesh yelled into the darkness over the tumult of voices and moving chairs. "Who cut the power? Jennings, if you're responsible—"

"It's not us," came Jennings' reply. "We tried. There's nothing to cut."

WE HEAR. WHO CALLS US?

"I—Mr. Smith! What should I do?" Mateo's voice.

We've got to tell them not to come. "Mateo! Science Master! Tell them not to come! Tell them we don't need them! Tell them we're—"

"No, Mateo!" Jennings shouted. "Don't try to communicate with them! They'll tear your mind apart!"

The ground rocked wildly, rock and sand falling, pelting everyone. Something toppled over and splintered.

"Mateo!" Sesh called, "Mateo, can you hear them? Can you reach them?"

Mateo didn't answer. But the Science Master did.

"I hear them!" she shouted. Then she sounded calm. "It's alright. I'm in contact with them. They want…they want…they want…"

"Yes? Yes? What do they want? Answer me, damn you!"

Her answer came a few seconds later: a shrill, piercing scream that rent the air and chilled his blood. A scream of suffering and insanity. On and on it went, until he heard a splash, and then nothing more.

Horace Jennings

I followed Mateo's voice in the darkness, imploring him not to do what I'd almost done in the basement of the lodge: reach the minds of those things and teeter into insanity. The ground rolled beneath me. I staggered forward. I reached the lectern just as it fell, and I fell with it. Mateo groaned beside me.

"Mateo?" I whispered. "Come on, son. We've got to get out of here."

He said nothing. I wondered if he was hurt. I climbed off the dais, felt my way in the darkness, pulled him after me.

From the opening in the ceiling, starlight fell on the reflecting pool, and standing beside it, the lunatic Science Master. She was telling Sesh she was in contact with the worms. I shoved past her and tripped against the bricked side of the pool. I nearly fell in, but Mateo steadied me from behind. We skirted it…

…And she began screaming, the soul-shredding scream I'd heard from Gertie McCaffrey in the lodge's basement, the scream of a tortured mind that would never heal. Fear and adrenaline pumped through me. Suddenly nothing mattered but getting Mateo to Helen and Harry, and getting all of us out of that cavern. I ran into countless people, shouldering my way, pain stabbing me as I kicked chairs and debris aside, never letting go of Mateo's arm. I called out to Helen and Harry, and eventually I heard them. We met at the passage to the entry cavern, a feeble green glow emanating from the other end.

"What happened?" said Harry.

"Something cut the power," I said. "This is our chance. Mateo, are you alright?"

"Yes, sir. I—"

"Helen, are you here?"

"I'm here, Professor. But—"

"But nothing. Let's get the hell out of here while we can."

We pushed past a knot of men in the passage, some running in, some running out. When we reached the entry chamber, the glowing moss actually seemed bright compared to the darkness of the convocation chamber.

"Can you find our satchels?" I asked Helen.

"Yes, they're right over there, but—"

"Get them! Mateo, go with her. Harry and I will be right here."

We waited for what seemed like an eternity, but was probably less than two minutes. Everything was there but our weapons.

"Figures," said Harry.

"Alright, up the ramp," I said. "This way!"

"Professor, wait!" said Helen.

But I wouldn't stop. "C'mon! Whatever it is, it can wait until we're outside."

We fled up the ramp. Harry was the slowest, limping, grunting in pain. Out we ran, into the night air, now cold and breezy, and a thousand stars overhead. Never was I so glad to be outside.

"Harry, do you think you can make it to the car?"

"I'll make it," he assured me.

"Stop!" Helen cried. "Do you hear that? Listen."

We all froze and listened. It seemed dead quiet at first. But soon I heard a sound—a susurrus, like wind through the trees. But this sound was different: deeper, steadier.

"What is it?" I asked her.

She opened my satchel and pulled out my field glasses. She trained them straight down the canyon, toward Powerhouse No. 2. When she lowered them, her gray eyes were pale in the starlight. The color had drained from her face, and she trembled like a leaf in a storm. She handed me the field glasses without a word.

There was a patch of brown at the far end of the canyon—brown and gray and white, hazy and moving, shifting like an amoeba, and growing steadily larger. Coming toward us.

"What in the name of—"

"The dam," she said. "It's broken."

The St. Francis dam—broken, just as Helen had feared it might, and Van Norman had assured her it couldn't. A wall of water a hundred feet high was sweeping down the canyon towards us. And we had no way out.

"Maybe five minutes," she said. "That's all the time we have left."

What could we do? Where could we run? We'd never make it to the car in five minutes, assuming we could find it in the dark; and even if we did, the flood would be upon us.

"We could take cover in the cavern," Mateo suggested.

"I'm not going back there, kid," said Harry.

"The ceiling has holes. We'd drown like rats," said Helen.

"Holes?" A grim laugh escaped me. "Physics, Helen. That water's going to rip those caverns away. Hell, the powerhouse itself is probably gone, and the generators with it. That's why the power failed."

"Well, what are we going to *do*?" she asked.

They were all looking to me.

"Our only chance is the colony."

"No!" said Helen.

"I'm definitely not going there," said Harry.

"No time to debate it," I told them. "It's the colony or death. Let's go."

We ran back in, down the ramp, to the cavern, where men were still conversing and running and trying to determine what had gone wrong, oblivious that death was only a few minutes away. We reached the wall inset with round, gray stone.

Helen found the pipes and inserted them into the holes, but Harry and I were now too weak to do anything but look at them. Helen exhorted Mateo to help her; but he was looking at the men in the cavern.

"Shouldn't we save them, too?" he asked. "They're good men, all of them."

"Men, or snakes?" said Helen.

"What's the difference?" Mateo asked.

Harry shook his head and looked at me, exhausted. "Jesus Christ."

I remembered the sea shanty, and my promise to the Almighty.

"Alright. Mateo, help Helen roll back that stone. I'll round up who I can. But that stone has to be closed behind us in three minutes, or we're all dead."

I started shouting at the men in the entry chamber about the flood, telling them to help Mateo move the stone and get behind it, but they looked at me as if I were as mad as the Science Master.

"They won't come!" I shouted back to Mateo. I felt the ground trembling slightly.

"Smith! Get Mr. Smith! They'll listen to him!"

"No time!" I shouted, even as I ran down the passage to the convocation chamber, colliding with someone as I emerged. Sesh.

"Jennings, I—"

"Sesh, the dam's broken—that's why the power failed. There's a wall of water headed this way. We've got to get everyone behind the stone door to the colony."

He hesitated only a moment. Then he nodded and shouted at everyone to follow him.

Back in the entry chamber, the sound of rushing water was now audible and growing louder. Sesh had a few of his men roll the stone back all the way. Helen, Harry, and Mateo ran in, then the men began charging through it like the running of the bulls.

The rush became a roar, and we could hear rock and debris impact the cavern roof, flung forward by the force of the water. We had only a few seconds left.

"Start closing it!" Sesh shouted, pushing his men through, though they hardly needed his help.

"Professor!" Helen screamed from beyond the portal, "come on!"

The opening was two feet wide. I looked behind me to see only Sesh. He put his boot on my rear and shoved me through, hot pain in my shoulder as my wound protested. I hit the ground and rolled over, to find him grinning at me from the other side, singing the last line of the sea shanty at the top of his voice:

"And it's time for us to leave her!"

The water struck, and he was gone.

CHAPTER 40

AUDIENCE

Horace Jennings

We all lay on the ground. The door had rolled closed, and the corridor filled with rock and dust as the torrent thundered by on the other side of it. Water sprayed in all around it, and from the ceiling as well. Here is our end, I thought: not fangs or worms, earthquakes or dynamite, but drowning.

We stood, coughing and gagging in the dust, wet sand and dirt caked on our clothes. When the dust settled and we could see the rest of the corridor, we stood gaping at what we saw: dozens of serpents tangled together, blocking our only path away from the deluge. The men we had saved.

Harry reached for his gun, which, of course, was somewhere beneath a hundred feet of water.

"Steady," I said. "If they'd wanted to kill us, they'd have done it by now."

And indeed, they had no interest in killing us. In fact, the whole spaghetti mess of them slowly untangled and slid away from us, in the only direction we could go.

We began a long trek down sloping passages lit by the ubiquitous luminescent moss—lichen. Mateo and Helen found it fascinating, stopping occasionally to turn on an electric torch and examine the geology of the walls, estimating our current depth. Harry fidgeted and muttered to himself. I gathered he didn't like confined spaces. As for me, I just hoped Susan—Shila—would be waiting for me, somewhere at the end of it all.

She wasn't. When we finally reached the end of our journey, it was a chamber with another rolling stone door. Serpents carrying spears ushered us into it. There, exhausted and bedraggled, we waited for whatever end would take us.

After many long hours, I heard the stone door being rolled back and a man's voice urging us to get up.

"Rise and shine!" he said.

I opened my eyes to find yet another strange sight on this odyssey of strange sights—this one particularly improbable: an aged black man in a Civil War dress uniform—a Union sergeant, by the look of him. He had a gold crescent painted in the middle of his forehead, cup up.

"Who the hell are you supposed to be?" said Harry, yawning.

That earned him a kick in his bad leg. "I'm the one who's gonna save your sorry ass, mister. That's who I am. Get up."

Harry did, slowly and painfully, as did we all.

But the old soldier was impatient. "C'mon c'mon c'mon c'mon! Let's not keep the king waitin'. Let me see those bags." He began pawing through mine. "What're all these papers?" he asked.

"Journals," I answered.

He began spilling out the contents on the floor of the cell. "And what this? And this? And this and this and this?"

I explained each item patiently. "Sir, if I may ask—"

"Don't 'sir' me!" he said. "You see these stripes?"

"I'm sorry…Sergeant. The Civil War ended sixty years ago. May I ask who you are and what you're doing here?"

"Alright," he said. "Who I am is Staff Sergeant William Thomas, 23rd US Colored Troops, Ninth Corps. Retired, if you ain't figured that out yet. And what I'm doin' here is taking you into the King's Hall to meet the man in charge. Now, are you all comin'? Yeah? Well, pack up that junk and bring it with you—he might want to see it. Let's move! Move!"

Having not much choice in the matter, we did as he asked. He led us down the passage and then into an enormous cavern with tiles and stone fixtures. At one end were strange ceramic tables with intricately painted tops; at the other was a stone dais with some multi-level, smooth ceramic fixture: either an elaborate stand for displaying fine pottery or a throne for a serpent king. The glowing lichen covered the entire ceiling and all the walls. Curiously, above the painted tables where we now stood were strings of electric lights, unlit.

I knew why, and I explained it to the Sergeant.

"The dam *broke*?" He gave a long whistle. "And where did all that water go?"

Helen explained the entry cavern and the convocation chamber, and how we escaped, which only begat more questions about the worms, which Mateo answered, and about Sesh, which I answered.

"Sergeant, we really should be discussing all of this with the king," I said.

"He's coming," he said. "Believe me, you don't want to rush royalty. You might have a wait ahead of you. Now, while we're waitin', why don't you take a look at our maps?"

He took us on a tour of the tabletops, which, in fact, were finely painted maps of California: deep green forests, turquoise rivers, brown mountains and deserts, crimson cities and towns, and a sapphire line depicting the Pacific Ocean. They were beautiful works of art, though somewhat outdated regarding the detail around San Francisco and Los Angeles. Mateo took pains to point out to the sergeant the inaccuracies of the former, while Helen handled the latter.

I grew more impatient by the minute. That Shila wasn't here concerned me greatly; it did not bode well. Finally, at the risk of bringing up our relationship, I asked the sergeant about her. He immediately wanted to know more, and I wasn't about to tell him.

"Have it your own way," he said, "but the king won't like getting half a story. You best consider that. Now, I'm gonna collect all your papers, maps, and what-have-you. He needs to see those. Then he'll come through that door," he said, pointing to a stone door at the far end, "and call you up. You get to him quick, and be respectful."

He walked out the door we came in with an armful of paper—including journals, Helen's USGS maps, the Tacitus scroll, and every other scrap of paper we had. It felt a little like robbery; and yet I found his uniform reassuring, even if it was worn by a serpent, and even if it made no sense.

We waited an hour. Two hours. Three. We were starving, tired, filthy, and irritable, getting on each other's nerves. Perhaps that was all part of the king's plan.

Eventually the door at the far end opened. But it was not the king who came out; it was the sergeant, carrying all of our paper. He plopped them atop the table where we sat.

"He's on his way," he said.

"'Bout damn time!" said Harry.

"You best stow that, mister. The king doesn't like attitude. Don't give him any." He smoothed his uniform and did an about-face.

A thought occurred to me. "Sergeant, you said you were with Ninth Corps. Wasn't that Burnside's unit?"

He stopped and turned to face me. "It was."

"Were you at Petersburg? The battle of the crater?"

He was silent for a moment. "Yeah, I was there. Knocked out for a while, but I heard what happened afterwards. The rebs shot us down like fish in a barrel. Even the ones who surrendered." He looked down at the painted tabletop displaying Los Angeles. "Stupid, what happens in war, isn't it? And afterwards, people forget. Hell, even I forget. 'Til I'm reminded." He walked out. That was the last we saw of him.

We made our way to the far end of the hall and lined up before the throne. A short time later, two figures emerged from the doorway.

First, an enormous serpentine creature of green and black—the largest one I had ever seen—a gold crescent painted above his yellow eyes; and second, Shila, her hair braided atop her head, in a faded Victorian dress more than half a century out of date.

    I ran to her, threw my arms around her, and we both wept, king or no.

CHAPTER
41

A PLACE TO SLEEP

Shila Ghiss

This is the happiest day of my life.

Horace and my friends live. They have brought Sesh's journal, proof of his plans against the king, and those of the Commander and Science Master as well. I am exonerated. Sesh's followers attest to the courage, character, and ingenuity of Horace and the others who have saved their lives.

It is the happiest day, indeed—until the king gives me his decision. My friends may not leave the colony for fear that they will reveal its existence. They must live out their lives here, with us; or, if they choose, they may sleep for one hundred years, by which time we will know which native species will rule the surface.

"Tell them," the king demands of me. "Translate. I have no wish to assume their form again. The memories of their war and enslavement make me ill."

I am overcome, weeping like a child. "I cannot!"

Horace holds me close. "Cannot what? Shila… what in the world is wrong?"

The detective senses the truth. "Here we go. Here's where it all goes into the shitter."

I explain it to them. They protest, plead, promise, rage, all to no avail. The king's decisions, as always, are final.

We are escorted not to a cell but to the chambers I shared with my father, spacious and comfortable, at least for me. I would trade them in a heartbeat for Susan River's room in Chinatown.

Helen and Mateo examine my father's murals with their electric torches.

"Look at this!" Mateo says. "Could this really be true? An entire civilization, chased from the surface by the dinosaurs a hundred million years ago? And then again by early man? It's incredible!"

"We've been through this already," Helen says. "Keep up."

"Is there no other way?" Horace asks. He examines the walls, turns up the oil lamp. "We can't possibly live down here."

"I understand," I tell him. "Now that I have been human, it is difficult for me as well. For you, it must be unbearable. I will show you the Chamber of Dreamers, where most of us are hibernating. Then, if you choose, I will place each of you into deep hibernation. You needn't worry, it is safe, and I am skilled at the science of sleep. It is my specialty. You will awaken one hundred years from now. It will be as if you have just awakened from a night's sleep. And you will be free."

"Free to live in a world ruled by humans or serpents?" Helen asks.

"There is no way of knowing," I tell her. "Perhaps both."

Harry Raymond sits on my father's desk, his head bowed. "A hundred years late for dinner. My family, maybe even my grandkids, will be dead and buried. The flood's looking better and better."

"And what about you?" Horace asks me. "You once told me that, before you met us, your greatest hope was not spending the rest of your days watching others sleep. But it looks like that's exactly what you're planning to do."

He takes my hands in his and whispers so that the others will not hear. "Have we really come so far only to lose each other at the end?"

His love gives me strength and courage. "Once I am certain that you are all doing well, I will turn my duties over to a new Warden of Dreamers. Then I will petition the king to join you in sleep. I am certain he will grant my request."

"That isn't very reassuring," Horace says.

Perhaps not. But it is all I can offer.

Horace Jennings

Shila took us to a chamber of hot springs, where we bathed separately. Harry and I padded to a nearby chamber hung with oil lamps. Two serpents had us lie on polished stone slabs. They examined our wounds and applied various creams and ointments.

Lying naked on a slab of stone before fanged serpents, their claws pawing at our skin, did nothing to reassure Harry about our coming ordeal. But by the time we left, his limp was gone, leading me to realize just how advanced this civilization is in life sciences.

All of us except Mateo needed replacements for our torn, bloodied, and muddied clothing. Shila provided us with replacements that might be appropriate for a turn of the century frontier town: a bustled dress for Helen, pants and a lace-up shirt for me, and a priest's frock for Harry. No doubt fashion would be different in another hundred years. It didn't really matter.

"You don't seriously expect me to spend a hundred years lying on a bustle, do you?" Helen asked Shila. "I'll be deformed, assuming I ever wake."

"There is no cause for concern," Shila told her. "The clothing is for when you wake. While you sleep, you will be naked, immersed in fluid."

We exchanged fearful looks. Helen just stood gaping. Harry spoke for all of us.

"Swell."

Clothing and belongings in hand, we accompanied Shila away from the interconnected chambers of the colony, down to a deeper level, where we saw few serpents. We walked through perhaps a mile of unused passages and natural caverns. At one point the passage narrowed, but had floor to ceiling openings to the left and right, like a fissure across our path—the halfway point, Shila told us.

Eventually, our journey ended at another stone door. A serpent coiled before it. It must have recognized Shila; it rolled back the stone.

Beyond the door was another cavern, this one dark and strangely cold. Stalagmites, stalactites, and other formations obstructed our torches, but the echoes of our voices told us the cavern was much bigger than any we had yet seen, though its ceiling was not high. There was no lichen, but our torches reflected the sparkle of various minerals.

"This is beautiful," Helen whispered. "A completely unspoiled natural cavern. It must be many thousands of years old."

"Yes," Shila said. "The cavern is ancient, but our use of it is new. You stand in one of our newest sleep chambers."

"But it's empty," said Mateo. "I don't understand. Where are the dreamers?"

Shila raised her arms, pointing to the ceiling.

I shone my torch at the ceiling directly above us prompting gasps from Helen, Harry, and Mateo. Between the stalactites hung translucent sacs—snakeskins?—filled with a yellow liquid. Within the liquid were dark, sinuous shapes, coiled into rings. There were all sizes of sacs and serpents, suggesting that the sleepers represented many stages of maturity. I swept my torch about the ceiling and saw that sacs were everywhere, as far as the eye could see.

"Good Lord! There must be hundreds…thousands…"

"Six thousand sleepers," Shila said. "Or, as we call them, Dreamers. You will soon be among them. Here you will sleep safely, monitored by those like me who lead our hibernation science. Wardens of Dreamers."

―⁂―

Shila Ghiss

They are frightened. Hibernation comes naturally to reptiles, but it is unknown to humans. And this hibernation—immersed in sleep fluid for a hundred years—is not natural.

None of them wants to go through with it, but neither do they want to live out their lives here, in the dimly lit caverns. Now that I have finally seen sunrise and sunset, and all the bright day in between, neither do I.

We walk to an empty part of the cavern where four sacs have been raised a few feet off the floor and filled with the yellow sleeping fluid.

Horace puts on a brave front for the rest of his friends. "I don't know about you," he says, "but I can't wait to see what humankind accomplishes in the next hundred years. We've mastered the forces of electricity and magnetism, and one day soon, we'll tame the atom itself. It will be a privilege to see it."

He disrobes while the others turn their backs, as human modesty demands, and steps into the sack as if he is getting into a bath.

We reptiles prefer hibernation cold; but knowing human predilections for warm baths, I have matched the sleeping fluid to their body temperature. It will cool soon enough once they are asleep.

"Ah," he says, his head and shoulders above the edge of the sleep skin, "this doesn't feel bad at all." But we all see that he is trembling, and not from the cold air of the chamber.

I explain to him what will happen. "When we draw up the ends of the sleep skin, you will be completely immersed in the fluid. You must breathe it in, take it into your mouth and lungs. Do not struggle. It will provide air and nourishment during your long sleep."

He grows pale.

"I will watch over you," I whisper to him. "Sleep well, my love." I kiss his lips, and despite long years putting Dreamers to sleep, I find myself growing sad and weak.

His voice is unsteady. "Goodnight, everyone. See you in a hundred years. Don't let me oversleep."

The new Warden of Dreamers, who occupied one of these sacs only a few weeks ago, takes one line, and I take the other. Together we pull down, and the sleep skin closes, pulled upward by its ends. Through the sleep fluid, I see the shape of Horace. He thrashes terribly for nearly a minute while his friends gasp and scream for me to release him. But I cannot.

"You've drowned him!" Helen cries.

"He is fine," I assure her, "as are all who sleep in this chamber. The fluid remains yellow while the sleeper is healthy; it darkens if they become unhealthy. It is a simple matter to monitor the color and test the fluid of any who appear to be in danger."

She is doubtful. But I have never seen Helen Parker surrender to fear. She is among the strongest and bravest people I know. She steps into her sleep skin, and Mateo kisses her goodbye.

"You'll be awake and driving a flying car before you know it," he says.

"Sure," she replies. There are tears in her eyes as she goes under the sleep fluid.

Harry Raymond is next. He looks pale but resigned.

"Well, no one's going to kiss me goodbye. Adios." He begins to sink.

"Wait!" I cry.

He pops up as if the sleep fluid is electrified.

I take his face in my hands and kiss him slowly, softly on the lips.

He smiles and shakes his head. "Crazy broad. Thanks." And then to Mateo: "You didn't see that." He slides under.

Mateo is the last. But he does not remove his clothes.

"Don't be afraid," I tell him.

"I'm not," he says. "But I have an idea."

CHAPTER
42

A LOOK FORWARD

Horace Jennings

I was cold. Mary had taken all the blankets again. I tried to pull them back to me, but I couldn't find them. My hands closed on nothing. I opened my eyes and tried to speak.

I was drowning in a sea of egg yolk.

I washed ashore on stony ground, freezing in the cold air. I coughed over and over, forcing the liquid from my lungs until I was exhausted. A warm covering fell over me.

"You're alright, Horace. You made it." A woman's voice—but not Mary's.

I opened my eyes to see Susan River smiling at me.

Then I remembered. A hundred years.

"The others?" I wheezed.

"We're here," said Helen. "Welcome to 2028."

I stood beside the open sac, wrapped in a blanket. I was still in the cavern, with all the other dreamers.

"Looks a lot like 1928," I said. And then, seeing Harry in the priest's frock, and Helen in her bustled dress: "Or maybe 1888."

"Whatever year it is, I'm just glad to be alive," said Harry. "C'mon, shake a leg, Jennings. There's a place nearby where you can wash off that goo and get dressed. Then we can get the hell out of here."

We left the cavern for the warmth of the adjoining passage, and I realized one of us was missing.

"Mateo. Where is he?"

"He awaits us at the fissure," said Susan—or Shila, I suppose. I was never going to figure it out.

So I washed and dressed up like Bat Masterson, and the four of us walked back through the mile-long chain of passages and small caverns until we came to the fissure in the connecting passage, where an oil lamp threw a small circle of light. It was very warm. Fresh air was blowing in from somewhere, as if a ventilation system had been installed.

Mateo was waiting for us, our satchels and supplies at his feet. He wore a monk's robe, complete with hood. He waved us over.

"Finally!" Helen said. "I was afraid you died in hibernation." She moved to embrace him, but he held up a hand.

"Okay, Brother Martinez, we're here," said Harry. "Now tell us what's going on."

"Alright," Mateo said, his face shrouded by the hood. "Now everyone, remain calm, and don't get upset."

"Mateo," Helen warned, "so help me—"

"Here's the deal. You've only been hibernating for two weeks. It's still 1928."

A brief pause, a collective "WHAT?", exclamations of joy, and then we heaped curses and threats on Mateo for putting us through the ordeal of hibernation. After that, we all had the same question: WHY?

"It occurred to me that the entry chamber is likely unreachable now, at the bottom of a river, or buried beneath tons of mud, or both," he said. "The serpents will eventually need to dig a new way out. And I thought, 'What if we dig one first?' Then we could just walk out."

"Dig our way through hundreds of feet of earth and rock?" I asked.

"Of course," Helen said dryly. "Why didn't I think of that?"

"Listen," Mateo said. "When we crossed this fissure, I had an idea. In that direction," he pointed to where the fissure disappeared beyond the wall to his left, "it stretches far from the colony, and in particular, far from the Dream Chamber."

"Chamber of Dreamers," Susan corrected.

By God, I thought, *Helen is rubbing off on her.*

"Yes, of course," he continued. "The point is, it's safe."

"Safe?" I asked. "Safe from what?"

In the next instant, we all understood.

He pulled back the hood of his robe. The left side of his face, neck, and scalp were disfigured. He'd been badly burned, though healed.

Helen gasped, then put her hand over her mouth. "Oh—oh, no! Mateo!" She ran to him, but stopped short, afraid to harm him further. "What happened to you?"

But I already knew. "Worms," I said.

He nodded. "I only had to summon one of them. But I got too close. Molten rock."

He'd used the two remaining cobalt pendants—his and mine—to summon a worm: one stone placed at the far end of the fissure, and one placed on the surface to draw it there.

"But how could you place a stone on the surface?" I asked. "You just said there's no way to reach it."

"So I thought. But no intelligent species would build a colony like this without sufficient egress. The fact that there'd been an evacuation shaft in Dream Chamber proved that. I reasoned that there had to be another way out. Shila made some inquiries and found it."

Shila nodded. "It was guarded, of course, but I am not confined here as you are. Once I showed them the three of you in hibernation, and Mateo preparing for it, they deemed it safe to let me pass. Mateo showed me where to place the stone."

"I used the USGS maps that Helen brought," he said, nodding to her. "Very helpful."

I was still aghast at the idea of Mateo communicating with those nightmarish creatures, and I told him so.

"Only one, Professor. And that was…enough. I knew from the scrolls not to engage them. They are…" his voice quavered. "They are…"

I grabbed his arm and shook him. "Don't. Don't ever."

Shila Ghiss

We walk single file into the fissure, Mateo leading the way with the lamp, Helen and Horace following with their dying electric torches. It grows hot, though the breeze of fresh air becomes stronger. Eventually, the fissure widens to a passage, and Mateo halts us.

Before us lay a hole in the floor with a fiery heat coming from it. It looks very much like the hole in the basement of the Sagebrush Lodge, and despite the heat, my skin prickles to gooseflesh.

Mateo walks carefully around it, holding the oil lamp high so we can see it clearly. "The bottom, if there is one, is molten rock," he says. "Don't fall in."

Harry Raymond comments on this advice using foul language.

We edge around the hole and find it much cooler on the other side, where a breeze of fresh air blows against us. Mateo shines the lamp ahead. There, in the wall where the fissure ends, is a smooth tunnel sloping up and away from us. Cool air cascades down from it.

The climb is arduous and takes hours, and the breeze grows colder the higher we climb. I imagine Susan River making this climb alone in the evacuation shaft, and I am filled with new respect for her.

We can see the light of the Father long before we reach the end. It strengthens us. Eventually, we emerge onto a mountaintop. The breeze becomes an icy wind, chilling me like nothing I have felt before.

My friends are thrilled. They whoop and cry and embrace each other. Horace says the air tastes like freedom. He hugs me like a bear, and I am glad for his warmth. He kisses me and tells me of all the wonderful things I have to look forward to: snow and a warm fire and holidays in the winter; flowers and green grass and pleasant days in the spring; long, lazy days and music outdoors in the summer; and a panoply of color when the school year begins each fall. Jazz music, "talkies", stargazing. Travel, art, and architecture. And all of it with fine friends, family, and bright students.

He missed these things, he tells me, long before we met. It began when his wife, Mary, died ten years ago; but it ends today, with me.

I excuse us from the others, their frock, robe, and dress flapping in the wind, and lead Horace aside to a rock where we sit in the sun.

"I can't go with you, Horace. At least, not yet."

"What? Of course you can!"

"I cannot. I am the King's heir. I have obligations, commitments. To my people. I cannot abandon them."

He looks down at the ground. I can see he doesn't understand. I must try to explain it to him.

"My people will eventually need a new ruler—but it cannot be me. I must help them make a new beginning, so that they are not burdened with another Sesh, another Commander, or Science Master. And there is hope. My father found a way for my people to take human form without harming you. I am living proof that it works. Perhaps it can offer us a choice apart from conquest or eternal hibernation—a way instead that will bring our two species together."

Horace looks back at me, the wind whipping his thin hair, and I can see that he is full of doubt.

"I don't know if I will succeed," I tell him, "but I must try. And once I have done my best to set things right, dear Horace…I will find you, I promise."

CHAPTER
43

RECKONING

Horace Jennings

We said our goodbyes to Shila in the cold wind and bright sunshine near the shaft. She embraced Helen, Harry, and Mateo, murmuring things to each of them that I could not hear. But Helen laughed, Harry smiled, and Mateo nodded at these final, private words.

Then came my turn. I needed no words; she knew my heart. A kiss, a final embrace, and then she began her long way back down. We watched as she disappeared into shadow. My heart sank with her; but I resolved not to give in to despair, as Sam Smith had done. It was the path I had nearly taken before the call from Mrs. Martinez.

We walked toward the road that runs along the canyon rim, discussing the past few weeks—our good fortune, darkest moments, and home. Only when we reached the road and looked down into the canyon did we see the scope of the destruction caused by the flood. The dam, the powerhouse, and every other human construct were gone; only mud and broken rock remained. We fell silent.

Everything in the path of the water, fifty miles from the Sierra Pelona Mountains to the Pacific Ocean, was destroyed. More than four hundred people were dead. People would one day call it the worst civil engineering disaster of the twentieth century. The century was still young, of course.

We were sobered and guilted, being saved by an event that caused the deaths of hundreds. That the rupture of the fault, had it succeeded, would have killed a thousandfold more, did not put us at ease. It was worst, perhaps, for Helen, who had seen evidence of the dam's flaws in the rock beneath Powerhouse No. 2. Van Norman had assured her, as no doubt William Mulholland and Stanley Dunham had assured him, had assured themselves and the public, that there was nothing to worry about. They were wrong, as great men—men with few peers—often are. I wondered then if my own mediocrity was perhaps a blessing in disguise.

We eventually found a ride, then a bus, then a trolley back to Los Angeles. The agent who rented me the Studebaker demanded proof that the car was lost. I told him precisely where he should look, while Helen tittered and Mateo blushed.

Our farewell to Harry Raymond was privileged: he invited us to his home to have dinner with his family. Of his wife, his two children, and his home life I shall respect his privacy and say nothing, except this: it was the closest I have come, since Mary died, to feeling as if I belonged to a family. When the evening was over and his wife was putting the children to bed, we had a few minutes with him on the porch.

"What does the future hold for Harry Raymond?" I asked him, with a flair of the dramatic.

"How the hell would I know, Jennings? Jesus, as long as it doesn't involve giant snakes or the end of the world, I'll be happy."

"But if it does," Helen asked, "can we still call on you?"

He thought for a moment. "I won't rule it out. In fact, maybe you can work for me."

Helen prompted Mateo to call his family to let them know he was alright. His mother and niece were overjoyed to hear from him, and ecstatic when they learned he would soon be coming home. I was glad for them, and for him. But his father had passed while he was spending time with Smith, who, in Mateo's mind, I suppose, was the father he'd wished he had. It seemed to sober him, age him.

Or, I thought darkly, was it his contact with the worm who enabled our escape? *A race of god-like beings living in the earth's mantle? The heat melts solid rock; the pressure crushes organic material into diamonds. What kind of creature could possibly live in such a place?*

The imaginary kind, I decided, despite what I'd seen.

Either way, Mateo was changed. Gone was the carefree, ingenuous idealist who would make the world a better place—the lad I'd always admired. In his place was a more somber, serious fellow. He wanted nothing more to do with geology.

We stayed a week in San Francisco, feted nearly every day by the extended Martinez family for bringing him home. The friendship between Helen and Mateo regrew and strengthened. It reminded me that age and distance had diluted the once close friendships I'd had with my peers—men like Charles Ellis. Making new friendships later in life was no easy feat—or so I told myself, briefly. For I soon saw that kind of thinking for the foolishness that it is.

So I made a promise to myself: that I would let neither age nor distance nor hubris stand in the way of friendships with people I knew and admired. I called Andrew Lawson while we were in San Francisco and invited him to join me for lunch and an afternoon at the de Young Museum. To my great surprise, he accepted, and we had a splendid time. We agreed to stay in touch.

Helen and I spent not just a few hours with Charles Ellis in Chicago, but an entire weekend, including an evening at a club with Louis Armstrong and His Hot Five and a trip to the Art Institute. Charles wanted to know everything that had happened in Los Angeles. We gave him an abridged version that included Shila but excluded her nonhuman aspect and compatriots. Anyway, I think Charles found the notion of me in a romantic relationship more incredible than he would the discovery of an alien race.

At our last dinner before our train reached Providence, Helen found me withdrawn and glum. The cause was obvious.

"Must I tell you again to have a little faith?" she asked.

"Faith I've got," I told her. "It's patience I'm lacking."

She raised an eyebrow. "You? A lack of patience? I don't believe it." She laughed and shook her head. "Sorry, Professor, but as we both know, patience is not my strong suit."

The next morning, I awoke in my own bed, in my own house. When I rose, I had tea, and Isis, looking down from the high shelf in the kitchen, seemed to judge me kindly. Outside, the air was fresh, as it had rained last night when our train pulled in. I marveled at the greenery and flowers that early April had brought, especially since my last evening in Providence had been in cold and snowy February. But that was then; this was now.

Once the hour became reasonable, I phoned my department chair.

"Jennings! This is a surprise. Where are you?"

"Home," I said.

"Home? I'm sorry to hear that. Did things not work out in Los Angeles? Did your sabbatical not go as planned?"

"It most certainly did not go as planned. But it worked out very well. It was everything a sabbatical should be, and more."

He paused. "Jennings, I'm hearing something different in you. Almost as if you have a new perspective."

"As always," I told him, "you are very perceptive. I do have a different outlook. This sabbatical has done me a world of good."

"But…it's been barely a month," he said. "What could possibly have brought about such change so quickly?"

"Sir," I said, "you wouldn't believe me if I told you."

Shila Ghiss

Horace's home is lovely. In the morning, the rising light of the Father blesses the foyer, parlor, and kitchen. It is spring, and there are vases of fresh-cut flowers everywhere. Horace tells me he has spent the past year learning to cultivate them.

Mary's presence is everywhere in this house, and I am glad of it. She brings to it a warmth that we must keep. I sometimes wonder if she is Horace's spirit guide.

I find him in the kitchen. He has set our places for breakfast. I sit, thank him, and he pours tea for me into an exquisite white cup with painted red roses and a matching saucer. There is sugar as well, and clotted cream. I reach for them.

"Oh, dear," he says. "I seem to have forgotten something."

He pulls a familiar cup from the cupboard—a heavy, ancient cup with three symbols. He places it before me and fills it with water.

Many lonely years are behind us, and many happy ones await. For now, we live this moment, content.

List of Real People and Locales Used Fictitiously

People	Locales
Clara Bow	Biltmore Hotel
Stanley Dunham	Culver Hotel
Charles Ellis	Del Monte speakeasy
Edwin Hubble	Dow Hotel
Andrew Lawson	Hudson River Tunnel
Guy McAfee	Lone Pine, CA
William Mulholland	Los Angeles City Hall
Gaius Plinius Caecilius Secundus (Pliny the Younger)	Menotti's Bakery
	Powerhouse No.2
Harry Raymond	Providence City Hospital
Kent Kane Parrot	St. Francis Dam
Dr. Seth Savage	Union Station, Chicago
Publius Cornelius Tacitus	Venice, CA
H.A. Van Norman	

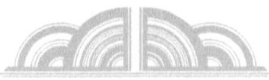

Acknowledgments

This novel—my first—is the realization of a long-deferred dream. That said, it happened purely by accident, inspired by a role-playing game with some old high school friends—Brian, Dennis, and Christine—and by Patrick Jenning's detailed history of noir LA, *The Long Winding Road of Harry Raymond: A Detective's Journey Down the Mean Streets of Pre-War Los Angeles*. There you'll find not only Harry Raymond but Kent Kane Parrot, who really did pull the levers at LA City Hall and who kept an apartment at the Biltmore. Thanks, guys.

Once I decided to write it, I was afraid that I might lose interest or give up. It seemed a daunting task. And it was. But the funny thing is, I fell in love with the characters. And once I turned the story over to them, the words came in a torrent. So when my first draft was done, I turned to my college and professional friends to review it. My thanks to all of you, especially Corbin, Carl, Cathy, and Jerry, for your invaluable feedback and advice.

My first draft was far from perfect. To quote Horace Jennings, when you want something done right, hire a professional. Enter Liz Monument, my editor, who balanced encouragement with critique as she showed me both what I was capable of and how much I have yet to learn. Thanks, Liz, and thank you, Jericho Writers, for introducing us and nourishing my passion.

Next came publishing. Only slightly less intimidating than the lottery that is traditional publishing was the prospect of learning how to self-publish as an independent author. Fortunately, Jericho introduced me to Debbie Young, a highly successful author and a leading authority on self-publishing. She took me from "Do I really want to do this?" to "I'm doing this, and it's nearly done." Thanks, Debbie!

Nearly done, but not quite. Books are judged by their covers, and I needed a professional to design not only the cover, but the book itself, and my publishing logo. Who better to do that than my good friend, David O. Miller, professional artist and expert in fantasy, sci-fi, and horror gaming? Look him up if you'd like to be amazed.

Finally, I circled back to two of the high school friends who were there at the start: Christine, for a final review of the manuscript; and Dennis, to produce my audiobook. Thanks again, guys.

That just leaves the three long-suffering people who have had to live with me during the writing of this book—my family. To Leslie, Emily, and Grace: thanks so much for your patience and support. But fair warning: the next book is well underway.

About the Author

A professional engineer and graduate of MIT (engineering and humanities), Michael Albergo writes character-driven speculative fiction rooted in real-life early 20th century locales, people, and events. He teaches at New York University and is an avid player of board games and role-playing games. *Native Species* is his first novel.

If you have enjoyed reading this novel, please rate it on Amazon.

For news and information about upcoming works by this author, please visit: http://MichaelAlbergo.com

www.ingramcontent.com/pod-product-compliance
Lightning Source LLC
LaVergne TN
LVHW041904070526
838199LV00051BA/2492